Rose and the Burma Sky

Rosanna Amaka

PENGUIN BOOKS

TRANSWORLD PUBLISHERS
Penguin Random House, One Embassy Gardens,
8 Viaduct Gardens, London SW11 7BW
www.penguin.co.uk

Transworld is part of the Penguin Random House group of companies
whose addresses can be found at global.penguinrandomhouse.com

Penguin
Random House
UK

First published in Great Britain in 2023 by Doubleday
an imprint of Transworld Publishers
Penguin paperback edition published 2024

A CIP catalogue record for this book
is available from the British Library.

ISBN
9781804991909

Typeset in Adobe Garamond Pro by Jouve (UK), Milton Keynes.
Printed and bound in Great Britain by Clays Ltd, Elcograf S.p.A.

The authorized representative in the EEA is Penguin Random House Ireland,
Morrison Chambers, 32 Nassau Street, Dublin D02 YH68.

Penguin Random House is committed to a sustainable future
for our business, our readers and our planet. This book is made
from Forest Stewardship Council® certified paper.

This novel is dedicated to the over a million African soldiers who fought in the Second World War, especially those approx. ninety thousand who served in Burma, and to my grandmother, who told me a little about her younger years and the young men who disappeared and never came back, one Saturday afternoon long ago.

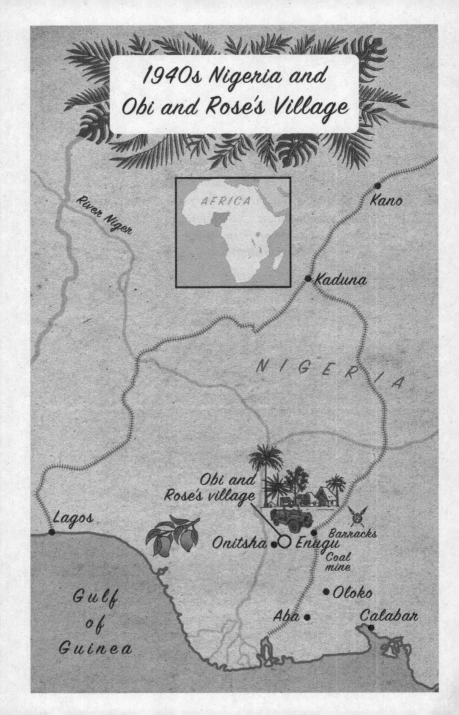

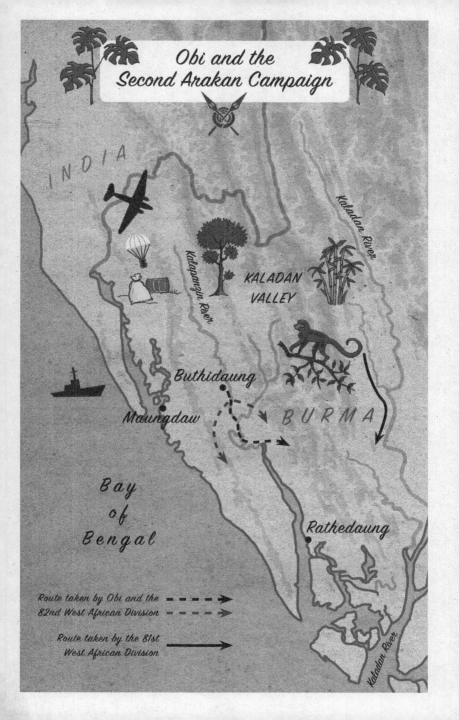

A fly that doesn't listen to advice follows the dead into the grave.

Igbo proverb

Prologue

The End

Burma, Hot Season, 1945

I DON'T KNOW HOW I arrived here, but the journey to this point has been long and arduous. I mean, how does a man get to the point of wanting to take the life of another? I would have to go back to the beginning to make you truly understand. Yet that beginning seems long ago, and despite the rage and the hot blood that throbs at my temples, I am weary, and so very tired.

I have seen many wicked deeds, so what difference will this one make?

Why should his death matter? For I have taken many a life in this godforsaken war. And yet I know deep down that it does. That to kill him would break the very core of me.

And so I lie on the muddy ground, leaves and twigs crackling beneath me, bamboo stems criss-crossing above my head, shafts of light poking through dense jungle, the sounds of the animals echoing in my ears, before gunfire breaks out once again.

I lift my rifle. My hands shake. The metal feels cool, solid, in my palm, and so I buck the butt against my shoulder, slide the strap out of the way, look down the barrel and aim. I see him. He stands cowering from the gunfire raining down on us, sparks flying every which way. I can just see his face as he glances over at me. I feel for the trigger with my index finger. I see him put out a hand and signal to the others.

I steady my nerves, sweat pouring down my temples, and take aim. I hear, feel, the pumping of my heart, and as I press down, my finger trembles.

When I started this journey I was young, full of hope, even promise. Rose once called me green. My sweet, dear Rose.

In the months I have been here in this jungle, fighting this war, I have learnt it is not good to feel, have tried not to feel. But the truth is, it is fear that has kept me going. I have lost many a friend, had to leave them to their fate, lying on the jungle floor where they fell. I heard their moans, and groans, and steeled myself, picked up my gun, my supplies, and kept walking. Did not look back, because it was either them or me.

Seeing Ifeanyi fall but a minute ago was the last straw.

We stood by the stream earlier and I watched him roll up his sleeves as he washed his face; we joked about home. I knelt beside him and did the same, then flicked water on him like we used to as boys.

I look over to where Ifeanyi lies on his back, staring up at the trees and scattering of blue sky, still gripping his gun. The sweat glistening off his arm. A hole where his heart used to be, the blood soaking his shirt, forming a pool on the ground. A Japanese soldier lying dead beside him.

I check around for the others, hear my heart pumping loud, and wonder if any are still alive. I stare at the dead bodies that carpet the jungle floor, but I cannot see all their faces. Five minutes ago I was speaking to them, joking with them; I even asked Ifeanyi to pass something or other to me.

And so I hold my gun, the bottom bucked up against my shoulder, pointing it at him. I lift myself slightly, aim at his heart. A heart for a heart, I think. I close my eyes, pull the trigger. Hear a sound. The final pieces at the core of me shatter.

I drop my head down to the floor, but then I lift myself to check, to see if he is dead. I cannot see, so I lift myself higher, and that's when I feel the full force of the bullets hitting my back. I drop my gun, lay my hands on the ground, cry out. I feel the blood gushing out, feel my shirt, my body, soak with my own blood. I turn over to lie on my back, look up at the trees and the sky, and the words 'For what does it profit a man' reverberate in my head. Reverend Nwachukwu shouts them from the pulpit of our makeshift village church. And I wonder how I could have done things differently.

'Am I not a man?' I say on the jungle floor, looking up into the blue Burma sky. Then I cry for Rose.

I see her sweet face. She is smiling. I reach out to touch her. But then, darkness descends.

1

The Beginning

Eastern Nigeria, Dry Season, 1929

WE DID NOT see it coming. How could we? For I was born in the hinterland, in a small village surrounded by African rainforest, not far from Onitsha and the Niger river, into a world that seemed so far removed from the war and all that it brought to us and our generation.

Looking back, I remember our shrieks of joy as we ran naked in the rain, our infantile faces blinking at the sky; we thought our joy would never end. I remember the heavy scent of ripe cashew fruit as we walked along the dirt paths, chatting as we ventured between compounds. The sweetness of Rose's father's guava fruit; we gorged on its pink stickiness when it was in season. I remember the exhilaration of picking big fat snails in the wet season to take home to our mothers' cooking pots. I remember our aunties, for we had many in those days, bent low, their heads bopping as they swept their yards clean. A group of neat parallel lines left on the ground, which went all the way to the village centre on market days. I remember the six of us, how we were, the day my mother didn't return.

My mother called the Niger 'Orimili', great water. But she was born into the old world, with the old ways, when the Umuada, the first daughters of our village, reigned. Back then, before the colonials, when our village elders governed everything, when the Umuada spoke, the men trembled.

I never truly got to know my mother, for I was a mere boy whose head was filled with play on the day she never returned.

They say my mother was a fighter, that she swung my little brother high above her head, his maleness dangling between his toddler thighs, swung him high, straight on to her back. Then tied her wrapper, well, well-o. Secured him, then the fabric at her bosom, before marching off, leading the women along the dusty road from our village to Oloko.

Well, they say the ground shook as she marched, that her feet pounded the red earth, the dust gusting up in a thick cloud around her feet.

They say that the tremors could be felt for miles around, that she woke villages as she, and the women, passed by. That their voices could be heard as far south as Calabar, ringing out loud, demanding to be heard.

And some women from those villages they passed stopped in mid-action, in the middle of pounding beans for breakfast or sweeping the yard, held their heads still, listened, and without hesitation put down the pounder or the broom in their hands. Began to bark out instructions to the rest of their household. They quickly packed water, food, gathered up the smallest of their children, the ones that still suckled their breasts, and ran out to join the women as they marched along that road to Aba back then, in 1929.

My mother was away for some time, had travelled south with the rest to protest against the threat of more tax; a direct tax on women implemented by the colonials after the great Wall Street Crash. Thousands of women went protesting, demanding their right to greater representation in the new system. No one expected it to turn into a two-month war, least of all my father.

They say my mother came from a long line of fighters, warrior-like women. That she could silence the village council with just a stare. That she was raised in the old ways, before Mr Kitson discovered coal instead of silver, before Lord Lugard, before the North was joined to the South, before the installation of colonial warrant chiefs and the colonial native courts, which pushed the women aside, silenced them in the new colonial system, way back then when Nigeria was born in 1914.

Well, at least before women like her were sent away to missionary schools; to St Anne's to the west, Holy Rosary to the east, to Queen's College and many more. Where they learnt to speak the King's English, primly pour English tea and don their white gloves to pose prettily for old studio black-and-whites.

They say my mother looked her shooter straight in the eyes, dared him, before falling face down to the ground. And that her blood flowed out on to the soil, a deep red, like palm oil, winding and parting like the Niger on the grainy ground.

They say that the women gathered round, saw the blood, heard the sky above give out a thunderous cry, screamed, then turned, in response to the cry from their god in the sky, to set alight the courts, the buildings and the shops of their colonial masters.

And why do I start this story with my mother? Because through understanding our women, even a little, you will understand what nestled at the core of my dear sweet Rose. What was hidden beneath her smile and her ever-so-gentle demeanour, how I fell in love, and why I lay on a jungle floor looking down the barrel of a gun. Both my mother and Rose were Umuada, the first daughters of our village; they had similar blood running through their veins. They were women who must be heard. I was born to and nurtured by such women.

But Rose was born into a colonial world, with new rules, new desires that shaped her, and shaped me. And it seemed that she was forever hiding between those two worlds. It felt to me, at least, as if she didn't quite feel enough in either, but underneath, at the core of her, she was Umuada.

I remember that December day my mother did not return.

There was something strange in the air that morning; I could taste it on my tongue. There was a heaviness in my heart that I could not shake. The four of us, plus the girls, Rose and Uche, had been in the cornfields playing like we always did. I looked up into the sky, saw an eagle, watched it circle, casting shadows over me. All of a sudden I was filled with such dread, as I watched it flying high, that I turned and ran.

'Obi, what's wrong?' Rose shouted after me.

'Nothing,' I shouted back, for I hoped it would be so.

'Where're you going?' cried out Emeka.

'What happened?' asked Uche, as they stood and watched me go.

I ran inside our compound, heard my baby brother's cry first. My father was standing in the middle of the yard; a group of people who were strangers to me handed my brother to him. I looked around for my mother but she was nowhere to be found, then turned back to my father who was handing my baby brother to Nnenna, his second wife. And I knew. My father stood frozen in the middle of the compound, nodded his head as they told him, but the women let out their terrifying wails. I looked around again for my mother, pleaded for her to appear, but she did not. And I knew.

News of the other mothers came later. They say that fifty-one of them died, gunned down by an automatic rifle.

That evening, the Umuada gathered in our compound. They filled our yard. I watched as more and more of them joined. I was somewhat confused, at a loss for what to do or say.

We, the children, sat by the fireside, outside our makeshift kitchen, trying to force down the food the women insisted we eat. Rose sat beside me. We looked on through the flames towards the centre of the yard as the adults tried to organize themselves. My father sat with the elders of the village, discussing what to do next.

Rose put her arm around me, pulled me close, rubbed my back, and although she was not more than a year older, she felt strong, so I leant into her, put my head on her shoulder.

'Why?' I kept asking.

We watched as a party was despatched to bring my mother's body home, then another to let any relatives further inland know.

The remaining women fussed and raged, calling out my mother's name as if that alone could bring her back. And when it got too much I bent my head and cried, and Rose hugged me.

Maybe that is where the seed of my love for Rose was truly born, because I knew her strength, had felt it that night. Yet, at the same time, as I got older I learnt to fear it, just as the colonials did who tried to control her, silence her, in the school she later went to, and just like my father before me had feared my mother's strength, and my father's father had feared my grandmother's.

If I could go back now, what different choices we all could have made. But mistakes are easier to see with hindsight, and hindsight cannot change what happened later between us all, or untangle me from the clutches of this love that just won't let me be.

2

Later

Eastern Nigeria, Dry Season, 1931

TWO YEARS AFTER my mother died, when I was ten and my elder brother was old enough to take over his farming duties, my father left to work in the mines in Enugu.

Things were never the same after my mother's death: a little joy left our corner of the compound, and although my father's pride would never let him admit it, I think her loss left a substantial hole in our family finances.

So we watched him, all thirteen of us and his two remaining wives, wheel his bicycle through the compound entrance, big bundles of his belongings secured on the back. We waved at him as he made his way along the route to open land, then on to the dirt path through the fields. The younger ones were excited, kept running back and forth, clinging to him as he went. Until he finally turned and gave one last wave, hugged the youngest of his children, and sent them back, before disappearing from view among the corn stalks.

And as I watched him go, I breathed out; it was a surprise, for I had not been aware I was holding my breath. My father was not an easy man. He loved the cane and used it on us, his sons, the most. So there was also a part of me that was happy to see him go.

Sometimes, particularly when my father returned on his short breaks from the mines, I secretly watched him at village meetings chaired by Rose's father, the former warrant chief of our village. Looked down on them from high up in our neighbouring mango tree, which bordered Rose's compound. My father was then as loud as the rest of them. I remember seeing them break cola nuts, share spirit and palm wine libations with ancestors long gone. I listened from on high, hid among the tree's dense leaves, looked down on the bald heads which shone with sweat below. They stooped on old wooden benches, which the womenfolk from both our yards brought out after sweeping the ground clean in preparation for the meetings; then, they quickly disappeared to attend to their own women's business. I watched my father – for even then he was something of a rebel – sitting among the group trying to decipher how best to use their pooled resources for our community, stand to make his point and draw a line in the sand, stamp a stick, point a finger, then stop for full effect, before uttering an old saying, like they did in the old days, before sitting back down.

And at the end of such meetings, when the spirit had freed all their tongues and the toasts began, my father would stand again, take the cow-horn cup and make a toast, remembering my mother, elevating her memory to that of a man's, before downing the liquor, flicking the horn and passing it on. And so I sat and watched my father in those moments after he sat back down, quiet again, solemn, lost in his thoughts, before he finally staggered home, like the rest of them, singing in the dusk, along the dusty paths, giving me a chance to climb quietly down from my perch and join the rest of the children already eating in our yard.

*

My grandmother arrived in our lives one morning, some months after my mother was buried. She emerged from the bush, walking stick in hand, heavy load on head, put it down in the middle of our yard, and called out our names. She demanded a stool and some water, having trekked through the bush to reach us after a dream. We brought them to her. She never went home again.

We loved our grandmother. She was a small woman with tough dark skin, which made her look older than her years. She had a sweet melodic voice, and would gently stroke and pat our heads as she sang us to sleep in an effort to soothe away the loss we felt, especially in those initial years after our mother was gone. Even now, a fully grown man, I still hear her singing to me, easing my sleep when the troubles of this world just won't let me rest. She was a widow, and had tribal scars on her upper chest and back, and when it was very hot she walked around our yard with her wrapper tied at her waist. Her flat, used-up pancake breasts free to the world.

I can see her now, her hand busy waving a plaited fan made from palm leaves, trying to cool herself in the suffocating heat. A very wise and yet funny woman, who I suspected had seen many changes, even horrors, in her time, but who never spoke of them, at least not to us, her grandchildren.

They say I look like my grandmother. We had the same high cheekbones and similarly shaped teeth. We were nothing alike, my grandmother, my father and I, totally different people, except in looks. We, the three of us, looked so much alike that people used to say that my grandmother spat my father out, and he in turn crawled upwards and spat me out.

I believe my grandmother could see things before they happened. She would suddenly look up into the sky and leisurely take the washing into our hut, while my father's wives looked on and pondered why she was doing it. Then the heavens would suddenly open, and they would have to jump up, run, and rush to take down their half-soaked clothes from the line.

Once, I saw her sitting under our pawpaw tree shelling pumpkin seeds for egusi soup. She suddenly stopped, moved her chair to the side, sat back down and continued shelling the seeds in her bowl, as a pawpaw dropped on the very spot she had vacated.

My grandmother, old and tired as she was, had a piece of land, given to her by my father, broken off from the land my mother had left behind. She farmed that small patch as best she could, sending me, or one of my immediate siblings, to the market to sell the surplus. We dutifully brought her back the money, which she tied up in cloth and hid. I often watched her as she turned her back on me and busied herself with hiding her little coins next to her stash of food: yams, rice bought from the market, dried corn and more. I used to wonder why she didn't spend a little on herself, but in time came to realize it was the reason we never went hungry.

Even during that year when my mother was still alive, and the men from our village disappeared, so half the harvest was ruined and all us children were forced to retire hungry to our beds, I remember my grandmother suddenly appearing in our yard with a bundle of food on her head. She put it down, called to the wives to come and take it, and later vanished once again back into the bush. That week my mother hushed us as we lay hungry in the dark, then secretly brought out her portion little by little in an effort to make it stretch and feed us. Two times that year when we thought we could take it no longer, when things were seriously dire, my grandmother suddenly appeared, as if she knew, bringing food to save us. Some say I inherited my foresight from her; I even believed them – that is, until I found myself among the bamboo stems, lying in a pool of my own blood, wondering if I was alive or dead. But the truth is I have had several revelations, and deaths, that brought me to the point of aiming my gun at him out there in the jungle.

3

Friends

W E, THE FOUR of us boys – Ifeanyi, Emeka, Michael and I – were in the same age grade. We were the best of friends back when we were children, before our troubles began.

Ifeanyi and I were the closest; we came from similar backgrounds. He lived in a mud hut compound like mine at the bottom of the hill, although his father only had one wife.

Emeka was the oldest of five, with two younger brothers, Ike and Nonso, who sometimes tagged along. They lived further up, between Michael and me. The family had spent a little time in the north but relocated when their father found a job nearer to our village; he had served as a clerk at the courts in Onitsha before his passing. Emeka's mother had high ambitions, and when his father died it seemed to me that Emeka was constantly trying to live up to them. We understood each other more in those days – having lost a parent young brought us close – but we were so very different in so many ways.

Michael was the son of the district doctor stationed in our village for a while; they lived the furthest up the hill in the big colonial house with the best of views. Michael was the tallest of us, a handsome chap. His family were not originally from our parts, but from another area of Igbo land, and his father had attended Howard

University College of Medicine in the States, a Black American university, where he met and married his wife. She was a fair-skinned Black American, with loose curly hair. A Carter by birth, a Garveyite by upbringing, whose mother had joined and marched with the UNIA women's division in Harlem back in 1919. I recall that, much later, when we were older, Michael's mother worked on one of Nnamdi Azikiwe's nationalist newspapers based in Onitsha, before Michael and Emeka also went on to work there part-time. She was unlike any of our mothers, but the sweetest of women whenever we returned to their compound from play. The first time she gave us homemade lemonade it slid down our throats, sweet and tangy. It was glorious, familiar and foreign at the same time. The liquid cooled our feverish skin after we'd been playing in the low grass chasing kites, which Michael showed us how to make from old newspapers, string, and sticks found in the bush.

Even today my mouth still waters whenever I think of those rowdy, boisterous days, when we roamed and ran through each other's compounds, letting out loud shrieks, pulling empty, rattling cans along the dry earth, playing football with balls we made from palm leaves or rubber we collected from the rubber tree. We gulped down the sweet lemony liquid with big toothy smiles between us, savouring the last drops once we were cool again.

As for Rose, my dear sweet Rose – who I knew as Nkem in those days – being neighbours, we played together the most. She would join the boys and me roaming the bush. She loved to race, but then she was much taller than us, except for Michael, so for the most part would always win. She climbed and fought and scrambled with the rest of us boys. Her father being a respected man, unlike many other former warrant chiefs, gave her, a girl, that privilege. A privilege that Uche just didn't have, meaning she spent most of her time attending to girls' things in her father's yard, but every so often would break away and join us.

Rose was very bossy, like eleven-year-old girls can sometimes be. We became very close after my mother died. I always felt happy in her presence, but maybe, even then, I might have already been a little in love. Maybe all of us were a little in love. Well, as much as children can be.

But Rose's father was different, their compound was different. Their house was built of brick and concrete. What people would call a bungalow nowadays, with a parlour, which I rarely got to see – it was hidden behind material, or a curtain, which they hung at the front door, so I caught glimpses of it as they would go in and out of the house – and with an elevated veranda, which I often saw the family sit out on in the evenings. Rose's father had only one wife, and four children. He was the son of a priest, a missionary, a freed slave who had made his way back from Sierra Leone. He had been made a warrant chief by the colonials. But, unlike many of the other warrant chiefs they installed, he had not been greedy and had stepped down on hearing of the death of my mother – before the reform of the warrant chief system, which was successfully brought about by the women's riots. They – his family and himself – were very respected indeed.

Rose and her father spent hours together just sitting and listening to their gramophone. The clipped English sounds were a wonder, an introduction to our mother country, England, over there, across the seas. The sounds reminded me of Mr Charles Archie Smith, our district officer. Sometimes, I would look through the stick partition from our compound, over to their elevated veranda, to check it was not Mr Smith breaking out into song, only to see Rose sitting quietly at her father's feet, listening to the gramophone. Other times she would sit just reading him the newspapers that came from Lagos or Port Harcourt through Onitsha.

Rose's father spoke the King's English very well, took afternoon tea on his veranda, and often entertained Mr Smith there. The district officer was a tall man with a thick black moustache, who seemed to tower over everyone. He was a British ex-soldier who had fought in the Great War. He spoke a little Igbo but often mispronounced his words, which caused much amusement among us children.

I often heard the two men, their voices drifting through the stick partition to where I sat on the ground on our side of the mango tree. As a small child I did not understand them fully, but wanted to be a very British fellow just like them. So, when I was lucky enough to attend our local Anglican primary school, I spoke English in a clipped manner, the way I remembered Rose's father and Mr Smith speaking, through my nose, in stop-and-start sentences. I would punctuate them with phrases such as, 'Listen, old boy,' or 'Jolly good, old chap,' as I had often heard Mr Smith say to Rose's father.

On occasion, Rose's father and Mr Smith would reminisce about the King's son the Prince of Wales's visit to Nigeria in 1925. And although I was only four at the time, I vaguely remember the excitement of that visit. The pictures in the newspaper of the battlecruiser anchored off the coast of Nigeria after his visit to the colony of the Gold Coast, and of him and his entourage boarding the train that took them to the north, to Kano, to meet the emir, and of the durbar held in his honour. We heard the chiefs were ordered by the commissioners to welcome him, and how some people even slept outside in readiness to see him. They said that everybody came out to line the streets and that the schoolchildren waved their British flags. We heard about parts of his speech, how the King had spoken about how we freely contributed to the common cause during the Great War that began in 1914, and how the Prince assured us of the King's unfailing interest.

We never forgot the pictures of the royal wedding, of the Duke of Gloucester, King George's third son, to Princess Alice in 1935. We sat in Rose's father's yard, on the steps of his veranda, looking at the paper: at pictures of the archbishop of Canterbury leaving Lambeth Palace to preside over the affair; of the carriages as they drove down The Mall from Buckingham Palace; and of the wedding party, which included the two little princesses, Elizabeth and Margaret. I decided that one day, maybe when I was older, I wanted to see the mother country, this England, and all its palaces.

Mr and Mrs Smith lived in Onitsha, a little distance away from our village, in the house specially built for them, among other colonials like them, not far from the port and the market, from where the colonials shipped out the palm oil and cash crops.

Mr Smith had a quiet yet determined way about him. His wife was a soft-spoken, nervous woman, who liked to grow vegetables in their garden. I know this as we, the boys and I, when we were older, used to like walking through Whitemen Quarters in Onitsha just to see how they lived. She grew neat rows of lettuce, tomatoes and other vegetables. We saw her once in the garden with rake in hand, directing her house help, or boy. Like her husband, she was very pale. She was known for often taking to her bed. It was rumoured she was often too sick to attend events with her husband. When I became a man I found out more about this strange sickness she had that caused much embarrassment to Mr Smith.

It is hard now, looking back, to believe that at that time I did not notice the differences between us all, and if I did they seemed so insignificant, especially with so many more trees to be climbed, bushes to be explored, rattling toys to be made and kites to be flown. And although my family was poor, in many ways they were good days, good days because I was ignorant of the ways of this world.

Our school days were very happy. When I was a young boy I pledged allegiance to the King and Empire. Stood in front of the flag, right hand over heart, and recited the words. I was proud of my British education, thought myself a very British fellow, a good scholar indeed. We marched into class singing at the top of our lungs the praises of the King. Learnt to speak English, leaving our primitive tongue behind.

It was always early but light when we left home, and we were fortunate enough that our school was not too far. Unlike some of my classmates, who had to walk for hours through the bush and morning darkness to make it in time to our little village school.

'Obi! Nkem!' shouted Emeka to Rose and me as he passed by.

'Coming,' I shouted, quickly finishing off my breakfast and throwing my school bag, an old rice sack which my grandmother had sewn handles on to, over my shoulder.

'The homework? Did you do it?' asked Rose.

'Yes, of course,' I lied, joining the two of them on the path.

Rose was always the first to join Emeka, even on days when I made a conscious effort to be ready.

Emeka gave me a look then turned to Rose. 'How did you work out the first questions?'

Rose began to explain something or other to him.

I made a face and hurried along in front of them. 'Come on, we will be late.'

We walked quickly and picked up Ifeanyi and Uche on the way.

Our classroom was open with half-walls on either side, so you could clearly see the school playing field, and fields of corn and yams beyond. It had a corrugated tin roof, which let out a chink, dink and rattle sound when it rained, like the sound of marbles falling on concrete. I remember the sweetness of the breeze heavy with the scent of red hibiscus in full bloom that drifted through the class, the air caressing our skin. And when it rained I loved to watch it pelt down, hypnotized by the drips and drops that fell from the edge of the roof; the noisy strumming beat would set me off into a sleepy nod.

We sat in rows on plain wooden benches and leant on narrow tables. Rose sat in the row in front, next to Uche, closer to the teacher; Emeka sat in the row behind them; and Ifeanyi and I sat side by side at the back.

Rose was Reverend Nwachukwu's right-hand girl, always ready to help, and even though she and Uche were the best of friends, they still jostled and argued for his attention – for although Uche was the brightest among us, always scored the highest when we had tests, Rose had a way about her, even back then.

We were mainly taught the four Rs: reading, writing, arithmetic and religion, but also about England, about the King, and about English customs, about afternoon tea and cucumber sandwiches.

We all loved our teacher, Reverend Nwachukwu, who was originally trained by Jamaican missionaries at Mary Slessor's Presbyterian mission in Calabar, before converting to the Anglican faith. And if the Reverend wasn't walking between the aisles monitoring our work, he was at the front teaching.

'*Echi*,' said the Reverend, standing to the side of the blackboard, cane in hand, pointing to a word. 'To-mor-row,' he then said in English.

'To-mor-row,' we chorused back at him.

'Again, class.'

'To-mor-row,' we said in unison.

'Again.'

'Tomorrow,' we repeated.

Then he turned. '*Azo*,' he said, pointing again at the blackboard towards a simple sketch. 'Fish,' he said in English.

'Fish,' we repeated like parrots.

'Again, class.'

'Fish!'

That is how we learnt, memorizing facts and half-facts, truths and untruths, as set out by our colonial and missionary education system. Until they all blended into one to become just truths and facts.

'And who discovered the River Niger?' said the Reverend.

'Mungo Park,' we replied in unison.

'Good, class, very good. Mungo Park discovered the Niger.'

We learnt without much thought or question, and were very grateful for this white man's discovery indeed.

'Reverend Nwachukwu,' I once asked, 'who were we before the white man? What were our customs? Were we not here before they came?'

'Obi, we do not ask such questions here. We are Christians now. We thank God we have left those pagan days behind.'

And so, in that answer, I learnt that who we were before was best not remembered. And so, like the Reverend suggested, as he had been taught, I too tried to leave what we were and who we were behind.

But, looking back now, Rose and Uche were hungry for the opportunities this learning could provide, opportunities to become one of the interpreters, student-teachers or clerks needed to feed the indirect-rule system. A cheaper system for the colonials to manage. I was too young really to understand, but even at that age I could see that Rose was focused; she never looked back at us, facing straight ahead with a determination to learn, or bending over to scribble on her board, as if somehow she knew that it could be a stepping stone to something greater. Maybe that was what was at the root of it, of what transpired between us all.

Soon, it was mango season, and at the weekend, or after school, when Ifeanyi, Emeka and I had completed our family chores, like fetching water from the stream, or scavenging the bush for firewood, we would join the rest.

We spent hours up in the trees near the fields, gorged on the sweet, sticky mangoes. Our legs dangled as we perched on separate branches, looking out on the green bush and farmland for miles around. Thin red paths could be seen weaving in and out across the land. Behind us were the tops of our parents' tin and thatched roofs, and looking forward, beyond the fields, in the far distance, we could make out the trunk road that led the outside world into our village, and would, one day soon, lead us out into that outside world.

4

A Decision

Eastern Nigeria, Wet Season, 1932

IN MY FINAL years of elementary school, the boys left one by one, until it was just Rose, Uche and me, and by then Uche rarely joined us. She spent most of her time in her father's yard, doing girls' things. We sometimes dropped by but her mother would always call for her to hurry up with something or other, and we would continue on our way, her eyes begging us to stay a little longer.

I will never forget the day we – the two of us, Rose and I – sat alone on the highest branch of our tree looking out over our village. It was past the hour she spent helping the younger ones at our local school. The rest, by virtue of being boys from families that could afford it, or because the community collectively saw promise in them and so were willing to fund them, like Ifeanyi, were away finishing up their first year of secondary school. I had secretly watched the elders from on high as they made that decision. They had argued back and forth, as they had limited funds. Some wanted to send Uche, who, as I said, was the brightest among us at our little school. In the end, Ifeanyi and another boy won, the brightest boys, but they were nowhere near Uche in intelligence. That day the elders decided not to fund girls as they would marry and take their knowledge to their husband's land, whereas the boys would stay. I myself was deemed not bright enough for such endeavours, as argued by one elder, Mr Eze, before he sat down and they swiftly moved on. Even I could not get angry at his words, as the Reverend often caned me because of something or other I had forgotten to learn or failed to recall.

So, we sat in the very top of our mango tree looking out on the world, as we had done many times before. The dark line of the trunk road could be seen clearly in the distance slicing through the landscape, and there was barely any room between us, and I heard and felt her heavy sigh.

'Obi, where would you go if you did not need to stay and farm?' asked Rose.

'I don't know. And you?'

'To school, like the boys.'

'You would miss me too much,' I joked.

She laughed. I liked to see her laugh.

We continued sucking on our mangoes, looking out over the land, the sweet juice escaping down the sides of our mouths, and we chatted and laughed at each other's silly jokes.

Then I looked at Rose, at her profile, her small nose sitting defiantly on her face, at the pepper grains of her shaven head, her blue cotton dress bunched up around her slim thighs, her legs dangling just like mine as she smiled out on the land in front of us, the messy, sticky juice leaving stains on the front of her dress. I just knew. The world seemed perfect between us.

So, that day, when I turned to her and she smiled back at me, the mango fibres stuck between her teeth, her hair very short and uncombed, I made up my mind that I was going to marry her.

Then we both turned back to look out on the land, over the

fields and the trunk road, and we both saw, at the same time, the car – what I now know to have been a Crossley saloon – making its way along the road in the distance. We could just make out its shape. It was Mr Charles Archie Smith's car.

As Mr Smith and Rose's father had formed a friendship over the years, his car could often be found parked in Rose's father's yard, either on a visit to our village or en route to more interior villages.

Sometimes he came and offloaded his bike, and other times he came with his boys, as he called them, and offloaded heavy bundles on to their heads, before trekking along the bush paths on their way to more remote places. Once, he even came with his nephews, who were older than us. I could not help but stare at them through the stick partition all the while they were there, for I had never seen children that looked like them before, with hair so blond it was almost white.

The car went winding up the main road, exiting on to the dirt path, the dust billowing up as it drove towards our home. I looked on as it bumped along the uneven road, and knew it was on its way to see Rose's father.

But this was later than usual and there was a feeling in the air that I could not explain as I watched the car come nearer.

Rose climbed down, waved me goodbye, and ran off to find out the reason for his visit. I watched as the district officer passed our compound, parked his car in Rose's father's yard, and got out in his green khaki shorts and white socks.

I watched as Rose's father rushed out of his house, with Rose by his side, his hand extended towards Mr Smith, a little look of surprise on his face. I watched as they shook hands, smiling at each other. Little did I know then what changes he was to bring.

5

Respect

Eastern Nigeria, Wet Season, 1938

LIFE: IF NOT for Rose, things might have been different. And yet, in reality, if I could turn back time, what decisions would I have made differently? For at the time I do not think I truly understood myself, or my place in this world, or my value. As a young man I was very naive. Maybe, if I had understood these things, maybe this in itself could have made the biggest difference to what happened that week.

I was always good at cultivating land. I used to enjoy the feel of the red fertile soil running through my hands, the sight of the yam hills in neat rows and the green leaves on the vines starting to turn yellow, signalling time for harvest.

It was end of the wet season of 1938. The sun was particularly hot, so harvest came earlier than usual. I remember the feel of the sun beating on my back as I bent with hoe in hand, I can still hear the crunch of the dry soil as I dug; my muscles ached as I used the hoe to free a yam from the soil, and it came forth into my hands like the earth was giving birth. I placed it at my foot, before standing to wipe away the sweat from my brow.

I heard it first, so turned, put my hand to my eyes to shield them from the sun, squinted into the distance to see a small cloud of dust moving along the road. As it drew nearer, it got bigger. I watched the dust cloud approach, until I could make out a jeep in the middle of it, and two figures in the front. The driver, a local man, was smartly dressed in army uniform; beside him sat a white army officer – taller and broader. I watched, then felt the full force of the air as they drove by. The back of the jeep was packed with uniformed soldiers. I laughed and waved. They smiled, laughed and waved back. I wondered where they were heading with such haste. My thoughts turned to Rose, as she insisted on being called by then. She had gone away to school with one name and returned with another. Her secondary school, like schools do in these parts, insisted she answer to a Christian name, not a heathen one like Nkemyochukwu ('the one I asked God for'). As I watched the dust cloud moving away, it made me think: would she consider me smart, even important, like the soldiers who went by?

I remembered how I had watched the district officer's car drive up the road, then on to the dirt path leading to our village; seen Rose as she climbed down and ran off into her father's house; peered through the branches of the tree separating our yards to see Rose's father emerge with her by his side, to shake hands with the district officer, Mr Smith, in his khaki shorts, white socks and sandals, an attire that I copied and later took to wearing when I was a very young man. Then they all disappeared together inside the house.

I had stood and pondered why the conversation on this occasion had to happen inside, when usually the womenfolk would be called upon to place chairs outside. I heard when Rose's father called for her mother to join them; this in itself was unusual.

As the evening crept in, and after eating my dinner with the rest of my household, I passed sideways through the gap between our

yards and went to the back, to find her sitting outside by the fire
with her younger brothers. The smallest of them lying with his
head in her lap. She had finished helping her mother in the kitchen, and sat poking hot coals with a rod in one hand and stroking
her brother's head with the other. I stood for a little while, watched
the flames flicker across her face, the slimness of her neck, her hair
tight to her skull and the sweet shape of her head, before she turned
her face up towards me and smiled.

'What did Mr Smith want?' I asked.

'He wanted to talk about school.' She moved, with her brother's
head still in her lap, to make room for me.

'What about school?' I said as I sat down.

'He told Papa I have a chance at a scholarship.'

'A scholarship!'

'Yes.'

'And will you sit for it?' I asked, holding my breath.

'Yes, of course. He said they – my mother and Mrs Smith –
talked about my schooling in the market. Said I was bright, that the
teachers at our school praised how well I helped out. Oh, Obi, can
you imagine?' she said as she beamed up at me; her white teeth
gleamed as the light from the fire passed across her smooth sepia skin.

But that was the problem: I did not want to imagine, for she was
the only one left. I had thought – well, imagined – that her being a
girl meant she would be around to keep me company, at least until
the boys returned from their schools.

And that is how I lost her, my first love, to that world beyond the
bush and green farmland. She must have sat for the scholarship, for
in no time her family and mine, as well as Uche, were standing by
the car which was to take her to her new future. They hugged, said
their goodbyes. I stood and watched from a distance; my heart
would not allow me to go closer. I was not prepared for my feelings
to leak out. So instead I climbed to the top of our mango tree and

watched her from there, watched as Uche reluctantly came forward on the ground down below and hugged her goodbye, to send her on her way to the prestigious girls' school in Lagos. And as I watched the two embrace, I could not help but think that if Uche had been born a boy, or even come from a different family, then she too would have abandoned me here alone on her way to such a school. Then Uche let go, her face forlorn. Rose moved away and began to enter the car.

I saw her stop and look around, almost as if she was looking for me. I wanted to climb down, to beg her not to leave, but I could not. I saw her open her mouth as if to call out, but then she closed it, turned and took her place in the back of the car. She looked out of the window, searching. I knew, I knew I had to let her know, and I began to climb down, to run to her, to let her know, and as I did, as I climbed down, I saw Emeka run out on to the road after her, dressed in his school uniform, having come directly from there. He must have left early that Friday. I saw him run after the car, saw him wave, saw the way she looked at him as she waved back, saw the tear in her eye as she drove away.

I watched them from our tree, as the car drove her away, along that dirt path; I climbed higher to watch it disappear on to the trunk road, taking her into the distance, towards her future, towards QMC Girls' College in Lagos. Where she learnt, like so many, to contain herself in starched cotton blouses and skirts that fell below the knee, and how to straighten and control her hair, arranging it so it looked more like her white colonial teachers', the shame of her natural tight curls wrestled out.

I continued to watch the trail of dust left behind once the car carrying her vanished along the trunk road.

I was a mere child when the trunk road was built and I have vague memories of watching the gangs of men in the distance, moving back and forth, like ants, clearing the land. Their faint chants sometimes reached my ears as I looked out from the top of my tree, from where I tried to search out my father and his brothers among them, or any of the men I could recognize from our village, but never could. The colonial army forcibly rounded them up and marched them off to work the roads. My mother, and the other wives, went several times to beg for their release but to no avail. The colonials told them they were entitled to the men's forced and free labour by colonial law.

Those were the years we went hungry, as there were no men left to work the land. That is, until they took my oldest brother, a prized Christian convert, after which Reverend Patrick, an Irish missionary, Reverend Nwachukwu's predecessor, marched to the district office and demanded his release. To my village's astonishment, they released him and my father. Seeing this, the rest of the village followed suit and started to attend church. The Reverend negotiated the release of more of the village men, and the village in return built the church and school in the centre of our community in honour of the Reverend's successful efforts, and I also think in part as a form of protection. As I grew I often watched the trucks, and people carrying heavy loads on their heads, passing back and forth along the road, carrying the palm kernels and cash crops from the interior, on their way to Onitsha and the boats that awaited them on the Niger.

That day when Rose went away I still knew her as Nkem, but when she came back she was Rose. A name given to her by the missionary headmistress, a very proper and strict Miss Broadwall from a place called Cumbria, partly because she could not pronounce her real name, but also, as I said before, because in Miss Broadwall's eyes it was nothing but heathen.

During the school holidays of her first year, we went playing in the bush, walking along the edge of the fields like we used to. I was behind Rose and she bent to pick up something from the ground. Her dress shifted, exposing the top of her back, the area between her shoulder blades, and poking out at the top were fresh pink scars which screamed out against her dark skin.

'What are those?' I asked.

'What?' she said, looking back towards me.

'On your back.'

She lifted her arm to touch the area between her shoulder blades, put her hand down and quickly fixed her dress. 'Nothing,' she said, and ran ahead to catch up with the others. I did not want to bring it up in front of the rest, so made a note to approach her later. I wondered about the scars, whether they were tribal, but this did not make sense to me for her family were not the kind to allow such a thing, and so I thought they could have been made at her school. But why?

Every time she came home for the holidays, the distance between us grew. She no longer ran through the compounds, or hitched up her skirt to climb our mango tree and look out on the lush green bush and farmland of our village and smile at me with mango fibres between her teeth. It seemed to me that over time Nkem was disappearing. But every now and then I caught glimpses of her hiding behind Rose's smile, or in a sudden look that crossed her face.

And so it was that I came, in time, to learn to silence my feelings for her. The little girl who held me that night my mother died, the girl I knew was hiding somewhere inside.

When we grew older, I would see her in her chair on their veranda, working the sewing machine. She sewed net curtains for the windows – my father's wives went next door to see her put them up – and made stylish clothes that made her stand out among the girls in our village. She even brought the papers from Lagos for her father, and fine plates which they brought out only when someone special, like Mr Smith, visited.

Her voice also gradually became quieter, until I did not hear her speak in public any more. She seemed only to smile sweetly and nod. But I heard her when she was next door, when she thought others did not hear, when she was behind closed doors. I listened from my yard on a morning, as her voice drifted over to me where I sat under our mango tree, contemplating the world. I heard her chastising her father, or her mother, or her siblings, because they had not done something as they should have. I smiled to myself then, for I knew the girl I had fallen in love with, my Nkem, was still there inside her.

But, thinking back now, there were always flashes, moments, which would suddenly reveal the layers of the woman she was yet to become, that caught me off guard, that sometimes unbalanced me, before she quickly corrected herself and they disappeared inside. I suspect that maybe – I can't be sure – there was more going on at her school than I will ever know.

Whenever she went off to school, I was left alone, the only one among the six of us left to run through our village with my rattling cans and walk through the low grass flying our newspaper kites. Even Uche eventually found a local secondary school. And so I had to grow up.

Each time Rose returned, she returned more womanly, more shapely, more knowing in that quietness. She stood out, was a modern woman indeed. I liked being around her, but I could never find the right words to say, never knew how to impress her, even as I sat there alone with her father on his veranda, listening to the gramophone, catching glimpses of her coming in and out of their house as she either brought her father's glasses or water, or came out to help change a record. And, on occasion, when Emeka joined me, and we went to visit and sat on her father's veranda to listen to the gramophone, just to be close, I knew from the way Rose's father asked Emeka questions, on what he was doing, on his future plans, that he was the more favoured one.

I joined my family farming the small plot of land we had, and on occasion helped out and taught English to the really young ones in my old primary school. For a few months before Rose left for her new school I had been her assistant, as she also helped out her mother at Michael's father's clinic on consultation days.

Rose was a diligent pupil-teacher, took her responsibilities seriously, unlike me. So, it was not a great surprise when, some months later, Reverend Nwachukwu called me aside and convinced me to focus my energies on farming. But in those days I still hoped that one day I would be able to further my education.

My older brother promised that when he finished learning his trade he would help with the cost of my studies, but instead, in the end, he set about building his own life. His promise to me forgotten under the pressure of raising his own family.

Over the years, just as Rose changed, the boys also changed, and although there was more of a distance between us as they progressed through school, it was not initially as pronounced. We still had things to talk about, places to explore. The older we got, when they returned during their holidays, the further afield we roamed. I would catch them up on village gossip as we walked along rough dirt paths on our way to the market square on market days, or as we trekked inland through the bush to the houses of old school friends who lived further into the hinterland, away from the main road. Once in a while when there were only three of us – Ifeanyi, Emeka and me – we would follow each other and hail a lift from a mammy truck or lorry along the trunk road, to run an errand as instructed by our families. We put our feet on a small platform and hung on to the outside of the truck for dear life, or climbed to the top to sit on the goods and see the world whizz past on our way to buy whatever was needed from the market, and later returned on foot with the supplies on our heads. And later, when we were older, we had at least a little drink in common. We would on occasion all disappear to a place in town, in Onitsha, to sit, eat, drink and catch up. We would sometimes walk past the pretty little gardens of the houses of the white colonials, or pass their stores as they kept a watchful eye on the locals who managed or served in them, or go past the catering rest-houses with tennis courts and golf greens. We watched them play through the fence, in their white tennis tops and shorts, lifting the ball high above their heads to hit it back at their opponent, and sometimes a few of the educated elite of Onitsha would join them on the court to play; this included Michael's father. On these occasions we would hitch a lift into town, before he drove on to the rest-house, and later on in the day we would meet him back at his car to catch a lift back home.

Soon enough it was Rose's last school holiday before returning for good to our village, for although she had finished her schooling, Rose was industrious and had found work as an assistant at her colonial school, but by then her mother was not well, and she was needed more at home. There was something about her, a restlessness. I saw it in the way she fidgeted and kept fixing her hair, or the way she perched herself on the edge of a chair when she was alone on the veranda, looking out into the distance, as if she was deep in thought, thinking of something or someone far away, or maybe just looking for something beyond their compound.

That last time she was home, I had tried to talk to her about my feelings, but it was not possible with her father there watching as I sat on the veranda trying to muster up words to say to her. But this last time, it was not a matter of not wanting to talk to her, it was as if I couldn't reach her.

*

As I watched the soldiers disappear in the dust cloud further up the road, I thought of her last visit. What would Rose and her father think? Would I be a more serious contender? Would he entertain me then, like I knew he entertained Emeka, think me more of a possible suitor if I had something doing? If I looked smart like them? Would he think me a more suitable match if I had more to bring to the table?

Watching the jeep become a speck on the road, I threw the hoe over my shoulder, marched up and down like I had seen the soldiers demonstrate in the market square a few days before. I tucked the bottom of the hoe under my arm like it was a gun and copied the march I had seen.

The white officer had arrived with five soldiers in tow. Our village was one of many stops on their tour of the area. Emeka and I had stood in the square among the crowd and watched their drill. The white officer's voice boomed out like a god's. The soldiers obeyed. They marched first to the left, then to the right, with guns down, guns up. It was a synchronized dance, and they carried it out to a drumbeat that I could not hear.

As I watched the Black soldiers marching to the colonial's commands, I wondered if Rose would think me important, smart, strong like them. I looked around and saw the quiet resentful respect on some of the men's faces.

The soldiers finished by kneeling and pointing their guns at the crowd. And for a second I held my breath. I heard a baby behind me fall silent, having felt their mother's fear. I looked at the soldiers pointing their guns directly at me and the crowd, waiting for their officer's command. No one moved, not the soldiers, not the crowd. The white officer's voice was suddenly booming out once again. The soldiers stood up, pointed their guns upwards, and fired their shots into the air. I felt Emeka flinch beside me, heard the awe from the crowd as the shots rang out. Their unspoken warning hung in the air.

'They call this recruitment,' said Emeka, leaning over to whisper in my ear.

When I was younger I had watched these drills as entertainment, but my father and uncles had watched in silence, and, like the baby behind me, I had also felt their fear. I came later to understand that these recruitment drives had a dual purpose.

'Let's go,' said Emeka.

I looked at Emeka, and then back at the expressions of the villagers standing around, noticed the fear on some of the women's faces, the begrudging respect on some of the men's, and although I knew Emeka had a point about the intimidating display, I suppose in those days I was desperate for some sort of respect, in whatever form I could get it. So I stood there looking at the soldiers in their smart uniforms, looking at the crowd's reaction to them, and wondered whether this could provide the answer I was searching for.

Out in the field that day, I tried on the possibility for size. Ifeanyi had told me that the pay was good, better than farming, but still I did not like the idea of fighting. But at that time there were no wars to fight, and things were peaceful. Besides, I needed the money, and one day I would need to be able to support a family, I thought. I was sure that farming a small piece of land would not provide well enough for the things Rose would desire.

I watched the soldiers disappear into the distance in their vehicle, then made up my mind.

6

The Dirt Path

THE NEXT DAY I left early. It was still dark and the compound was just beginning to stir with morning coughs and shuffles.

I did not tell anyone where I was going or what I had planned. It would be an hour before they realized I was not there for breakfast, but they would be too busy with their own chores to think it significant. I walked along the dirt path, then the bush and farmland trail to where I could hitch a lift on the mammy trucks on the main road to the temporary recruitment station. I was lucky that morning; I did not have to wait long. I walked along in the dark, and the first lorry I hailed stopped and picked me up.

There was already a queue at the gates of the recruitment station. There were young men looking for work as barrack boys (washing clothes, running general errands for the soldiers, that sort of thing), and one or two, like me, wanting to join up.

When they opened the gates we went in different directions. I joined the recruitment queue. There was a row of tables lined up in the open, and a local soldier standing beside the tables asking us new recruits questions, before ticking a sheet and ushering us on to the white officer sitting down behind the desk, with two other Black soldiers standing up behind him.

'Name?'

'Obi Nwogo.'

'You wish to sign up?'

'Yes, sir.'

'Take the Bible,' he said. 'Use your right hand, boy.'

'Yes, sir.'

'Repeat these words.'

And so I did.

'Place your thumbprint on the paper here.'

'I know how to sign my name, sir – I can read.'

'Oh, jolly good, splendid, we need more recruits who can. Listen, go with . . .' He looked around. 'Yes, go with the private here after your medical, see if we can't use you as a clerk of some sort.'

'Yes, sir.'

I followed the private into the tent for my medical with the local male nurses, took off my shirt for them to prod and poke me, before they signed and handed me a medical certificate clearing my health. I then followed the private to another shaded half-tent where I waited for them to make arrangements for written tests, before finally joining other recruits in outdoor exercises.

My eldest brother was the first to hear the news. I told him on my way back from signing up at the temporary barracks. He thought me a fool, and advised me to tell them it was a mistake, but I told him there was no need to worry, that there was no war to be concerned about. He shook his head and shouted hurtful words at me, particularly about our mother; that is, until I could no longer take it and I was forced to tell him home truths, that if he had done as he had promised I would have had no need to sign up. Ever since then, we have never been close.

It was my eldest brother who had left home first, then my older sister, who eloped to marry a travelling salesman from Owerri, a man of whom my father did not approve, and who she ran away from eleven years later with five children in tow.

Being next in line, it was therefore not a great surprise when I came home to deliver the news to my father and his wives that I also would be leaving.

He was home that week from the mines. He was silent at first, then nodded and wished me well. As I said before, he was a man of few words, but I think in a way it must have been a relief. One less mouth to feed. He had other sons coming up who could take over my farming duties, and as my mother was dead he did not have to feign any great sense of loss. So there was no big fanfare the morning I packed my belongings in my bag, threw it over my shoulder, kissed my grandmother goodbye as she cried, and walked down the dirt path towards my future.

But the youngest of my father's children, including Nnenna's, my father's second wife, lined the route as I left. They ran out to wave and shout their goodbyes. Seeing the look in their eyes, I knew they would miss their big brother. Particularly the treats I occasionally brought home, or the mangoes and pawpaws that I would climb up to get and throw back down into their expectant hands, and me gently chastising them for not being quick enough with fetching the water, or the firewood, for the household. Rose's father also came over. He stood at the entrance of our compound as I came out, patted me gently on the back, wished me luck and handed me a food package prepared by his wife. I looked over at their house. She stood on the veranda, in the doorway, the curtain behind her pulled to one side. I waved. She smiled and waved back.

7

Quick Step

Eastern Nigeria, Wet Season, 1939

SEVEN MONTHS LATER, Rose's mother died. I got the message scribbled on a piece of paper, sent by one of my younger brothers via a friend to the training barracks in Enugu. It was straight after morning drill, and I was sweating and exhausted after exercises in the hot midday sun, and irritated from the Sergeant's shouts as we tried to jump over an obstacle in full army attire, gun in hand, the sweat streaming down my face and threatening to drip into my eyes.

'Lift those monkey hoofs,' he shouted. 'LIFT THEM!!'

His mouth was wide enough to see his tonsils. His face a fresh dark pink from the effort, and from standing so long, stick under arm, uniform perfectly starched, beneath the harsh African sun.

When we first arrived, we did not understand Sergeant Fowler's shouts. It seemed like he was continuously angry, but the more we understood his words, the more we wished we didn't.

Sergeant Fowler was an older, more experienced soldier with tattoos down his upper arms, on show when he took off his shirt and stood in his vest. We often saw him, on an evening after duties, settle in his deckchair just outside his quarters and read a book, or watch the sun go down, just before his barrack boy laid out his clothes for dinner in the officers' mess, where all the white colonial soldiers dined. I watched them from outside in the dark. I sat on a dry log in the field, gazing up at the stars, before glancing over to them through the open mess window. The mosquitoes buzzed around the dim yellow light in the room; the officers' chatter, the clink of cutlery against ceramic plates and their alien sounds washed over me.

But when Sergeant Fowler was among them he fell silent. I never heard his voice among their chatter, although I knew he could shout the loudest of any of them. At the time this was strange to me, as I had not developed a good enough understanding to differentiate between them. I just knew that their ways were different to ours, for in my culture age was very important: the more senior a man got, the more we respected his wisdom and treasured his experience.

The Sergeant was the closest we ever got to the British officers; they were always somewhere in the background, and if not in their offices, they were gathered in small groups, looking over what each company was doing, or down at the papers between them, pointing off in some direction or other, giving orders or instructions to fellow officers, who would in turn run and give these orders to Sergeant Fowler, who would pass them on to the African sergeants, who would in turn give the orders to us. So I used to like sitting on my dry, crumbling log on the edge of the field at night, looking up at the stars, contemplating my world, thinking about Rose, about the future, about how and when would be the best time to approach the subject of marriage, now I was earning a wage and could in time support a wife, but also secretly glancing sideways at them in the officers' mess, as I found them fascinating. Rarely did I see them laugh, or joke around, or see them show emotion like we did, unless there was drink between them, like on the evenings I watched them from my log, after the mess meal, or when they returned from town after socializing at one of their places.

Captain Miller, our company commander, spoke in a more refined way. The captain was a slightly younger version of Mr Charles Archie Smith, our district officer, and although I knew he was green I afforded him respect, for I assumed that he must have some greater knowledge or skill for these white colonials to have put him in charge. But still, although Captain Miller was in charge, I knew that if I had to make a choice between the two men to lead me in battle, I would have chosen the Sergeant. However, this was not wartime but training, and quite frankly I found the Sergeant a very rude and uncouth man indeed.

I think this is the reason why his barrack boys never lasted, for he had a tendency to shout at them, and often in Hausa, which they did not understand, as he had spent a little time training Muslim soldiers in the north before being transferred to the south-east. Well, that and the drink. He was not a pleasant man once full of drink, and every so often, on an evening, he would return from the colonial rest-house drunk, and his boy, as they liked to call the barrack boys – although most of them were fully grown men with families back home to support – would get the worst of his behaviour and insults.

One evening, I was sent to fetch him as they, the officers, had decided to gather earlier than usual due to guests coming for dinner.

I stood outside his quarters, having jogged over. 'Sir, the officers have already gathered in the mess,' I said, short-winded.

'Damn!' he said, getting up from his deckchair. 'Hurry up, boy!' he shouted back at his barrack boy as he went inside to finish dressing. 'Or I'll kick your black arse into tomorrow.'

'Yes, sir!' said the barrack boy, a man of a similar age to my father, as he hurriedly finished pressing his shirt, then took it inside to help the Sergeant dress.

'Not that one, you idiot.'

His voice drifted out from the room. I stood and listened to the Sergeant barking instructions at the barrack boy, who scuttled around fetching whatever it was the Sergeant wanted. A minute later the Sergeant emerged fully dressed, with his khaki army jacket on, trousers pressed to a point, shoes with almost a mirror shine, and headed towards the officers' mess to join the rest of the colonials.

I watched him disappear before turning to the so-called boy, who somehow reminded me of my uncles, and addressing him in our language.

'Why do you let him speak to you like that?' I asked, but heard the stupidity of my question when I said it aloud. I paused, stumbled over my words then rephrased the question: 'I mean, why don't you leave like the others?'

He chuckled a little, looked at me. 'The lizard would like to stand erect, but his tail will not permit him,' he said, uttering an old Igbo proverb.

I wrinkled my brow at him, a little perplexed.

Then he smiled and said, 'One day you will understand,' and proceeded to get back to his duties. As I left, he laughed and shook his head after me.

I continued to the stores to collect a bottle for the meal. An officer had sent me to retrieve it from the store clerk.

'Quick, quick,' he had directed, clapping his hands.

So off I went.

Having collected the bottle, I returned and entered the mess. They had already sat down and were chatting among themselves. It was a surprise to see Mr Smith on the opposite side of the table, but not unusual, as the army and colonial service networked with each other and Mr Smith was an ex-soldier.

I took the wine over to the servers, accidentally eavesdropping on the Captain's conversation. He was sitting behind us at the head of the table, with Mr Smith beside him on the left and Lieutenant Richards on the right. The officer was one of Mr Smith's nephews, transferred from the barracks in Lagos. I recognized him from the days they used to visit Rose's family with Mr Smith, when we were children. His hair was still blond, but not white as it had been back then.

I tried to make eye contact with Mr Smith, but knew he would not notice me. Colonials rarely did, particularly if you were outside the setting they knew you from.

'Well, old chap, I know Arthur from my Cambridge days. A good chap indeed, good with the ladies, too. I read Geography with him, played a little polo with his brother. What's his name? Can't recall the fellow's name. He was one of your lot, based in Lagos.'

'You mean Charles?' said Lieutenant Richards to the Captain, his brow lifting as he asked the question, with a little of a twinkle in his young green eyes.

'Yes, that's it: Charles Ewins,' said the Captain. 'Pleasant enough chap, but didn't think he was suited to the army like his brother. Now, Arthur, his brother, he's an excellent soldier.' Then the Captain turned to Mr Smith and said, 'You know their father.'

'Do I?' asked Mr Smith.

'Yes. Major Thomas Ewins. You know, the one with the pointy moustache.'

'So I do,' said Mr Smith.

I gave the bottle to the head server and quietly left the room.

I settled into army life. It was tough, but somehow I got through the basic training. I got used to the scraping of my head, not a strand or spike left, as bald as the barber could possibly get it without removing skin. I had no choice but to line up with the rest of them and begrudgingly pay the Sergeant his fee, which he insisted he collected to compensate the civilian who came in regularly to perform the job. I heard from others that the Sergeant took a size-able commission out of the fee.

We woke at five thirty for morning exercise, ran five miles, did push-ups and sit-ups, all before breakfast. After this we settled into the continuous drills under the scorching sun, which seemed to bully and taunt us with every quick step, slow step, eyes right, eyes left, rifles up, rifles down. The sweat poured from my brow, but I had to ignore it for sheer fear of breaking a command, and the tor-rent of insults that could be levied at me by Sergeant Fowler, or his non-commissioned African subordinates. In those initial weeks, during training, my muscles seemed to ache with the intensity of each new exercise. For although I had been a farmer, and so used to physical activity, I was not used to the relentlessness of it, or the shouting which was done as if we were not human beings. They seemed to shout more the higher the level of education you had, or if you simply showed some sign of intelligence. There were four companies in total in training, and our company was comprised of the most educated; the rest were more or less illiterate, so we seemed to be treated the worst. We did these drills from morning to even-ing, with only a break for lunch. We did them so much it became almost like a dance; I even practised them in my sleep.

If it wasn't march drill, then it was weapons drill, then rifle drill, or bonnet training, or wireless training, and on and on.

I remember the first time I held a gun in my hand. It was strange, even stranger when I fired it. I lay flat on the ground, pointing the gun at the white target board ahead, pulled the trigger and was not prepared for the pull back; it startled me and knocked me off bal-ance, bruised my shoulder.

Sergeant Fowler stood above me, gave a shake of his head, swore under his breath, then shouted, 'I don't know how I'm supposed to train you ignorant sods.'

I was so angered by this that I was determined to master the gun.

The drills were relentless, but thank God for our local non-commissioned officers, who sometimes translated and re-shouted Sergeant Fowler's words, for due to them we were able to master the drills quickly enough. I know this as at the end of six weeks Sergeant Fowler looked surprised at how quickly we had picked them up. I was glad when my training as company clerk and driver started, as this gave me some time away and relief from the midday sun.

I was in the barracks changing my sodden top after exercises before heading out again for lunch in the open with the rest of my company, when I got my brother's scribbled message. One of the barrack boys from the Captain's office brought the letter. He waited while I opened up the paper and read it. I did not know what to do with the information disclosed within the letter. I wondered about Rose, about her father, and the arrangements that needed to be made, about how best to get home in time for the funeral. I was in that state of contemplation when the barrack boy cleared his throat and informed me that the Captain wished to see me in his office. This in itself shocked me, so I walked down the hall and knocked on his door with trepidation.

'Come in, Private.'

I walked into the room, my head slightly bowed, cap in hand. It was a simple room, cool, its walls bare concrete with red-painted floors. The Captain sat behind a wooden desk, a filing cabinet to his left, the window behind him and young Lieutenant Richards standing almost on guard to his right. He was a tall fellow, just like his uncle.

'Lieutenant Richards here tells me that the former warrant chief of your village has just lost his wife.'

'Yes, sir,' I said, wondering how Lieutenant Richards knew this, and why Sergeant Fowler wasn't in the room.

'Sad state of affairs,' he said, then looked down at a letter on his desk. 'Sorry to hear. Well, I have a letter from Mr Smith here.'

'Yes, sir.'

By this time I knew that Mr Smith and Captain Miller knew each other well. So it was not unusual that my captain should have correspondence from Mr Smith. But what was unusual was me being called to his office, and him sitting there talking to me directly, without the message being sent through Sergeant Fowler, and then on down through his subordinates. But even more than this, what struck me as peculiar at the time was why Mr Smith was concerning himself with such matters. But this was fleeting, and quickly pushed aside, as Rose's father and Mr Smith were to some extent like family friends.

'Mr Smith has requested, if it is possible, for you to pick up Mr Okoro's daughter, Rose, at the truck park in Onitsha and take her to the family home.'

'Yes, sir,' I said, wondering how best I was going to do this, for it was a bit of a journey using the mammy trucks, even longer if I collected her by bicycle to travel from Onitsha to the village.

'You can take an army vehicle for the purpose, but be back here ready to report for duty at eight a.m. sharp on Wednesday morning.'

'Yes, sir.'

'We need the vehicle for special operations.'

'Thank you, sir.'

And so it was that my superior gave me leave to attend the funeral, but also to pick up Rose from the truck station and accompany her home. He had also loosely known Rose's mother from the work she did on women's associations; some of the members were market women and soldiers' wives.

I waited at the bus station to collect her, looked at my watch a thousand times; she was very late that day. She was meant to arrive at one, but didn't turn up till after three. As I waited I fidgeted with my uniform, fixing my collar, my cap, the sleeves, looking at myself in the wing mirrors of cars and trucks. Rose had never seen me in uniform; I wanted to look my best, make a good first impression. I hoped she would find me dashing, hoped that the uniform made me look important, like someone with something doing.

The last time I had seen Rose had been over six months ago. Then, I had been bent over harvesting the land; I had heard the car speeding along the road first, then the car horn, and from the sound of the engine I knew it might have been Michael driving his father's car recklessly again, so I had stood up to see him, but instead saw Rose waving at me from the passenger's side as they drove by. Uche was in the back, looking a little subdued, as usual. I guessed they were on their way to the bus station.

We, Rose and I, had argued over the weekend, so I had not been in the mood to say my goodbyes to her, but as they passed, seeing her smile at me out of the car window, I could not hold my anger at her for long, so I waved and smiled back.

At the weekend I had squeezed through the partition, like I always did as a child. Waved at her mother and father sitting on the front veranda talking quietly to each other. Then made my way round to the back to find her sitting there by the fireside, like she used to as a child, but this time she was alone, her brothers inside. I took my seat beside her. I knew she was in one of her moods that night, so I waited for it to pass, for her to reach out and talk to me, but instead she seemed to get angrier, shifting and agitated, poking the coal in the fire a little harder as we sat.

'What do you want?'

'I just came to see you before you leave tomorrow.'

'Couldn't you have changed your clothes?'

I looked down at what I was wearing; it was no different to what I normally wore on an evening. 'My clothes?'

'Yes.'

'What's wrong with them?' I asked, looking down again and pulling on them.

'Why do you always have to look so wretched? Why can't you find something doing other than that farm?'

I was silent for a little while, confused, then said, 'What's wrong with you?'

She stopped, opened her mouth as if to say something, but then her shoulders slumped and her eyes glazed with what I assumed to be frustration, and I saw her withdrawing inside herself, so I asked again.

She shook her head. 'Nothing.' Then, as if she had a change of mind, she said, 'My mother wants me to marry straight after school.'

'Why so soon?'

'I don't know.'

'Did she tell you who she wants you to marry?'

'No. But that's not the point.'

'Sorry, what is the point?'

She was silent again.

So I pushed her a little more.

'There's got to be more. Obi, tell me there's more,' she said, looking up at me, seeking an answer.

I scratched my head. 'But isn't that what most girls want, to be married?'

She turned her face away, continued poking at the fire.

'But not you? So what do you want?'

'Obi,' she said, still looking at the fire, 'I don't know.' She turned to me and smiled sadly. 'Obi?'

'Yes.'

'Do you remember when we were children?'

'Yes.'

'When my father used to send me on errands to drop off notes or letters at Michael's father's house, and you used to tag along with me?'

'Vaguely. I don't recall the errands, but I remember we used to go over there to play.'

'Well, do you remember his father's office, the one where he saw patients on clinic days, where I used to help out?'

'No.'

'Well, maybe you boys were too busy playing and fighting in their backyard. I used to like going over there to peek in on his father's office. I remember you boys were always so rowdy when you played, you hardly missed me when I disappeared. Well, I used to like peeking in when the door was left ajar and there was no one else around. There were so many things to see; I recall there was a skeleton in the corner, and I remember a blue globe on his desk, and books that just seemed to go on for miles.'

'And?'

'I used to – when his father wasn't in – like to go in and run my fingers over his books, imagine all the knowledge and places they contained. His father caught me once and . . .'

'And what?'

'I was just thinking, that's all.'

'Would it be so bad, marriage?' I said.

She looked at me incredulously.

'I mean,' I said, and cleared my throat, 'I mean, what if . . . if I was the one?' I put my hand over hers, which was resting on the bench beside her, looked into her eyes and said, 'What if it was me?'

For a moment we sat on that bench looking at each other, and as if my words had sunk in, she jumped up and laughed nervously.

'Why are you laughing?'

'Are you serious?' she asked, looking down at me.

'Well, I . . .'

'You can't seriously think my parents will consider you?' she asked. 'You're still a boy, and besides, have you looked at yourself?'

I looked down at my clothes and my tattiness.

'You don't look like you could rub two guineas together, let alone think about marrying a wife.'

I looked at her looking back at me, and for the first time I saw myself through her eyes. I could not find words, for I knew there was truth in what she said. It cut deep, so instead I closed my mouth, looked at her and lied. 'Well, I was only thinking about you, that is all, just trying to solve your problem.'

'Oh. Thank God for that! I thought you were serious for a minute.'

'No,' I said, shaking my head. 'No!'

'Good, because you really need to sort yourself out before you even think about that. You can't farm that little plot of land all your life.'

I was silent while she rattled on. For the first time I saw myself the way she saw me and didn't like the reflection, didn't like the fact that in her eyes I was a joke. I stayed a little longer with her just so it didn't look like I was running away, but inside I died so many deaths. Until I came to the realization, in that moment, while sitting at that fireside, pretending I was OK, that something had to change, that I was going to have to change. And although she did not know it, I made up my mind that she was going to be mine. That I was going to be the sort of man she could not laugh at. So that was why, late that summer, I joined the army.

8

A Better Way

Rose disembarked from the mammy truck that day at a little past three. I saw her in the distance stepping down, the conductor giving her a hand to jump gently to the ground, and like on the days I looked up to see her climbing our mango tree, she jumped off the truck just as beautiful, but this time a womanly kind of beautiful, which called to the man in me. Then she waited for her luggage, which the conductor put down beside her, and stood searching me out in her black mourning dress, with a belt that pulled her in at the waist, black heeled shoes, a black bag and gloves to match. Her hat sat pretty on her curled hair, with her dark-red lipstick perfectly in place. I looked at her and couldn't decide which one I loved more: my Nkem, who I fell in love with up in our mango tree as a child all those years ago, or this modern woman standing there before me now that I was a man. I adjusted the fit of my jacket, straightened my back and walked towards her, and as I walked I saw her head still moving around, looking for me somewhere beyond me, and I knew she did not recognize me.

'Rose?'

'Obi?'

I smiled back at her.

'Is that you?'

I smiled again, bent to pick up her luggage from the ground.

'Oh dear Lord, when did you join the army?'

'Six months ago,' I said, and took her by the elbow to lead her to the car.

'I didn't recognize you,' she said as we weaved our way through the other people in the yard.

'Do I take that as a good or bad thing?'

She smiled, remembering our last conversation. 'A good thing,' she said.

I quickly put her luggage in the boot, then came round to open the car door, smelt her sweet perfume as she lowered herself into the passenger seat.

'I don't see you for a few months . . .'

I made my way to the other side of the car.

'. . . and you go and join the army,' she said.

I smiled a third time, started up the engine and headed out of the yard; the crunch of the tyres driving over gravel and dirt rang in my ears. I took another quick look at her in the seat beside me as I drove out of Onitsha on to the main road leading to our village. The thick grassland, trees and bush were now on either side.

Everything about her was perfect, not a hair out of place, not a crease on her dress, despite days of travelling, but I noticed a strain around her mouth as she smiled at me. I watched her open her bag and take out a cigarette, noticed a small ring with a jaguar on her right hand.

'I hope you don't mind?' she asked, holding the cigarette to her mouth.

I shook my head. 'No, of course not,' I said, as if it was the most normal of things for her to do, as if this was the sort of thing that our girls did. I looked away, straight on to the road ahead, tried to hide my shock. Then stole a quick glance back again, decided it must be the strain of losing her mother.

She tapped the cigarette twice on the back of her bag which lay flat on her lap, then bent her head slightly to take a drag as she lit it, and puffed the smoke towards the gap at the top of the window.

'You won't tell?' she asked.

I understood her request and nodded.

'What's that?' I asked.

'What? Oh, this, just a ring,' she said, 'a puzzle ring,' then proceeded to take it off and put it in her bag. 'So when exactly did you join the army?'

'Not long after you left.'

'Oh,' she said and gazed back out of the window.

'What do you think?'

'What do I think of what?'

'Of the uniform.'

'I'm sorry,' she said, then turned her head to look me up and down. 'You look handsome.'

I laughed, then focused on the road. 'So how have you been?'

'As well as can be expected. How are my family and the preparations?'

'Your father is struggling a little, but your aunties have come and the elders are helping and working things out. But they still need you.'

'Yes,' she said and fell silent, staring out of the side window, as if she was trying to stop the tears.

We drove along in that silence. All the while the atmosphere got thicker, and she seemed to get paler and paler.

'Please, stop the car.'

'What?'

'Stop the car.'

I pulled in where I could beside the thick grassland.

She immediately jumped out. I saw her run to the edge of the bush. A car passed us, and on the opposite side of the road a group of women walked by carrying loads back from the market. I watched her bend and throw up. I got out of the car to help, but at the same time, although I didn't know exactly what it was, something about it felt familiar. 'Are you OK?' I asked.

But she threw up some more, then waited a little to make sure there wasn't more to come.

'Can I help?' I asked while handing her my handkerchief.

'Thank you,' she said and wiped her mouth.

'Are you all right?'

'Yes. Yes, of course, must have been something I ate,' she said, but her eyes didn't meet mine.

I nodded, followed her back into the car.

She sat quietly, her arms folded.

'You OK?'

She nodded.

I started up the car again, checked for oncoming traffic and drove back on to the road. We remained in silence the rest of the journey.

That afternoon I dropped her off at her father's compound and went in my uniform to visit old friends and family from around the village. Clapped my hands twice outside each hut and dwelling, to be greeted with shrieks of delight. Chairs and palm wine were brought out in celebration of my return and, of course, in honour of my fine uniform.

So I was slightly drunk when I made my way back through the village; it was dusk and I thought I spotted Rose, with a friend, with Uche, holding a small kerosene lamp in the distance. I shouted out to them, but they did not hear; they suddenly veered off the path into the bush, on to a much smaller dirt path, and in my half-drunk state I decided to follow them.

The path got narrower, the bush denser, as I walked along, until all I could make out in the distance was the little light from their kerosene lamp. And as I searched the darkness ahead for the spot of light, a tree branch, or some other type of vegetation, would hit me in the face. I stumbled a few times as the ground was uneven and covered with thick shrubs and broken branches. I do not know why my drunk self did not turn back at the beginning, but the deeper I followed the light from their kerosene lamp, the more I became afraid that I would not find my way back out again. Finally, the small light disappeared, I felt a little panic, and I stopped where I was to really search the bush ahead. My eyes adjusted and I could make out a bigger light in the distance flickering on the ground; I assumed it to be from an outside fire at a homestead. My ears adjusted too, and I heard up ahead a woman's voice greet them in the dark, and knew for certain that there was a dwelling there. I recognized the woman's voice as Mama Nkoli's.

I hid in among the vegetation, stared at them from my hiding place. I could make out Rose, Uche and Mama Nkoli from the edge of the bush. The light from the outside fire illuminated them as they spoke. And I suddenly sobered up. Mama Nkoli was notorious for sorting out women's problems. I was a mere five-year-old boy when I remember making such a night visit with my older sister and an older female cousin. They had used me as cover and lied about me getting lost in the bush. My cousin had rolled around in agony for days afterwards, and has never been the same since. Then, I thought of Rose in the car as we drove back home, blowing smoke out of the window, her hand shaking slightly, remembered her bent over, throwing up by the roadside, and, having grown up in a compound filled with women and children, a part of me knew. Shock mixed with anger, but still I did not want to believe it was true.

They went into the hut.

I could not help myself. I ran from the bush. Called her name. Yanked the material covering the opening of the hut aside. All three sat on a mat in front of me. They looked back in shock.

'Rose!' I shouted.

She stared back. Her eyes glazed with tears, and the answer I did not want to see was in her gaze.

'Rose!'

'This is no place for you,' said Mama Nkoli. 'This is no place for a man.'

I ignored her, turned to Rose, wanting to know who the father was, but there was something about her that looked defeated. I had never seen her that way before, and the desire to protect her took over as I knew Mama Nkoli's was not the safest place, had heard rumours, including of the troubles my cousin now had, and so I said, 'Rose. Please, come.' I reached out my trembling hand to her, felt Mama Nkoli pulling on my other arm.

'Obi, please just go,' said Uche.

'Rose, come with me,' I begged. 'Please!'

She sat up as if contemplating my words.

'There is a better way,' I said.

She stared back at Uche, at Mama Nkoli, then I grabbed her arm, pulled her up from the ground where she knelt with all sorts of things laid out in front of her. I dragged her out of the hut, dragged her away, into the bush, back into the vegetation. Mama Nkoli and Uche stood behind us, screaming for me to let her go.

It was only after a while that I realized I did not know where I was going and stopped to assess my surroundings. Rose's crying rang in my ears and I let go of her arm and stood silent.

I looked back at her; she knelt on the ground crying, rubbing her wrist.

'I'm sorry,' I said, 'really sorry.'

She continued kneeling there. I knelt beside her, put my arms around her, kissed her head.

'There has to be a better way,' I said. But her shoulders shook.

'Is there?' she said, looking up into my eyes.

I sensed she wanted me to give her another way out, so I said, 'Yes, there is. Come,' and I reached out to her.

She looked at my hand like she was contemplating whether it was a good idea to take it.

'Come,' I said again.

She grabbed my hand and stood up.

'Do you know how to get out of here?'

'Yes,' she said, and led the way.

When we got to the main path and I orientated myself by my surroundings, we walked home in silence. I accompanied her to her veranda, stood looking up at her as she went to go in.

'Trust me,' I said, 'there is a better way.'

I didn't know what it was at the time, but I was convinced that there was a better way than putting herself and her future at risk.

'But Obi . . .'

I reached up, put my finger on her lips and silenced her. 'We can talk about this tomorrow. It is late. You still have time to go back to Mama Nkoli's if you decide to before I drive you back to Onitsha on Tuesday. But let us talk in the morning.'

She nodded and I watched her as she entered her parents' home and closed the door behind her.

I watched her go and hoped that sleep would give me the answer.

9

My Little Nkem

T HE BURIAL WAS simple, well attended by most of the people in the village.

Rose's aunts washed her mother's body in the morning, so I was told. They rubbed her down with camwood, as is our custom, dressed her in her finest clothes, then placed chalk marks in Nsibidi script on her hands and head for the next life. Her mother's people came playing the drums to pay their respect, and the women elders of our village came wailing in empathy at their joint loss.

It was strange looking down on her mother lying there in state, her head surrounded by white fabric, her eyes closed as if asleep in the middle of their front parlour. Rose's mother looked like the woman I had known in life, and yet again not. Her skin was so much darker than I remembered. I filed past the coffin like the other mourners, paying my last respects. They had taken out their furniture and replaced it with benches that lined the walls. Rose sat with her brothers on the right. I reached out to console them as I went past, circled the coffin, before heading back out of the front door, the curtain taken down for the occasion, and walking again on to their veranda and into their yard.

*

We, Rose and I, had met in the very early morning when all were busy with morning chores and preparations for the funeral. I had signalled to her from across the fence, and we had met in the dark shadow of the mango tree, talked in quiet whispers.

'How are you feeling?'

'Fine,' she said, then looked back at her father's house, and back again at me, like she was afraid of being overheard.

So, I said no more.

We stared into each other's eyes. I could see her tears begin to build, and I remembered that night my mother died, when she was there for me, so I pushed aside my disappointment and reached out. We stood in the darkness and I squeezed her hand tight. I did not know whether her tears were for her dead mother, the predicament she found herself in, or both. But I could feel fear, uncertainty, in the hand that I held. I waited for her trembling to subside, wondered at this Rose I saw before me, remembered the sophisticated one who had sat in the car smoking like a movie star the day before.

'You OK?'

She nodded, gave a sad laugh.

Then there was silence while I mustered up the courage to ask her the real questions that needed to be asked.

'How did it . . . happen?'

She looked down.

Silence.

I cleared my throat. 'How far gone are you?'

'Two months,' she barely whispered.

'Two months? Whose . . . Who is the father?'

Then I felt her pull her hand away, her chin jolt up, and Nkem was back.

I tried again. 'Who is the father?'

'It's not your concern,' she said, taking a step away from me and folding her arms across her chest.

'I am only trying to help.'

'So help,' she spat back, and unfolded her arms, placed her hands on her hips.

I looked down at my shoes.

'Last night . . . you said . . . you said there was another way. What other way?' She looked up and searched my eyes.

I could see her wanting me to save her, and suddenly the gravity of the situation overwhelmed me and I stammered, 'I . . . I just meant . . . there's . . . there's always a better way.'

Her face changed and she looked into my eyes in anger. 'You dragged me through the bush to tell me this?'

'I . . .'

'Are you trying to ruin my life?!' she said through clenched teeth.

'No.'

'Then . . .'

'Hush, keep your voice down, your father will hear,' I said.

She looked at me, then back at her house, lifted her hand up at me, the other on her hip, went to say something, thought better of it, and then turned and walked away.

'Rose!'

They buried her mother in a corner of their yard, under her favourite tree. Our Anglican priest, Reverend Nwachukwu, said his prayers as they put her in the ground. They killed a goat, which they used to feed their guests. The women, including those from my household and the Umuada, out-cooked themselves. And when all was done, they took Rose with her siblings to shave their heads for their year of mourning. She emerged a little while later on to the veranda, no longer that modern woman I had picked up from the station, or the one who had gone away to school, or the one who had stomped off that morning, but my little Nkem. Her head bald, the skin shining like it did when she was a child and it was freshly shaved. She looked just like the girl who laughed and climbed and ran with me through our yards with rattling cans in tow. My beautiful Nkem. I stood to the side looking at her, as she curtseyed in front of each elder, paying respect. I watched her and wondered what had happened – how did she, a respectable girl, get herself into such a predicament? – wondered about the type of life she lived there in Lagos, remembered her smoking and wondered did I even know this woman making her way through the guests. I knew what would be the outcome if they – the elders, her father – should find out this news, and I wondered why the hell I had intervened the previous night.

She made her way back to her father's veranda, sat down and looked out on the people in the yard.

I walked over, looked up at her diamond face, her brow crinkled as she gazed over the heads of the guests to something in the distance, far away.

I tried to see what she was looking at, but there was nothing there. 'Are you OK?'

She looked down, nodded, then gave a sad laugh.

'I'm sorry,' I said. And in that 'sorry' I was saying sorry about the night before, about her mother, and for the many things that were to come once her family heard her news.

She laughed again drily, then lifted her hand to her bald head.

'It will grow back.'

'Will it?'

'Yes, it will. You'll be fine,' I said.

'Will I?'

I was silent, did not know how to respond, for I knew what she was really asking. I saw her father's anger, the backlash from the elders and the rest of our village, and before I knew it, the words had come out of my mouth.

'You know, despite everything, you're still beautiful.'

I hoped she understood what I was trying to say, but I heard the words, listened to them like it was someone else speaking them, and I knew them, deep inside, to be true.

I wanted to see her smile, for there was too much sadness in the air. 'You will always be beautiful to me.'

I think, looking back now, that in those words a part of me was letting go, that in that moment I realized that even if I didn't know or understand this Rose, I knew that at the core of her was still my Nkem, and whatever happened, the little girl I fell in love with up in our mango tree would always be beautiful to me.

She laughed another little, sad laugh. 'That's just like you, Obi,' she said, fighting back the tears. 'You always see things in . . . in such simple ways.'

'Do I?'

'Yes. You do.'

'Well, aren't they?'

She laughed again, the tears overflowing.

'What are you two talking about so intently?' interrupted her father.

We both jumped; I had not seen her father join us.

'Nothing, Papa. Nothing. Obi was trying to reassure me that things will be OK,' she said, wiping away a tear from her eye and getting up from the veranda where she sat.

Her father looked at me, and I saw a broken man.

'Thank you, Obi. Thank you for your kindness.'

'Yes, sir,' I said.

'I hope you're right, for I don't think I can take any more of what life has to throw at me right now.'

'Yes, sir.'

'Rose, your aunties need you in the back.'

'Yes, Papa.'

I watched her disappear into the house. I took one last look at her father, knew he was barely standing; I had never seen him like that. I thought of the smiling, joking man who I had seen through the partition greeting Mr Smith of an evening. I wondered about Rose's news, wondered whether this would finally break him, then turned to join the rest of the boys in the yard.

We – Emeka, Ifeanyi, Michael and I – helped out by bringing extra benches from the neighbouring compounds for the guests to sit on, and fetched and carried things as required, while drummers played into the night.

When it was quiet, after returning the benches to their respective owners, the four of us gathered in Rose's yard. We sat on the ground, waiting to see if the family needed us before we dispersed. Our kerosene lamps stood between us; Michael and Emeka leant against our old mango tree, the dry crackled bark pressing rough against their backs. The crickets chirped and creaked, hiding in the dark. The mosquitoes buzzed and sang around our ears. Outside, fires from the neighbouring homesteads flickered through the bushes. We sat fanning ourselves, reminiscing about the days when we were children. The low, encouraging, wise murmurings from the elders sitting beside Rose's father on the porch washed over us.

It was the beginning of the end. Ifeanyi would soon be off with Emeka to find work in Lagos. Emeka was to transfer to nationalist newspaper the *West African Pilot*, which was based in Lagos and run by Nnamdi Azikiwe, a second cousin on his mother's side. Michael, on the other hand, was to follow in his father's footsteps, and would be setting off to Sierra Leone to board his boat to America to study medicine. We sat together watching the last of the mourners.

'How did we get here?' asked Emeka.

Ifeanyi and I looked at him sitting beside Michael and nodded.

'It's the second funeral this month,' he said.

'Our parents are getting older,' said Michael. 'It is our time.'

'Our time for what?' I stupidly challenged him, for Michael had a tendency to make grand statements that on closer examination had little meaning. At the time, I had always thought Michael's talents lay in politics rather than in medicine, but maybe I was not the best person to judge, for there was still so much that I had to learn, and my feelings towards Michael were ever so confusing: on one hand I admired him, and on the other there was a little . . . I don't know, maybe irritation.

Michael rolled his eyes, looked at me and said firmly, 'To make our mark in this world, to add what we will.'

I looked away.

Then Ifeanyi said beside me, 'There is so much to do, to become, there are too many teachers, lawyers and doctors needed in this land. It is daunting.'

I understood his words, for we were both the first generation in our families to receive a formal education, unlike Emeka and Michael, whose parents were educated but to varying levels, Michael's parents being part of the educated elite, the ranks of which I knew all three of us wished to join. And yet in that moment I thought of my grandmother, of her wisdom, for in our village she was often called upon for her guidance and counsel; being an elder, she held the knowledge of our traditions and old beliefs. But beyond our village, out in the new world we were going into, she would be seen as a mere illiterate, which denigrated her, and me by association. I thought back to those days, after our mother's death, when she rocked us to sleep with her sweet lullabies, lullabies that spoke of the past, and of who we were.

'If you did not need money, what would you be?' Michael asked Ifeanyi.

'Maybe a teacher, for we need teachers, or a lawyer to help our people manoeuvre through the confusion of the colonial laws . . . I don't know. All I know is the future of our people depends on us and the decisions we make today,' said Ifeanyi.

I watched him and felt the earnestness in his words.

'And you?' asked Michael, directing his question at me. 'When you have overcome your madness of the army, what do you wish to be, or even become?'

We looked at each other and in that moment I had nothing to say, for it dawned on me that maybe I had no ambition. Well, what I really mean is not like them, for my ambition was much simpler; it had been to marry my childhood love, and this dream was now in pieces. This was not something I was willing to share with them, so I laughed, felt an ache in my chest, bent my head down to hide the turmoil, to think what to say.

'Well,' Emeka interrupted, 'I cannot wait to start at the newspaper . . .'

I watched and fed off his energy, the ambition they all shared for a better world, and inside I thought of Rose and her predicament, and tried to think of a solution, for although I was hurting, she was also a friend and I was very anxious for her. Then it came to me. It was the sight of my father's second wife interrupting the elders and giving Rose's father her condolences before retiring to our yard that finally gave me the solution.

We boys talked on till late. Michael was the first to make his excuses, then Emeka. After a while Ifeanyi and myself decided to call it a night and said our goodbyes.

I mustered up the courage and went in search of Rose in her backyard, but as I went round I saw her and Michael in deep, whispered conversation. I stopped, watched them from afar; something about them seemed more intimate than it should have been. I waited, wanting to interrupt, wondered if Michael could be the father – but when could it have happened? She was all the way in Lagos. I stood watching them and tried to calculate when her last visit home had been, but then I heard Ifeanyi calling me from my yard. I quickly backtracked, hoping they did not see me, returning to my own yard to see what Ifeanyi wanted.

'So what were you and Michael talking about last night?' I asked her that Sunday morning, once again under our mango tree, three hours before we needed to leave for church.

'What are you talking about?'

'I came round at the end of the evening to say my goodbyes and the two of you were in deep conversation.'

'Obi, you can't think—' She looked sideways, like she was thinking of what to say, then continued, 'Look, Michael and I are friends, like we are friends.'

'Is that all?'

'Yes.'

'Are you sure?'

'Of course.'

'It's just the two of you seemed close.'

'He was giving his condolences.'

'Is that all?'

'Of course.'

'Does he know about the child?'

'No!'

'Are you sure he is not the father?'

'Obi!'

'Well?'

'No! Of course not.'

I looked at her and wanted to believe her. Besides, from my calculations, I did not think it was possible for him to be the father; she would have been in Lagos and he here in the east. 'Well,' I said, 'it's just that I have been thinking.'

'About what now?'

'About your predicament.'

'It is no longer your concern, Obi. I am a big girl, I will take care of it.'

'Just listen! I've been thinking.'

'And?'

'Well, I thought the best way forward is for us to marry.'

'To what?'

'Yes, marry.'

'I don't think—'

'Hear me out.'

'I can take care of it myself,' she said.

'It's not that simple. We both know what damage can be done.'

She was silent, looked up at me. 'I am scared, Obi.'

'I know.'

'I didn't want to be there the other night, so when you suddenly appeared I wanted to believe you, wanted to find another way.'

She was silent again, her arms folded around her stomach. 'Obi, why do you want to help me in this way?'

'Have we not always been friends?'

'Yes, we have.'

'So what do you think?'

She was silent for a while, then said, 'It would help get me out of this hole.'

'So?'

'Yes. Thank you.'

'I was thinking we could make the announcement this evening or on Monday, before we leave first thing Tuesday.'

'But Obi, it is not fair on you,' she said. 'This is not your problem.'

'Never mind me. Are we not friends? It will buy you time and take the shame from your father's eyes.'

She nodded, looking down at the ground, contemplating what my offer really meant.

'Besides, remember I can have more than one wife, so the sacrifice is not too great.'

She lifted her head, still sad, and smiled, then said, 'Thank you.'

10

Vicky's

O N THE MONDAY, that last summer when Ifeanyi, Emeka and Michael returned for the funeral, we took one last exploratory trip into Onitsha. But this time, instead of walking or trying to hitch a lift along the trunk road, we went in Michael's father's car. I sat in the back with Ifeanyi, with the windows wound down. Our shirts billowed in the breeze as Michael shouted back at us and merrily sped along. Once or twice I held my breath, as I was convinced he was going to crash into the back of a truck, before he swerved and overtook it. His father had lent him the car to run errands and pick up items from the pharmacy in town, but I wondered if his father knew how reckless a driver he was, as he never drove that way when he was around.

We went to our favourite eating place by the river, called Vicky's. It was no more than a little shanty erection cobbled together from four wooden corner posts, open on all sides with a rusting tin roof above. It was the ideal place to sit and watch the world go by, in the comfort of its shade.

It was way before lunchtime, so relatively quiet. I used to like to watch the river ferries slowly crossing the Niger, bringing the people across from Asaba to the ferry landing below. Loved the sight of the canoe boys gliding by in the background on the water, pushing their produce-laden canoes further downstream to market. Liked to observe the people disembark and make their way up the incline, some carrying huge loads on their heads, while others strolled casually, as if they too had come across to meet friends. And as we sat there drinking our refreshments, I thought about Rose. About how she'd looked that morning when she waved us goodbye from her veranda, when Michael drove by to pick us up.

Michael was the tallest and oldest of us; a dapper chap, he seemed to charm everyone, including our local girls, who lost their sharp tongues and became coquettish whenever he spoke to them. In our parts, among the children of the village he was a little like a movie star, and he spoke English with a slight American twang. Michael was everything I was not: polished, well educated and handsome, with a straight nose like the colonials. The truth is, if we had not been friends from childhood, I doubt whether his family would have allowed him to be friends with us mere locals. I looked over at him laughing and talking away with the others, pointing out a pretty girl or two disembarking from the ferry below.

Emeka sat beside him, Ifeanyi and I half facing them, straddling our benches, so we too could look out on the view while we conversed. I felt the slight breeze cooling my skin, turned around and took a sip from my drink, and secretly watched Michael, his charm, his sophistication, thought of Mr Smith, of Michael's father, and desperately wanted to be like these men, for surely this was the type of man that Rose would want and deserve.

I looked at Emeka hanging on Michael's every word. Remembered the way Emeka had run out on to the road that day, so long ago, when Rose had left for school, or the way, over the years, I would suddenly spy him on the steps of her veranda, and remembered the looks they exchanged when it was time to say goodbye. He was shorter than me, with a gap in his front teeth, a broader nose than mine. I looked at him, and although he was fair, polished in many ways, thought his features to be too local, and so did not even consider that it could have been he who had fathered the child. Then I turned my attention back to Michael.

I pondered the conversation I had secretly walked in on between Michael and Rose two days before. The way Rose had responded to him, I knew instinctively that it was Michael who was really my main concern, and not Emeka. I had a quiet nagging feeling, but what could I do but believe what she had told me, as I had always known Rose to be honest.

I looked towards town, watched the action, the market boys pushing barrows, shouting for people to get out of their way, thoughts of Rose standing on the veranda this morning filling my head. She had looked pretty in her black mourning dress. I wanted to spend more time with her alone, to find out more, but this was practically impossible: with her being female and me being male, it would only have set the village tongues wagging, and especially with Ifeanyi, Emeka and Michael back for this final summer before we embarked on our various life journeys, there were too many goodbyes to say.

I knew that, like me, they too, in their own ways, were in love with her. But if one of them was the father, it would kill me. It was best I spoke to her alone. Being next door meant I could slip through the partition to speak to her later when there was no one else around.

I looked beyond the market, towards the colonial shop and big warehouse, at the white men outside attending to business, then towards the river port in the distance, to the ships and barges docked there, to a colonial standing on top of boxes on a ship, pointing and directing, shouting at a local foreman to do something or other. I marvelled at his command, at the vastness of the barge and the ships and the cranes, felt unease at the primitiveness of the canoes, which glided by in the background. Then looked over at the silvery river that sparkled, the sun's rays reflecting off the moving water. It blinded me a little, so I turned back to face Michael and Emeka.

I cast my eyes down, bowed my head, wondered at these godlike men, their power, their authority and knowledge, looked at the old newspaper on the table in front of me, which I had brought along. It had been given to me by Rose's father that morning, after he was done with reading it himself. A ritual he had begun to carry out whenever I was home, as soon as he had found out I also liked to read the papers. And once I was done with it, I used to hand it back to Rose's mother, and occasionally to my father's wives, to make use of it either in the kitchen for wrapping food in, or for some other purpose. On the front page there was news of the impending war in Europe. I began to read.

'Obi.'

I did not hear him calling me at first.

'Obi.'

He snapped his fingers at me.

'Sorry.'

'I don't understand why you are continuing to follow this news so closely,' said Michael.

'It's important,' I replied. 'Besides, I am in the army.'

'Yes, indeed. Only God knows why you were stupid enough to sign up.'

Ifeanyi coughed loudly, twisted in his seat and said, 'Listen, is it really necessary to talk to him in that way?'

'I am only pointing out what we are all thinking,' said Michael. 'Even you, Ifeanyi, had enough sense not to sign up to their army, yet look at Obi here, whose mother died at their hands.'

'Michael, leave Obi alone,' said Emeka.

'What? Let's not talk about his stupidity?' said Michael.

'Look, we are meant to be having a good time,' said Emeka.

But Michael continued, 'I watch you sitting there smiling, looking admiringly at every white man that walks by, while you ignore the plunder going on behind you.'

'What are you talking about?'

Michael laughed. 'The problem with you, Obi, is you are like a man grateful to a thief who knocks on your door to sell you cheap shiny trinkets, and meanwhile, you are so engrossed that you don't notice your home being ransacked and emptied of its belongings behind you.'

I looked around, spread my arms wide, revealing the sights behind me to the rest of them, and said, 'All I see are the ships and docks they built.'

Michael shook his head and said, 'One thing, my friend: our colonial masters are business-minded, so rest assured that these things would not have been built if there was not a lot more for them to gain.'

I opened my mouth to speak but Ifeanyi interrupted.

'Listen, old chaps, I just came for some food and beer,' he said. 'Not really in the mood for this; it's our last visit here before we go our separate ways.'

'You're right,' said Michael. 'Just ignore me. In that case, let's raise a toast.'

I was relieved to see him calm down so quickly.

'A toast? To whom?' asked Ifeanyi.

'To us. This is our last time here before we head off in our various directions.'

'That's right,' said Emeka. 'Obi is now in the army; Michael, your father is sending you off to America to study medicine; and I am off to Lagos to work at the *West Pilot*.'

'Yes, a toast,' said Michael, 'to us.'

'To us indeed,' chorused Emeka and Ifeanyi.

Michael and I remained silent for a second, defiant, as we gazed at each other, then lifted our glasses. 'To us.'

On our way back we passed the shops owned by the white colonials. There was something in the air; they seemed distracted, unsettled. They did not have that all-knowing look about them like they usually did. And as we passed by shopfronts I overheard a conversation between one of the owners and his workers.

'Why are you all sitting there like fools? Do you not know there is a war coming?' said the white colonial.

The men dusted themselves off and got up from where they sat to re-enter the shop and get on with their work.

Then I heard one say to another in Igbo, in a hushed tone once the colonial had disappeared inside, 'And so? What has it got to do with us?'

'What do you mean?' said the other.

'What has the white man's war got to do with me?'

The other said, 'Well, if there is war, there is war. This Hitler fellow, who is he? Is he not white like them?'

As my father was away at the mines, I made our announcement later that evening to my uncles, who were at first sceptical about my determination to marry Rose. They initially objected due to my age, but once I convinced them of my seriousness, and that she had already said yes, this was met with great approval, for Rose was from a very good family indeed. The truth is, in normal circumstances this match would have been a lot more difficult, but these were not normal circumstances.

I told them that Rose and I would be travelling back to our jobs in Lagos and Enugu in the morning; we might not be able to get time off for maybe a month but would want to marry then, so were keen to get her father's approval as soon as possible. They understood the urgency, but felt that it was not the right time to approach her father due to the burial of her mother that weekend. So, as my father was away in the mines, we made arrangements for them to visit her father the following weekend to register our family's interest in Rose, and they dutifully agreed.

In the early morning of the next day I drove Rose to the truck station in Onitsha. We stood beside the army vehicle that had been loaned to me, saying our awkward goodbyes. I cleared my throat and said, 'In a month's time – we will marry then?'

'Yes,' she replied.

'Will you be able to get the time off?'

'I will have to,' she laughed. 'I want to be married before I start showing.'

'Yes, of course.'

She lifted her hand to dust something off my uniform. 'In a month, then,' she said.

I nodded. 'And, Rose, don't worry; everything will be OK.'

She laughed a little again. 'Thank you, Obi,' she said. 'You know, you've always been able to make me feel better, even when we were children.'

'Everything will be all right. Am I not right?' I asked.

She paused, then said, 'As usual, you always see the world in such simple terms.'

'Well, the world is simple.'

'Is it? Is it really?' she said as she looked up directly into my eyes, questioning, as if she needed to understand my logic.

'Yes, it is.'

She looked away as if she wanted to cry, bit her lip and stared into the distance. 'Sometimes you can be so green.'

'Rose?'

'Don't mind me,' she said as the tears began to stream down her face, then took a handkerchief from her bag, wiped her eyes and plastered on a smile. 'A month it is, then,' she said, reached up to kiss me on the cheek, then walked away.

And so I watched her board the mammy truck on her journey back to Lagos. I stood aside and waved as it pulled out of the yard, the gravel crunching beneath the wheels. She looked back at me and smiled as the truck went by. I watched it disappear on to the road, leaving a trail of dust behind. Little did I know, so little did I know of what was to come.

11

Wedding

I SETTLED BACK IN at the army barracks in Enugu, and at the weekends – not often, mind – I walked the hour it took to visit my father at Coal Camp.

My first ever visit was out of duty. After all, sons were expected to check in on their fathers, and as I was to be married I thought it best to tell him face to face. Besides, I could not go home and say to my uncles and grandmother that although we lived in the same town, we did not see each other, and therefore I had not informed him of my news. It was hard to find him on my first visit, among the bush houses, uneven paths and natural gullies that made up the camp roads. I stopped many a man as they walked by, asked them if they had heard of a Mr Nwogo and did they know where he lived, but to no avail. I went deeper into the camp, passed by the migrant miners' dwellings, jumped over wide ridges in the ground, wondered why I had even decided to come and find him in the first place. But I got lucky, the gods were kind, for one of my father's friends saw me pass by, stopping people, and as I am almost the exact replica of my father, he guessed I must be his son, and led me to his dwelling.

'Obi, is that you?'

'Yes, sir.'

He laughed, and called his friends to come and meet his son, the third-born of his children. It was the first time I had ever known my father to introduce me with such pride. It was almost as though in this setting he was a different man. And for the first time we sat outside his dwelling, on chairs he had brought out, side by side, man to man, watching the world go by, calling greetings to men he knew as they passed by, and every so often he called them over to introduce me to them.

'How is the army, my son?'

'The army is the army,' I said and leaned back in the chair, looking out at the rest of the camp.

'You look well.'

'Do I?' I said, and lifted my arm to stretch the knots from my shoulders, caused by the daily drills and exercises.

'Yes, you do,' he said in earnest.

I was silent, bowed my head to look at the ground, to give me time to think what to say, for that was the first time that I had ever sat side by side with my father, watching the world go by. It was strange, but despite this, felt the most natural thing to do. He sat back relaxed in his chair, like he wasn't the man who never spoke when we were at home, and whose only form of talk was through the cane.

'Take some,' he said and nudged a bottle of schnapps with a glass perched on top towards me.

'I don't drink spirits.'

'Take,' he said again.

I went to reject his offer but decided it was best to take some and pretend. I did not want to change the new mood between us.

So we sat in silence on our chairs that first visit, not saying a word, passing the schnapps between us. And when I saw that the day was beginning to end and I could not delay it any more, I cleared my throat.

'Rose and I are to marry.'

He stopped midway while lifting a glass to his lips. 'Really?'

'Yes. She agreed last time we were home.'

He made a face. 'And what does her father say about this?'

'I don't know; your brothers are calling on him tomorrow.'

He laughed. 'I am sure he will politely entertain them and curse them once they are gone.' He laughed again and then slapped me on my back. 'Well, my son, you do aim high.'

'I thought I'd best let you know.'

He laughed once more. 'Thank you,' he said, picking up the bottle, 'then let's make a toast,' and poured some on the ground for the ancestors to partake of, and some into my glass and his. 'To her father's response,' he added, laughing even more.

'To her father's response,' I echoed, a little irritated.

We downed our drinks, looking at each other above the rim of our glasses, his eyes challenging me on Rose's father's reaction to the news.

'It is getting late,' I said, getting up and dusting myself off. 'I must go. I will come back again another time.'

He nodded, got up and walked me part of the way, to a point where I could get my bearings, then waved me goodbye.

That is how I began to build a relationship with my father, to start to understand him and see him through adult eyes. Every so often I would visit him, take a little of what he liked to drink with me, and each time we sat side by side on the chairs he brought out and watched the world go by. I began to understand what I had not in childhood: that my father only knew how to be a father to men and did not know how to speak the language of children.

My uncles sent a message, and, as my father had predicted, Rose's father was not happy with the match. That was until Rose turned up a week before we were due to marry, to show him the urgency of the situation. Rose told me there was much anger and many words thrown at her that day. She could not bring herself to tell him the whole truth: that I was not the father. So, he always blamed me for his daughter's downfall. From that day on he always spoke to me through others, even when we were in the same room, right up to the day we soldiers packed the trucks and left, not knowing if we would return home alive.

He had no choice but to agree to the match, one that he told me in anger, the day before the wedding, was far beneath her, but I held my tongue, for Rose's sake.

I stood in his front parlour and clenched my teeth while he went on, dutifully bent my head so he could not see my eyes, cap in hand, and just at the point when I could not take any more, and I opened my mouth to tell him the truth, Rose came in and broke up everything with her crying. Her father sat down and reclined in his chair, looking ahead, while Rose knelt with her head on his lap, sobbing. Her crying must have moved him, for suddenly he put out his hand and patted her on the head, before he finally gave his blessing.

The wedding took place on a bright sunny Saturday morning. Everything seemed right with the world, and although our marriage was an arrangement, to protect her, I think that deep inside I held a small hope that everything would work out.

That morning I shaved the sides of my head, made a single side parting with a razor and wore my uniform for full effect. I looked in my father's cracked and mottled mirror, which I had borrowed from him the night before, and was pleased.

My uncles arrived early and my father toasted the success of the events of the coming day. He was proud of me obtaining such a good match for the family and that we would soon be related, at least by marriage, to Rose's father, our former warrant chief.

I followed the entourage; the youngest of my brothers carried the drink, cola nut and items for the bride price on their heads at the back. My father and his eldest brother led the way. We clapped our hands outside Rose's father's parlour door. They beckoned us in. Five of us entered for the proceedings; the rest remained in the yard with the other guests.

It was exactly six weeks to the day since we had buried her mother, and she was beginning to show, but maybe it was only her father and I who noticed, for I noticed everything about her that day. The loose clothing she wore to cover her belly from prying gazes, the sadness that sat around her eyes, how smooth her skin felt when my hand brushed hers as she passed me the cup to drink from, the smile that didn't reach her eyes as she tried to pretend that it was the most joyous of days, the grateful glance she cast my way when it was all done.

Rose's father was subdued, quiet throughout it all.

And on our wedding night we sat in my hut, on the bed opposite each other. She sat at the head, I at the foot. The air was static, the silence awkward. I saw her look around, at the dirt floor at her feet, gingerly spread her fingers above the old sheet that covered the mattress, the best of my sheets, then recoil, look up at the ceiling, then down at the few shabby possessions that I had stacked in the corner, and begin to cry.

For the first time I looked around the hut as she was doing, the place that we – my brother, sister, grandmother and I – had shared for years, that had been a place of solace after my mother was killed, and in that year they had taken the men to work the roads and we almost starved, and felt shame.

In all the years we had played together I had never thought of our differences, but there in that room, on our wedding night, I looked around and saw the room as she did.

I felt the bed shake with her crying and reached out to comfort her. My hand hovered over her shoulder, but no words came; I hesitated, then withdrew it, felt the weariness move through me. I sat at the edge of the bed, not looking at her, but listening to her sobbing. I picked up my blanket.

'You have the bed,' I said to her, and made a place for myself on the mat on the floor, covered myself with the blanket, turned my back on her and looked straight at the dirt walls of my mud hut while she sobbed.

'I'm sorry, so sorry, Obi,' she said.

But eventually, I heard the creak of the bedsprings as she lifted her legs on to the bed, fully clothed, and fell asleep on the edge.

Then I turned on to my back, looked up at the thatched roof and wondered how this was going to work.

12

War Ahead

THE RADIO HAD arrived early in 1939. It sat on Rose's father's veranda for special broadcasts and was the only one for miles around. The villagers sometimes liked to gather in his yard to listen to the occasional programme transmitted directly from the BBC in England. After the initial excitement at the new entertainment, life had continued as usual in the village.

All during the summer months we continued to hear rumours that there was a war brewing in Europe. At the time it did not mean much, just something that was happening over there, across the seas. And although by then I had been in the army for almost a year, naively I did not truly comprehend what it had to do with us; besides, my mind was preoccupied with other things. But I understood this much: this Hitler chap was not good news.

I was almost twenty that summer and Rose almost twenty-one. I was a private, waiting for a posting, having completed my training at the 2nd Primary Training Centre in Enugu.

Looking back now, my friends and I might not have fully understood, but I suspect that my grandmother did. I think she knew what was to come, for whenever I went home to visit Rose, to see how she was coming along, my grandmother was not her usual self. She seemed somewhat agitated, and was always asking me questions on the impending war in Europe.

She and Rose became allies, they gravitated towards each other, and as my grandmother had had many children she was a source of womanly advice now that Rose's own mother had passed.

Each time I came home there were changes in the little hut that I had once shared with my brother, sister and grandmother. New clean curtains at the entrance, a new mattress, a small table and chair to the side where Rose would sit and sometimes write, a sewing machine sat comfortably beside my belongings in the corner. Everything seemed much more organized and neater to my eyes. She seemed much more focused, determined. The crying Rose I had left behind had gone, and in her place was this woman who I felt I knew from long ago somewhere in the shadows.

I watched her working away at her desk, that first long weekend I returned home, knew she had spent the morning helping at Michael's father's clinic and wondered if she was assisting him with his inventory, as she sometimes did.

As the daylight faded she struggled to see. The kerosene lamp flickered, casting shadows across the side of her face, letting off faint fumes which made their way over to me lying on the bed. Its light provided a yellowish glow around the desk, making her look like an angel.

Eventually she stretched and gave up, as the last embers of light had faded in the sky outside almost an hour ago, and she sat at the desk, looking into thin air, deep in thought, fiddling with her jaguar puzzle ring, which was now on a chain around her neck. She was showing much more by then and wore a loose blouse that she must have sewn while I was away.

I lay quietly on the new mattress and starched white sheet,

watching her, listening to the children laughing and clapping along to old folk songs outside by the open fire, like we once did.

'Your ring looks like it should have another part to it,' I said.

'Obi, are you still awake?' she asked, turning slightly in her chair, then listened to the children singing outside on the other side of the compound. She laughed. 'It does.'

'Where is it?'

'Somewhere,' she said, then smiled and turned back to pack away her papers in a neat pile. 'I thought you fell asleep after your journey.'

'I did. What were you writing?'

She hesitated. 'Nothing much. Just a course.'

'A course? In what?'

'It isn't important.'

'I didn't ask whether it was important,' I said, a little annoyed. 'What type of course?'

She walked over to the corner of the room to her trunk, picked up a bundle of white cotton yarn and two needles with the partially made booties she was crocheting for the baby. 'The Cambridge certificate,' she said with her back to me.

'What?' I asked, for I was confused. 'Are you not going to be a mother?'

'Yes, but I thought—'

'How are you going to be a mother and study at the same time?'

'I don't know,' she said, walking towards me. 'I just know this is something I have to do, especially with the baby coming.'

And for some unexplained reason I suddenly said, 'I demand that you stop with this nonsense and focus on the baby.'

She bent her head, laughed a little, gave me a strange look and signalled for me to move over. 'I think you're forgetting this is not a real marriage.' She brought her legs up and leant her back against the wall, her crochet work resting on her lap.

'Obi,' she said, looking down at me and stroking my head.

I looked up into her sweet eyes, her face hovering above mine, felt her hand caress, soothe my temple.

'I have always known you to be different, not typical, so I can't take this sudden change seriously,' said Rose.

I turned my face and looked up at the ceiling, a little frustrated, for although I had set out to help, I truly had not thought things through. I had thought that Rose having the baby of another man would help take away my feelings. I had not imagined the effect that having her so close, in my hut, in my bed, touching my temple, would have on me.

'Don't you know I'm in love with you?' I blurted out.

She was silent for a little while, picked up her work and started crocheting. 'Obi, you're not in love with me,' she said with a sad smile, 'you're in love with the type of love you have seen in the movies.' She then got serious, put down the booties and leant her back against the wall again. 'God, I could do with a cigarette right now.'

'You know that would be an abomination around here.'

'Don't I know it. Don't worry, I am getting pretty good at playing the dutiful wife. I think I've managed to convince your father's wives, especially Nnenna. Your grandmother – she is lovely, and so very helpful, however . . . I know she's a different matter.'

'Mama loves you.'

'Does she? Well, I love her too, have loved her since I was a little girl,' she said, smiling again, 'but she still watches me when she thinks I'm not looking.'

'That is just her way.'

'Is it?'

'Yes.'

'So how long have we to keep this up?'

'I haven't thought that far ahead.'

She nodded. 'I wish we were children again. Our biggest problem then was making it home in time for dinner.'

'Speak for yourself,' I said, remembering the year of hunger, the day I got the news that my mother had been killed, and the subsequent years without her.

'I'm sorry, I forgot.'

Once again the differences between us and our families poked their heads up between us. 'You remind me of my mother,' I said.

'Do I? In what way?'

'There is a strength, a fight about you that reminds me of her.'

'Really?'

'Yes. I watch you sometimes. I see you smile and bow your head like the wind could blow you over, but underneath I know there is a will of rock. It excites me.'

'I'm not sure whether I like your description of me.'

'That time, when I saw you and Michael talking, you never did tell me what you were talking about.'

'Just this and that.'

'There you go again.'

'He was just telling me about his studies in the States.'

'Why would you be interested in that?'

She did not answer and looked away.

'OK, just promise me this: the child you are carrying, promise me it is not his.'

'I promise. It is not his.'

She said it with such earnestness that I believed her. 'Then, we will figure this out together.'

'Have I said a proper thank-you for helping me?'

'No, you haven't.'

'No, I didn't, did I?' She laughed.

'Instead you repaid me by crying throughout our wedding night,' I teased.

'I am really sorry. I *am* grateful,' she said. 'Thank you.'

'The certificate? How are you going to do that and the child? You're due in a few months.'

'I don't know, but what I do know is I will figure it out. It's not the first time I've had to fight to get what I want.'

'Have you had to fight?' I asked, a little perplexed, as to me Rose was very privileged indeed.

'Yes.'

'For what?'

'Do you think I got into QMC Girls' College by accident?' she said, flinching as she felt a kick.

'You all right?' I reached over, put my hand on her stomach, felt the baby kick again. I looked up into her eyes in astonishment. She smiled back at me, her hand over mine.

But then we heard one of my father's wives call her name outside in the yard, and a clap outside the cloth-covered entrance.

'Ms Rose, Mama said you should come and get the food for your husband.'

'Thank you, Chichi. Tell your mother I'm coming,' she said, then turned to me. 'I'd better go and play your dutiful wife,' she joked.

She got up and I watched her waddle out of the hut.

And so it went on. Each time I returned home I left in even more of a muddle, and it always took time to untangle the confusion of emotions inside me. I worked even harder to shake the ache, for I think that with each home visit I fell in love a little more, and a little more. I hoped I would not do, or say, something that I would later regret.

Naivety can lead you deeper and deeper into places a wise man would avoid.

My grandmother, on the other hand, seemed very distracted, like the white colonials. She spent most of her time either eavesdropping on Rose's father's meetings with Mr Smith, the district officer, who arrived more frequently than usual, or searching out news in discarded newspapers, even though she could not read. She pestered me numerous times to read sections from the papers, which she thought contained important information.

I was on a long-weekend leave that September 1939, picking up a few supplies for Rose's baby from a German-owned colonial shop in Onitsha, when I was accosted by two Englishmen as I came out of the store and went round the corner.

'Boy!' shouted one of the men.

I flinched on hearing him, but quickly composed myself. I even contemplated ignoring him, but decided, particularly as I was in civilian clothes, that it might create more problems than it was worth.

'Boy!' he shouted again.

I looked around.

'Over here.'

I had no choice but to cross the road to see what they wanted.

The two men stood beside a black Wolseley. They motioned for me to come over to the driver's side. So I did. One of them leant up against the vehicle, smoking a cigarette, watching passers-by, almost like he was the lookout guy, while the other drew in close.

'Did you notice anything unusual going on inside that store?' he asked. His voice firm, authoritative, like he was used to getting answers.

This in itself was unusual: for one white man to ask me, a native, about the business of another white man. I quietly looked them up and down, and decided that they must be some sort of policemen dressed to look like businessmen. This was not the sort of entanglement I needed. So I smiled my most charming smile. 'Well, sirs, I am glad you asked me that question. Do you know, I was the only man in there buying baby things. Do you think it is right that

I, an African man, should be sent to buy such things? This should be women's business. It is not right. I have a mind to throw this wife out and get a new one. What do you think?'

They looked at each other and one of them asked again, 'Did you see anything unusual in that store?'

'You mean apart from me alone shopping in among the women? No. Is that not bad enough? Do you think I should get myself a new wife?'

'OK, boy, move on.'

'But sirs?'

'Move on.'

And so I did.

It seemed that there was something in the air that weekend, something not quite right, and when I walked past Reverend Nwachukwu on my way back from Onitsha, he told me about the broadcast on Sunday. As I passed by I even overheard some village men, who had gathered on the green near our village church for a gossip, and, I suspect, to get away from the nagging in their households, talking about the broadcast. So, that Sunday, having left Rose at home following a restless night, I headed straight to her father's yard after church to listen to the radio on his veranda.

To my surprise, many people from the village had had the same idea, so when I got there, Rose's father's veranda was already filled with a number of elders sitting on the steps, and around the radio. I climbed our mango tree, as I used to as a child, to look at them and listen to the radio in a little more comfort; the only thing was that as I climbed, three of my younger brothers were already in the tree a little further up, so I took my seat on the first branch. I saw Ifeanyi, Emeka and Michael when they entered the compound, looking at all the people in surprise. After a short delay to his plans, Michael was due to leave for the States on the Monday, the next day. I whistled to them and they came over to join me in the tree.

Our legs dangled and swung from the various branches as we looked down over the yard, waiting; Rose, having rested, was standing by the radio in a flowery cotton maternity top, trying to tune it in. They must have called on her for help. It was past eleven in the morning, but before midday. Her father was in his usual seat, two of her younger brothers standing in the doorway of their house with the curtain closed behind them.

The radio crackled, then we heard the presenter's voice, the elders quietened everyone, and we fell silent and listened.

'This is London. You will now hear a statement by the Prime Minister, Neville Chamberlain.'

His voice was clear above the low crackles. 'I am speaking to you from the cabinet room at 10 Downing Street. This morning the British ambassador in Berlin handed the German government a final note . . .'

I looked over at Ifeanyi; his head was bent, listening intently.

'I have to tell you now that no such undertaking has been received, and that consequently this country is at war with Germany.'

We heard the bells ring out from the radio.

'Now, may God bless you all . . .'

There was silence. A few of the elders shook their heads. And although I sat there with what felt like half my village, it was as if the true impact of that broadcast was on a time delay. I truly did not understand what war in Europe really meant to us all the way over here in Africa, nor, at the time, did I truly appreciate the grave impact that it would come to have on me and my friends. But I think maybe my grandmother understood, because as Rose's father's yard began to empty, and my friends and I waited in the tree contemplating the news, my grandmother continued to sit there in silence, like she was lost in time, somewhere in her own head.

I looked at Ifeanyi, at Emeka and Michael; they smiled back at me while we waited for everyone to depart. We did not realize that this would be the last time we would gather together like this in our tree. We peered down at our elders slowly making their way out of the yard, we chuckled fondly at the sight of them; naively, we looked at them and thought we saw our future too.

Once we had climbed down, I let my friends go ahead, waved them goodbye, and went to check on my grandmother still sitting on the steps of the veranda.

'Are you OK?' I asked.

She looked up at me blankly, shook her head.

'Here, let me help you.'

I put my hand out, helped her get up from the steps.

'Will you be able to make it next door?'

'Yes,' she smiled. 'Obi, you are a sweet boy,' she said and shook her head again, her brow creased, several lines formed on her forehead. 'A very sweet boy.'

I smiled back at her. 'Why are you so sad?'

'My dear Obi, I am an old woman, have seen many things in my lifetime, but it seems the world does not change, just keeps repeating itself.'

'What do you mean?'

'I was a young woman when the last war happened and younger still when the colonials came with their guns and boats to take over our land. And I have lost many people along the way.'

'Yes, but surely this is not our war?'

'Oh, my child. You are too young to remember the last war and the devastation of it. Maybe I have done too good a job of protecting you, so much that you do not understand that what starts over there will eventually make its way here.'

'But . . .'

'But nothing, Obi. Leave the army, leave it before it is too late, go and hide.'

'But, Ma,' I laughed.

'You think my words funny?'

'No!'

'I am too old and too tired,' she said, 'and you are too green. Please listen to me. I do not want you to become a killer of men.' Then she pushed away the hand I was using to help her and waddled off in the direction of our compound.

I watched her, laughed a little, then got serious; I knew from experience that it was best to listen to my grandmother's warnings.

I watched her back as she walked off, a little unsteady, into our compound, her words still ringing in my ears.

13

Fatherhood

Eastern Nigeria, Dry Season, 1939

R OSE GAVE BIRTH three months later.
I was home in time that Friday, just by chance, after travelling on the first truck from Enugu for a long weekend. I got in early, a few hours after her waters broke.

I sat outside the hut, the hot midday sun beaming down, waited anxiously, heard the baby cry as it came out into the world. My uncles patted me hard on the back and congratulated me. I looked at them as they celebrated the new arrival; one of them ran quickly to his home next door to fetch some gin and came back to give libations, pouring some on the ground in thanks to the ancestors for the newborn. I did not know what to say or even what to feel. The woman I loved lay inside my hut having given birth to another man's child. It was as if I was outside my own body, looking on at myself smiling, playing happy families, while I was dying inside. Over those six months I had tried to convince myself that maybe Rose was right, that I wasn't in love with her, that I was only in love with being in love, like in the movies, but hearing that baby cry, it killed me.

They brought the child to me, put her in my arms, still warm and steaming. It felt awkward. I looked down at her. She was the palest child I had ever seen, so I looked up to question it.

'There are albinos in the family,' said my aunt.

'Oh,' I said. There was a long pause, but I did not have the heart to tell her the truth.

The child wriggled, demanded my attention, stretched out her arms, opened her mouth, exposed her toothless gums and the little tonsils at the back of her mouth, and screamed. Yet, for all her screaming, she was small, fragile. I rocked her gently to soothe her, went to adjust the cloth she was wrapped in, and she grabbed hold of my thumb, squeezed it with such a strength that I knew instantly she was Rose's child.

I froze, looked at her small hand grabbing mine. She should have been my child. A tear escaped my eye, and I felt the slap on my back.

'You're a father now,' beamed my father's oldest brother.

Her delicate baby smell reached my nostrils, and I could not hold her any longer, so I walked with her to our hut to give her to Rose.

Rose sat up on the bed and gave a tired smile as I entered. My grandmother and Michael's father, the district doctor, were beside her. And as much as I didn't want to acknowledge it, in that moment she still looked as beautiful as ever. I walked over, handed her the child and walked back out again, went to the only place I could. I climbed up the old mango tree and sat on the top branch staring out on the old familiar trunk road in the distance, tears streaming down my face. The elders looked on at what they considered to be my strange behaviour, shook their heads at what they perceived to be my modern ways.

I sat there. The army no longer seemed important. My grandmother's words rang in my ears.

'Obi, leave the army, leave it before it is too late.'

*

'How are you feeling?' I asked Rose much later, when all had gone. It was night again, just me and her in that confined space. It was hot, sticky, made worse by the heat from the kerosene lamp. She sat up in the bed as I entered, the baby asleep in the basket by her side. I brought out my mat to make my bed on the floor.

'Much better,' she said quietly, looking at me. 'Where did you go?'

'Just somewhere to clear my head.'

The child made gurgling sounds. Rose turned to pick her up, and discreetly put her nipple in her mouth; the little one sucked away greedily, and I sat down beside them both, watching the interaction between mother and child.

'She is a little pale,' I said.

'Yes, she is.'

'Are you sure she is well?'

'I don't know. I hope so.'

I sat silent for a while, watching them both. 'I thought my grandmother was going to sleep in here with you?'

'I told her to rest as I would need her more in the morning.'

'You look drained.'

'I am.'

The child made a sound and pushed away her breast; Rose tried to feed her again, but she would not latch on and started to cry.

I could not help myself and said, 'Give her to me.'

'What?'

'I said, give her to me. Remember, I am used to children, maybe even more so than you. This yard is full of them.'

She handed over the child to me; I rocked her, stood up and paced with her. The little one went quiet.

'Go back to sleep,' I said to Rose.

'Where are you going?'

'We are going outside to look at the stars.'

We didn't go back in until the child was asleep in my arms and Rose was fast asleep on the bed.

'Now that she is here, are we going to talk?' Rose said, following me around the room with the baby in her arms, as I collected my things to go back to the barracks that Sunday morning.

'Talk about what?'

'About what we are doing here.'

'What is there to talk about?'

'What are we to do next? I can't continue to live here for ever.'

'Why not?'

'I've been thinking,' she said, 'once I am fit enough I will be going back to Lagos.'

'To do what?'

'Uche said that they are looking for trainee nurses in the hospital she works in. At least till I can figure out how to do what I really want to do.'

'And the child?'

'I have an aunt who has promised to take care of her. I can send money home.'

'Does she not think it strange that you want to leave the baby with her when you have a husband?'

'Then I can leave her here with your grandmother and Nnenna, until I have settled in and I can send for her.'

'Rose, what do you want me to say?' I lifted my bag and threw it over my shoulder.

'Obi, you have to understand. I am grateful, but I told you a long time ago I want more.'

'So you keep telling me.'

'Just because I am a woman doesn't mean I have to settle for less.'

'But Rose, you already have more, the problem is you just don't know it.'

She paused, looking at me, searching for words.

'I have to go,' I said.

'I will write,' she shouted after me. 'Let you know when I go and when I am settled in.'

I waved back at her and kept on walking down the path, through the fields, to catch a ride back to the barracks on the trunk road.

We christened the little one a few weeks later, before Rose left, stood in our makeshift village church, pretending to be a very happy couple indeed, and baptized her in front of our family and friends. Rose dressed her in a lace and cotton christening dress, with a hem that went far beyond her chubby feet. She had sat up all night sewing it from a pattern she had picked up at the colonial stores in Onitsha. Reverend Nwachukwu cradled the little one gently in his arms, pulled his black-and-white robe out of the way, and poured water over the loose curls on her head. She gave a strong cry, as if she was demanding that she be handed back at once. I named her Little Rose, after her mother, who allowed me to name her. It was her way of saying thank you.

14

Letters

Eastern Nigeria, Wet Season, 1940

A ND, TRUE TO her word, she sent letters.

Dear Obi,

I hope this letter finds you well and in better spirits than the day I left. As promised, I am writing to let you know I have arrived safely. The hospital is very modern and well equipped for the most part. The majority of the patients are colonials, many from the army, but we do occasionally get others.

There is so much I wish we had talked about before I left. Sometimes I wish I could be more like you, see the world as you do – things would be simpler then. Uche says I am spoilt, that I don't understand the real practicalities of this life. I do not agree with her, for as you know, I have already made my fair share of mistakes. It's not that I don't want the things that you offer, for I love my child and you are a good man, as well as a dear friend. It is just that working at Michael's father's clinic has taught me that there is much to learn and do in this country of ours and I have a great need to play my part. I hope you understand.

Anyway, things here are fine. We are forming a nice little group, especially with four of us now in Lagos. I am trying to learn a little Yoruba but I am not very good at it.

I will continue to write and keep you abreast of the happenings here. Please take care of yourself. Ifeanyi, Uche and Emeka send their regards.

Yours faithfully,
Rose

Her letters were filled with descriptions of her hospital life, and the antics of her recently arrived white colonial chief nurse, and the foolishness of the other nursing staff around her. I felt her excitement, her energy come through the pages whenever she wrote. Her pen seemed more fluid, it seemed to skip and glide across the page, as if she was in a hurry to get her words on to the paper. And I sat on the edge of my bed in my sleeping quarters, at the end of a long day, staring at her words on the lined page, wondering how to reply, for I could feel I was losing her.

Dear Obi,
Hope all is well. I woke up this morning missing our night-time conversations. I assume you are busy for I have not heard from you, despite my letters.

Things here are good. The other day I got to assist a doctor with minor surgery, like I used to assist Michael's father. It felt like old times. All the white nurses were busy; they had no choice but to use me. The doctor was impressed, said he would call on me again.

Well, it seems the war in Europe is beginning to affect supplies. The ships have been delayed. I suggested to one of the sisters that we use the aloe vera plant or the hibiscus rosa growing in the grounds to dress wounds. At least till the supplies arrived, like we did at the clinic. Do you know, the silly woman laughed at me and said, 'We are not in the bush now, nor do we practise your witch-doctor medicine here. We are civilized.' What is it with these colonials? I really had a job holding my tongue at the ridiculousness of her.

Anyway, I cannot continue to write with no response from you. Please write soon for I will have to take it as a sign that you no longer wish to continue to hear from me.

Rose

And so for a little while, in an attempt to silence the wants nagging away at the core of me, I tried to forget about her. Started to see other girls near the barracks; there was no one around who knew me well enough to tell them I was married. Besides, it didn't seem important – after all, it was not a real marriage – and I tried my best to come to terms with the fact that maybe Rose and I would never be.

And whenever I went home, the hut was quiet, sad, like it missed them as much as I did. Although Little Rose was merely a few feet away, in the hut opposite mine, looked after by my grandmother and my father's second wife, who I heard sometimes sing her to sleep, like she used to do to her own children. I checked in on her, every now and then. I knew Rose sent money home for her upkeep, but – I don't know why – I felt a sense of responsibility for her, or maybe it was just to keep up appearances, but I also took to giving money to my grandmother for her.

And as much as I tried, those nights back home in our village, I lay in our bed, looking up at the thatched roof of our hut, at the suitcases she had left behind, remembering her smile, feeling the sheets she had lain in against my skin, missing her.

My dearest Obi,

It was so wonderful to finally get your letter that I just had to sit down and write back straight away. I take this as a sign that you have forgiven me.

There is so much to tell you but not enough time to relay it in this letter, as we are preparing to go to some new eating place that Emeka has discovered, and an acquaintance will be leaving in the morning for Enugu and has promised to deliver this letter to you. I will write with more details later. But I just have to let you know that I am now helping the doctors in the minor-surgery clinic, a few hours a day. I now appreciate how much I learnt in our little clinic, and miss our small village, but the practices are still so much more advanced here in this big hospital. I do wish you were here with us.

As I write, Uche is flustered, trying on all sorts, and I need to get back to helping her. I only ever see her get like this when Emeka comes to pick us up. If I didn't know better, I might think she is a little in love with him, but that would be ridiculous as she is too serious-minded.

Anyway, please take care of yourself.

Yours faithfully,
Rose

15

For King and Country

THE WAR CREPT up on us at first. Each time I returned to my duties, after my visits home, the energy in the barracks seemed to change. It began slowly, a small gathering here, another gathering there. It built up until there just seemed to be a lot of secretive activity among the colonial officers. We watched on, wondering what it would lead to.

Then the army started to ask for volunteers. Posters were pinned to the side of buildings. I saw many people stop to look. In one poster, angular-jawed white men from all three forces marched with rifles on their shoulders, with an Indian and then an African soldier at the back. It was captioned with the words 'The British Commonwealth of Nations – Together'.

But few came forward, and so the requests got more urgent. The village chief, who had been installed after the warrant-chief system was disbanded, had no choice but to send men. He chose the oldest and weakest of the men he could find, who were subsequently rejected. My grandmother, seeing this, and having lived through the First World War, was one of the first to quietly pack off the oldest of her male grandchildren, those over ten, to relatives who lived further into the hinterland. It took them two days of trekking through the dense forest to get there. In time, my father spent longer at the coal mines, as the railways required more coal to export the raw materials, such as tin and rubber, needed for the war. And eventually, when Uche came home, she arrived complaining of food shortages in the hospital and schools near by.

It was not until news came that the colonials had confiscated the land of the German company operating in Onitsha market, and had detained them as prisoners, that we became aware that the enemy was not far away. This was the very company I had visited for Rose's baby supplies, months back, and where the two officers in civilian clothing had accosted me.

Then the messages came through about the army, sent from friends in neighbouring villages, saying that they were going from village to village combing through for able-bodied men to help in the fighting. My family heard and prepared, chose whom best to hide, and waited in apprehension as the officers scoured the neighbouring villages, moving ever closer.

Mr Smith visited my old village primary school. He stood in front of the pupils, stick under arm, in full colonial uniform, apparently, with Reverend Nwachukwu beside him translating his words for those who didn't understand. They lined up neatly outside, excited at his visit, eager to hear what he had to say, and he told them about the white man's war in the faraway lands. He told them that everyone had to contribute in order for Britain to win, that the young men who usually tended the land were either away, or would be away, in the army, or doing other essential jobs, and so my siblings and their friends did as Mr Smith requested and collected the wild rubber from the forest, and the overripe palm kernels that the young men would have farmed, then walked the long walk along the trunk road to Onitsha, and delivered them into the yard of the Niger Company.

The army finally arrived at our village. Interviewed the men, examined the ones left behind, then – to the village's surprise – turned their eyes on the older boys in our village primary school, those in their final year, and conscripted the biggest of them into military service.

I saw more and more of our local men arrive at the barracks, which was surrounded by a barbed-wire fence and guarded by loyal soldiers; even Emeka's younger brother Nonso came through. And also some who were not so local, from different tribes, from the Igala, Ibibio and so on, including a few Yorubas living in our area, and northerners, Hausas. The colonials' preference was always for the northerners, and there were many more of them recruited in the north. Michael told me once that they preferred the northerners because we, the southerners, asked too many questions. But this was wartime and so they recruited whoever they could to make up the numbers, and they needed more of us educated southerners and easterners to meet the higher demand for administrative duties.

Some of the men came willingly, ready to fight for King and country, but others arrived dazed, confused, from the army sweeping the town streets, and others just because they happened to be in the wrong place at the wrong time and naive enough to fall into that trap. Many were poor illiterate bushmen, unable to speak the King's English like the educated recruits such as me. Many arrived frightened they wouldn't return home alive to their loved ones, and some just couldn't get used to the regime of army life, so they ran away.

I watched them run. Heard the caning and saw the defeated souls on their return from military confinement. I was torn between joining them in running, the advice of my grandmother ringing in my ears, and a sense of duty as a man and soldier. Every now and then I would find myself outside the Sergeant's office to request leave from the army. I would hover, pretending to be interested in the noticeboard outside his door. Once I even stood right in front, lifted my hand to knock, then wondered about the alternative: I could not go back to work my father's land – that in itself would be a sign of failure – and besides, what were the chances of Sergeant Fowler granting me such a request? And so I thought better of it, and turned away. At night I dreamt of escaping, maybe to the city, to Kano or Lagos, maybe to join Rose and the life she wrote of in her letters. But I didn't.

During our breaks between army exercises, we took our rest under the shade of a tree. I got to know the new recruits better, even shared a story or two. There was a young boy called Chuks, who didn't look much older than thirteen to me at the time; there was something about him, about his eyes, that made me want to take him under my wing. That first day we met, he was sitting among us, lost, and so I asked him, 'Why are you here? Shouldn't you still be at home among the women?'

'I didn't have a choice in the matter,' he answered. 'My chief offered me up to the army.'

'What do you mean?'

'I was asleep and they came for me, and a few of us young ones in the village. They knocked on my father's door. Told me to dress and loaded me into the conscription truck with the other poor souls and brought us here. I keep seeing my mother running behind the truck screaming for me.'

I nodded. 'And you?' I asked the other young boy beside him, who we called Afam.

'They told me they had work and were looking for boys to help serve the officers. I followed them and this is how I ended up conscripted into the army against my will.'

Well, a week later, he and Chuks attempted to run away, but they caught them and brought them back. I wish now, looking back, that I had helped those boys escape. The last time I saw Chuks he was lying dead, face up, an enemy bullet in the middle of

his forehead. His eyes wide, staring up at the sky as if his death was
a surprise to him. His head cushioned by the twigs and vegetation
on that Burma jungle floor. I closed his boyish eyes, took his gun
and kept on moving. I remember thinking as I moved away that it
was a good thing his mother was not there to see what happened to
her little boy.

It got to the point that so many boys and men had run away that
a few of us educated soldiers, who could speak English very well,
were called into the office by Lieutenant Richards, Captain Miller's
underling. We stood watching him walking up and down, slapping
his swagger stick against his leg, a look of concern on his young face.

'Listen, old chaps,' he said, with sweat glistening off the top of
his pencil moustache, 'I understand from the Sergeant here that
there has been a little unrest among the new recruits.'

We stood, backs straight, eyes forward, lined up side by side,
questioning why we had been called into the office and whether to
answer. We all must have thought it better not to, as there was silence.

'Yes, sir,' answered Sergeant Fowler behind us on our behalf.

'Well,' said Lieutenant Richards, pushing back a strand of his
greased-back hair as he spoke, 'soon you will have the opportunity
to serve your King and empire abroad.'

We continued to look straight ahead.

He circled us. 'You know, there will be great rewards awaiting
you on your return. You will be paid generously,' he said, 'through
your gratuity pay, and pensions.'

I felt his breath faint on the side of my cheek as he spoke, before
he moved round to face us all.

'Enough to set yourselves up for life. Purchase some good
farmland.'

My ears pricked up at this news. I thought of the neighbouring
lands to my father's; to be able to farm my own land and build my
own home on it was my dream. I thought of Rose, immediately,

standing there telling me she wanted more – well, this would definitely be more.

'And you will be handsomely decorated. You will have to fight the women off,' he said persuasively.

I took a quick glance at him. I don't know why, but there was something about him that I trusted. Maybe it was the glint of naivety that I sometimes caught in his smile, or the way he always made an effort to greet us in our language, or the fact that he was Mr Smith's nephew – I don't know, there was just something different about him. I looked at the others and I could see they too were excited at the news.

'Yes, sir,' said the Sergeant, again on our behalf.

'Yes, sir,' we repeated. 'Thank you, sir.'

We had heard rumours of this, but to be called into the office and told this meant that the rumours were true.

'Now, I want you to let the others know.'

'Yes, sir.'

And so we did. The message passed through the barracks, about the medals and the army money awaiting them, a form of confirmation of previous rumours they had heard; the Sergeant even repeated them, and the men's running away reduced.

I myself packed away the thoughts of escape, silenced my grandmother's voice in my head, and wondered how bad it could really get over there.

'What will you do with yours?' asked Afam, as I rolled over to sleep in the barracks that night.

He had told me he was from a neighbouring village to mine; he was no more than sixteen, a boisterous and humorous boy. I liked him; he reminded me of my younger brothers. I lay on my bed looking up at the ceiling, contemplating the question. I remember thinking at the time that I might even be able to convince Rose to stay with me, once I owned land.

'Don't know,' I answered instead. 'Go to sleep.'

Hmm, the ignorance of youth.

In our quarters, across the way, I overheard two soldiers, sons of the educated elite, like Michael, talking about how there was a new prime minister, a Mr Winston Churchill.

It seemed like a lifetime ago, but I remembered we had met these two outside the catering rest-house in Onitsha once, way back then, when we were boys. At the time I remember stopping and waiting for Michael and the two of them to finish talking; they had nodded their heads at us. A quick, efficient nod. The same nod they gave me each morning from across the way, sitting up in their beds, as we all woke to the early sound of the bugle.

And so I settled down, obeyed the orders of the colonial officers, of the Sergeant and NCOs. At the time this seemed the most natural order of things, a continuation of civilian life, for back then I looked upon the white man as almost a magical being – that is, before this war opened my eyes.

The war brought opportunities for me as many of the colonial soldiers were required for duties elsewhere. I was among the few who had received a full primary education; we were trained to work in the office, and to teach the new batch of soldiers to use the wireless set and the Bren gun, releasing more of the colonial soldiers for other duties. In time, we – the soldiers who had joined before the war, and who had received a very British education – were promoted and assisted the more experienced soldiers in training up the young men passing through the barracks in ever increasing numbers.

In our leisure time, when we got the chance, we played football; it became a regular thing among us educated and more experienced ones. I got to know those two dapper fellows from across the way very well. I think one was the son of a district lawyer; the other I am not sure. They reminded me of Michael. In time they passed on their old newspapers to the rest of us.

In June of that year, those of us who could, read about the fall of Paris and the French surrendering to the Germans, including the atrocities that the Germans were said to be carrying out in their own country against their political opponents, resistance groups, Gypsies and Jews. We also read news about the thousands of Senegalese soldiers who had been taken as prisoners of war over in France and were being mistreated and killed in camps, due to the Germans' hatred of the Black man. It was written about in a small article in the paper. I would have missed it, if it hadn't been pointed out to me.

And so we sat in the evenings, sometimes playing cards, just before bed. In the midst of slamming cards down between us we discussed many things: Hitler's *Mein Kampf*, in which he talked disparagingly about many, including us, the Black man; about the German policy to take no negro prisoners of war, hence the massacre of the Senegalese soldiers; about what they could be doing in their concentration camps. And so, like the rest of them, I began to look upon this Hitler fellow as a not-very-good fellow indeed, and began to have more resolve to fight against this tyranny.

Earlier that month, news had also come through that the Italians had joined forces with the Germans and declared war against Britain. The activity among the colonial soldiers increased, and training and recruitment stepped up. I became increasingly busy. I was needed more, to help with training, and also in the office, and I overheard news about a great number of training centres being set up here and abroad, in the Gold Coast, in Sierra Leone.

Then we got news that soldiers would be needed immediately to fight in East Africa following the Italian invasion of British Somaliland. It was then that I realized that this war was actually on our doorstep and it began to feel real.

They gathered us out in the open, stood on the steps leading into their offices, unfurled a map of East Africa marked up with red flags. The Captain stood with a pointer in one hand.

'Men, the time has come for you to fight for King and country,' he said, then turned to point the stick at the map pinned to a board. 'The Italians have invaded British Somaliland, and it is time to fight. Men, are you ready?'

'Yes, sir,' a few called out.

'I said, men, are you ready?'

'Yes, sir,' we chorused.

Not long after, I watched from the sidelines as the army trucks filled with soldiers, including a few officers. Waved them goodbye as the convoy drove by on its way to the trains, to join the rest of the division in the battle for East Africa.

'Sir, will they be back?' asked Afam as we watched the trucks roll past.

'I don't know,' I said under my breath, distracted.

'Afam, why do you have to ask such a question?' asked Chuks.

'All right, the Sergeant wants you both in the stores. Now!'

'Yes, sir.'

The two reluctantly walked off. At that time, I was glad that my appeal to the Sergeant to keep Chuks and Afam behind had not fallen on deaf ears.

I turned back and watched the dust swirl as the last of the vehicles drove out of the compound. I made eye contact with the two dapper chaps in the back of a truck, nodded at them with that efficient nod. One lifted his cap in a salute, smiled at me; I smiled back as he went by, mouthed for him to come back safely. He never did.

A part of me wanted to be with them, on my way to see action, but the powers that be had decided I was needed more at the barracks, helping to train the new recruits. And even as I watched them go, I still could not have imagined then what was to come, or the cost of it. But even so, even as busy as I got, despite what was going on around me, at night, alone in my bed, when we were hunkered down for the night, when I closed my eyes I saw Rose; I could not shake her from me.

My dearest Rose,

It is a beautiful day today and I write thinking of our one-year anniversary. I still remember our wedding day with much fondness. I enclose a picture of us posing in the photo studio in Onitsha. You look pretty in your wedding dress with a bunch of flowers in your hands. I also include some pictures of Little Rose. They were taken in the same studio a few weeks back, when I was home. She is a strong and healthy child.

Unfortunately, I have some sad news. My great-uncle's second wife, Auntie Nollie, died a month back, but the good thing is she lived to a grand old age.

Things are getting tougher here in the east with food shortages. Last time I was home there was much complaint about the hardships this war has brought. Much of the food has been diverted to feed the army and there just aren't the young men around like before to farm the land. The good news I can give you is that Little Rose is still with Mama, and as usual she had the foresight to prepare somewhat for these hardships. Do not fret — Little Rose is in safe hands.

There is a lot of activity among the colonials nowadays. We got news today that the 3rd Nigerian Brigade has been deployed to join the British and their allies to fight the Italians in East Africa. Some of our men left early last week to join them. The soldier in me wishes that I had gone with them, but I was informed there was greater need of me here.

I must say that your letters about hospital life have amused me, particularly your tales of the peculiarity of the other nursing staff. But I often wonder about you and your life in Lagos. Please tell, have you found the 'more' you went searching for?

Things seem to be escalating with this war, but one day when all this is over, I hope to improve my lot. I had hoped to do so to be more worthy of you, but I am beginning to understand your wishes – well, for today at least.

Hope you are taking good care of yourself; I was told TB was circulating in Lagos.

Please give my regards to Uche and ensure you rest, for I know as usual you are working hard and putting others before yourself.

Yours faithfully,
Obi

Dear Obi,
I hope this letter finds you in good health. Thank you for the pictures of Little Rose. I have missed her so very much and cried with joy on seeing how round she is getting.

I have been so very busy these days in the hospital that this is the first time in two weeks that I have found a moment to reply to your letter.

Yes, I am finding the 'more' I came looking for. I cannot explain it, but inside me there is an urge to live a life that is not too commonplace. Sweet of you to ask. I intend to drive myself on like always, for there are many here who need the help that I can offer, and I am very happy in my work.

I don't know if you heard but Ifeanyi has joined the army. We tried to tell him not to but he would not hear any of it. He has always been such an egalitarian, even to his own downfall. There are rumours that he may also be shipped out to fight in East Africa. We are all praying that this is not the case.

Obi, I really wish that you would not express your feelings as you do, for if it wasn't for your kind help I would have been shamed, and it is really me who should be wishing to be worthy of you.

Please take care of yourself. Uche and Emeka send their regards.

Yours faithfully,
Rose

16

Hardship

Eastern Nigeria, Dry Season, 1941

'KNEES UP! EYES front!' I shouted. 'Quick march. One two, one two.' And the new recruits obeyed, marching off around the field as I had taught them. The dust lifting from the dry ground as they quick-stepped around.

I had spent over two years in the training barracks, progressed to lance corporal, helped out the sergeants with the new recruits and with paperwork in the office. Learnt to drive, and to ride a motorcycle, together with a few others, to run quick errands and despatch paperwork between the colonial offices in town.

But every time I went home, which was not often, that's when the hardships hit me; for being in the barracks was almost like living in a bubble. There were fewer and fewer goods to purchase in the local market, and the imports from abroad were no longer available as the Germans were patrolling the seas – and as for locally grown produce, like rice and yams, more and more was being diverted by the colonial forces to feed the army that they were building up to fight in the war. I began taking what I could home with me, making sure that I left as much as I could with the women to take care of Little Rose.

We also got news from the north that the colonials were forcing people to work in the tin mines and that many were losing their lives. We worried what effect the colonials' need for more raw materials for the war would have on the coal mines, and my family worried about the conditions that my father could be working under.

Dear Obi,

I was home this last week and I wanted to thank you for your generosity towards Little Rose. I really don't know how to thank you for all that you have done for us. I feel truly blessed to have you in my life. You really are the loveliest man I have ever known.

I hope and pray that army life is treating you well. This war continues to rage on. Uche is thinking of joining the army medical services; I was thinking of maybe following her, but maybe I am too much of a coward. All we can do is pray for the safe return of Ifeanyi and the rest from East Africa to us.

Please, please, take care of yourself.

Yours faithfully,
Rose

My dearest Rose,

It is really with pleasure that I am helping out with Little Rose. She is a jovial child. Although still very pale. My father's wives think that it is because of the albino trait in our family; I did not tell them that this could not be. Please let me know, does her father have the trait or is he from the Imo side of Ibo land?

We got good news today: we heard that our troops helped win the battle in British Somaliland and could be on their way home soon, and pray God Ifeanyi is with them.

I was also sent news from home that Michael has joined the army over there in America. I am surprised at this and will not believe it till I see it with my own two eyes, but then again Michael has always had a way of surprising me.

Some of the sergeants here were passing around newspaper articles on the East African campaign today. Our own soldiers were upset, as they could not see any of our Nigerian Brigade in the pictures, only the white South Africans. They say our troops fought a long and arduous battle to win Ethiopia, only to be held back outside the city of Addis Ababa to allow white South African troops to enter the capital first. The articles barely mention our troops. Surely, this cannot be right. I do not understand this at all.

Well, things still seem to be escalating in Europe, and the white man seems intent on including us in the troubles he has made, but one day when all this is over, I pray that we will all be together again, like the old days. Please give my regards to Uche. I hope you and Uche will consider carefully this joining of the medical services, as you wrote about in your last letter, for this white man war does not appear to be ending any time soon. Take care of yourself.

Yours faithfully,
Obi

17

Us

Eastern Nigeria, Dry Season, 1942

IN JANUARY WE got news that the Japanese had invaded Burma, mere weeks after their attack on Pearl Harbor and the day America declared war on Japan.

I was in the mess pressing my uniform with the hot iron, the coal embers glowing through the small gaps at the top, when I looked up to see one of my colleagues burst through the doors to share the news. He had overheard the officers gathered together in the boardroom talking about it. He seemed to be excited by the news as he relayed it to the others. I listened, but continued with the task at hand, as it was not significant to me at the time.

That week I noticed that the activity among the officers increased even more. They met frequently behind closed doors. I overheard their muffled and sometimes, it seemed to me, frantic discussions, watched them from my desk as they went in and out of each other's rooms, while I filed away inventory documents. I was sitting waiting to be relieved from my duties by the other clerks, when the door to Captain Miller's office suddenly opened. Captain Miller was standing in the doorway, looking around, then spotted my superior and called him into his office. Five minutes later he came out of Captain Miller's office and straight over to me.

'Lance Corporal Nwogo.'

I stood immediately. 'Yes, sir.'

'We need someone to do something important.'

'Yes, sir.'

'We require someone to courier some documents to the 4th Battalion in Lagos. These are extremely important. Do you think you're up to the task?'

'Yes, sir,' I said, thinking straight away of Rose.

'Good. We don't have time to waste. Go and collect a few of your personal belongings and be back here in five minutes. Private Okafor will take you to the station; there's a train leaving in an hour to Kaduna. You can make the connection to Lagos there.'

'Yes, sir.'

Private Okafor got me safely to the station; the buzz of the motorcycle engine faded as I watched him drive away. I bought my ticket, watched the crowd of vendors on the platform, awaiting the arrival of the next train to sell their goods of yams, plantain and all sorts. I looked down the tracks; they seemed to wind and curve into the distance, disappearing into the green bush. It was a hot day and I brought out my handkerchief to wipe the sweat from my brow. I heard the train whistle first: its broken, discordant toot-toot rang out, chorused by the chug-chug of the wheels riding the tracks, and I readied myself to board as it came into view.

I climbed on to the train along with the buzz of other passengers, the case of documents firmly in my hand, my personal items in a bag thrown over my shoulder. I found a seat near the window, felt the cool breeze fan my skin as the train sliced its way through the grassland. The palm trees waved in the yonder, and my head was filled with the excitement of seeing Rose again.

*

Having successfully delivered the documents into the hands of the officers at the 4th Battalion, I had made my way to the hospital. I was now off duty, but still dressed in my uniform. I had taken off my cap and asked for her at the entrance, and they had directed me to this part of the hospital.

As I passed a number of wards, I looked in through each doorway; the mid-afternoon light was still shining through the windows. I stopped at the ward where they had said I would find her, peeked in. It was a long room; metal-framed beds were lined up on either side, the white patients set an equal distance apart; the ceiling fans were in a row in the middle, spinning on their down-rods. I bowed my head in greeting as each colonial nurse walked by. One stopped; I assumed she was the sister for the ward.

'Can I help you?' she asked.

I held my cap in my hand. 'I'm looking for Rose, ma.'

'Rose? Oh, of course.' She turned. 'Rose, there's someone here to see you.'

Then suddenly I saw her, in the distance, assisting one of the nurses. I walked further into the ward. She spotted me and her smile widened; it spread over her face like daylight spreading at dawn.

She turned to the nurse she was assisting, mumbled something and then came over, all the while looking straight at me. I could not take my eyes off her, held my breath as she approached.

'Obi!'

'Rose!'

We stood looking at each other. There was something different. A new energy between us. She had never looked at me before in the way she looked at me that day.

'Being away from me seems to have done you good,' I said, breaking the silence.

'What are you doing here?'

'Running an errand.'

She laughed. 'I'm so glad to see you.'

'I'm glad to see you too,' I said.

'I will be off duty in an hour.'

I nodded.

'Can you wait for me outside? I will be with you as soon as I can.'

I waited on the steps of the hospital, all the while wondering what had just happened between us.

She came out an hour later. I stood up, watched her as she walked towards me, smoothing down her skirt.

'How long are you in Lagos for?' she said, reaching my side.

'I catch the train back tomorrow morning.'

She nodded, looking up at me. 'How is everyone? How is my baby, Little Rose?'

I put my hand in my wallet. 'Here, I brought you this.' It was a small box containing a little of her baby hair and another picture. 'Ma cut her hair last time I was home. I put a little in a box for you. As for the picture, I forgot to send it to you; it was taken a month or two after the last ones I sent.'

She took the box and picture from me, looked at them both. Her hand shook a little and when she looked up her eyes were moist.

'My baby has grown even fatter,' she laughed.

'Indeed,' I said.

'Thank you. Thank you so much. This is just like you.'

I looked on as she tried to wipe away a tear from her eye.

'Are you OK?'

'Yes. Come, I told Uche you were in town. She has invited Emeka to meet up with us as well. It will be like the old days,' she said, excited, grabbing my hand, and I had no choice but to throw my army bag over my shoulder and run after her, to catch a bus to meet up with the others.

*

We met up at a little eating place, where the food was good and the drink flowed.

The street was wide, on one side lined with bungalows with rusty tin roofs and brown-painted shutters, on the other with two-storey colonial buildings, and a scattering of cars which sat like fat bulldogs lounging in the sun by the roadside.

We ordered some light refreshments, and watched the women returning from the market, their heavy white loads steady on their heads as they turned and conversed with each other. We observed the languid amble of the men as they strolled up and down the street. Occasionally we heard the ting-ting sound of a bicycle bell before a man cycled by. The smoky smell of suya swirled and twirled through the air from the vendor at the corner, and I marvelled at the ease and joviality of city life.

Emeka was on good form, forever the charmer that night. Uche did not take her eyes off him, but laughed at each of his jokes, no longer the serious-minded girl I had known back home in our vil-lage, but dressed up in what I recognized to be one of Rose's outfits. Music began to flow from a window above, the sound of Tunde King and the Jolly Boys Orchestra filled the air, and we danced a little, joked a little like we used to, under the window at our eating place.

And in those moments I watched on, a quiet contentment sit-ting in my stomach.

'How is army life?' asked Emeka.

'Fine,' I replied, putting my drink down on the table between us.

'It suits you,' said Uche, leaning forward in her chair, reaching out to squeeze my left arm. 'I've never known you to be so muscu-lar; even your jawline is more defined, more manly,' she added, then leant in to whisper in my ear, 'Rose is a very foolish girl.'

'Rose, watch out, Uche has her sights on your husband,' joked Emeka.

'Well,' Rose laughed. Leaning in on my right, her elbow resting on the table, hand cupping her chin, eyes sparkling into mine, she said, 'This one she just can't have.'

I was taken aback, could not look away, and so we sat there staring into each other's eyes, an unexpected electricity sparking between us. I had never felt it before.

Uche feigned indignation on my left and removed her hand.

Then Rose suddenly looked away, her brow creased, almost like she had caught herself. I had no choice but to turn too, did not want to be seen staring into the emptiness she left behind. Emeka sat directly opposite, and I caught an expression on his face that unnerved me, before he quickly hid it behind a smile. Then I turned to see Uche looking at Emeka with an expression of . . . I don't know, maybe anger, before she too composed herself.

There was something in the air that night, something that rattled me, but I just couldn't figure it out. Maybe it was the drink, or the allure of Lagos, or the kittenishness of that eating place that cast its spell. I just don't know.

'The papers say that the Japanese have driven the British out of Burma.'

'Emeka, please!' said Uche.

'What? Don't you care about this war?' asked Emeka.

'I care,' said Uche, 'but please, not tonight.'

He continued, directing his words at me as if the two of them, Rose and Uche, were no longer there. 'There are rumours they may send troops out from here to fight in Burma.'

'I've heard the rumours,' I said.

'They want more of us to join. What do you think?'

'Please, Emeka. Is life not tough enough here without reminding us about what is happening in Europe and in Asia? Isn't it enough that it has taken Ifeanyi from us to fight in East Africa?' said Uche.

Emeka was silent for a little, looking at me for an answer.

'Uche is right,' I said, 'tonight is for merriment.'

The music changed, the beat more up-tempo.

Emeka looked towards the dancers under the window, who gave out a small cheer in response to the change. He shook his head, looked back at us, and said, 'Maybe you are right.'

'I would love to dance,' said Uche in a soft voice, her hand on Emeka's lower arm.

Emeka laughed, got to his feet, put his hand out. 'Would you do me the pleasure?'

Uche smiled broadly, put her hand in his and followed him to where the group were two-stepping under the window.

When they were gone I turned to Rose and said, 'So this is Lagos, the city you wrote so much about in your letters.'

Rose smiled. 'Yes, this is Lagos.'

'In your letters you implied you have found the "more" you came looking for.'

Rose looked at me and laughed. 'Yes, I am beginning to find it.'

'And are you happy?'

She sat silent for a while, contemplating my question. 'Yes,' she said, staring into my eyes, 'but I think I miss us.'

I choked on my drink.

But she looked away and continued like she hadn't said anything, and for a moment I thought that I had imagined her words.

'Maybe it's the hospital that makes me happy. I don't know why but it makes me feel alive, closer to my purpose.'

'Purpose?'

'Yes, purpose. I am not doing what I want to do, but I know I am getting closer.'

'Isn't your purpose with your child?'

'Yes, it is, and it will be once I have figured out how to make it work.'

'And what about us, where do we go from here?'

'Is there an us?'

There was silence between us; her question hung in the air. I could see her thinking, like she was considering something.

I spoke to try to lighten the mood. 'You know, by tradition, you are supposed—'

'That is what I love about you, Obi: you are not a traditional man.'

I laughed a bittersweet laugh and said, 'Sometimes, I think it would be easier if I was.' I took a sip of my drink. 'You know, you as a woman – you should know your place,' I teased.

'Why must I know my place?' she said. 'Why can I not have it all, like a man? If I was a man, my wife and child would have moved with me to Lagos. If I was a man . . .'

'If you were a man, would you have married a woman carrying another man's child?'

'I'm sorry,' she said and looked away.

'So, does he know?'

'Who?'

'The father.'

'Yes.'

'And he chooses not to come forward?'

'As Uche said, not tonight. Not tonight. Tomorrow you go back to your barracks, but tonight is for merriment.'

And so we got up and joined the rest to shuffle and two-step to the music. Someone must have shouted up to the apartment above, which belonged to the proprietor, because the next thing we knew, the gentleman had poked his head out of the window, smiled, raised his thumb and changed the music. Rose kept smiling across at me whenever I caught her eye, but I knew she also stole little glances when she thought I wasn't looking, her brow creased as if she was quietly contemplating.

At the end Uche sat back down beside me and leant across, spoke in my ear. 'Emeka is walking me back to the hospital. I have taken some of my belongings from our room already. I will sleep in with a friend tonight. If I don't see you tomorrow, have a safe journey,' she said and half hugged me.

'Wait . . .'

'You're a married couple, you need some privacy.'

There was nothing I could think to say in response that wouldn't have embarrassed Rose. Besides, I felt that Uche was in a hurry to be with Emeka. So I nodded, and hoped they had some sort of mat for me to make a bed on the floor.

She then turned to Rose and said, 'I will see you in the morning.'

'Where are you going?' asked Rose.

'They want to give us privacy,' I said in her ear.

'Privacy, for what?' she said.

'Aren't we married?'

'Oh! Oh,' she said, 'yes, of course,' and fell silent. Then she turned to say her goodbyes to them.

And as Uche dragged Emeka away, I saw that look cross his face again. I thought of the look that had also crossed his face all those years ago when we were children, when Rose drove off to school, and wondered about Rose, about Emeka, and whether Little Rose had any resemblance to him. My stomach tightened, but I dismissed it as a ridiculous thought.

We walked home slowly that night. There was a cool breeze in the air, and people were in good spirits as we passed them; a few vendors were out at the evening market, some shouted for attention to their wares, and every now and then Rose and I would be forced closer to each other as a bicycle went by. Once I reached out to steady her as a motorcycle almost drove us into the open gutter, felt the electricity charge through me. It seemed there was magic in the air, an intensity between us that hadn't been there before.

'Are you OK?' I asked, as I turned her towards me to avoid her falling in, and felt the sweat on her shirt at the small of her back.

'I'm fine.'

We stood there for a moment, with the dust swirling in the motorcycle's wake. I looked down into her eyes, felt the heat of her body against mine, lost myself in the smell of her perfume and her sweat, stared at the sight of her red lipstick on her parted lips. Then she pushed gently against my chest and I was brought back into the world.

'Uche was right,' she said, 'the army has done you good. Come. This way,' she called, hurrying off.

The room was small and hot, with one bed on either side. As we went in, I put my bag down on the floor. But maybe the room wasn't small, maybe it was the tightness in my chest as I held my breath that evening, trying not to betray myself, watching her as she lit the kerosene lamp for us to see by. We seemed to bump into each other as she manoeuvred around me, and so I took a seat on the bed I assumed to be Uche's to get out of the way, but still it seemed awkward. I watched her as she quickly put away a few of her things, then she sat down on the bed opposite to face me.

'So which one do I sleep in?' I asked. 'This one?'

'Yes,' she said, looking at me like she wanted to say something else. 'Obi, you seem different.'

'Different in what way?'

'I don't know, you seem more grown up. More like a man.'

'I don't know whether to take that as a compliment or not.'

'It is a compliment,' she said.

And there was silence again as we stared at each other.

I broke the stare first, tired of wanting something I knew in the end I just wouldn't get. 'So, how are we going to do this?' I asked.

'Do what?'

'Change for bed?'

'Oh, yes. We should be used to this,' she said with a nervous laugh.

I turned away from her, got up and looked in my bag for my chewing stick to brush my teeth, pulled off my shirt to ready myself for sleep. Stood there looking around the room for water to rinse my mouth. That's when I felt her face against my back, and her hands encircle me.

'Do you remember when we were children?'

'Yes,' I said, feeling her heat on my back, my heart beating so fast I could hear it, looking ahead while she hugged me from behind.

'Do you remember our mango tree and how we used to race to the top?'

'I do.'

'For so long I have only been able to see you as that little boy I used to beat.'

She kissed my back.

'And?'

'And I guess this last year, seeing you with Little Rose, receiving your letters and going out tonight, has made me realize things that I didn't want to admit.'

'And?'

'And I want there to be an us.'

I turned to her, held her in my arms, looked down at her. 'In what way?'

'I want our marriage.'

'And what about the father of Little Rose?'

'He is no longer important.'

'Then, if you want me, show me. Because I am tired of playing games with you.'

She reached up and kissed me.

We made love for the very first time that night. We did not sleep, watched the arrival of the day through the window. I did not want to go, but I had to.

We stood on the platform making sweet promises to each other, and I assured her that I would try to get a transfer to the barracks in Lagos so we could be closer. Maybe even bring Little Rose to join us. Finally be a real family. Then she took hold of a leather talisman she had hidden under her blouse and put it around my neck.

'For your journey and protection,' she said, beaming up at me. 'Come back to me.'

'You can't stop me,' I said, then smiled, turned, boarded the train, and waved at her through the window as it pulled out of the station. She got smaller as the train chugged away.

18

A Body

I WAS OUT ON drill that day when they called me. We had just finished a five-mile run in the midday heat, and I was drying the
sweat from around my neck and chest when I saw one of the NCOs
run across the field to Sergeant Fowler. At first I paid them no
mind, but maybe it was the way in which the NCO huddled with
the Sergeant that caught my attention, or how the Sergeant seemed
to look up and stare at me from that distance, then turned and
called one of our African sergeants over to him to huddle in quiet
conversation again. Both men looked up together and I could tell
that they were both now staring at me.

'Obi!' Sergeant Ibeh shouted and waved at me.

I waved back and he signalled for me to follow him.

He took me into one of the offices and made me sit down before
telling me.

I turned numb. The blood started pumping through my ears so
loudly that I could not hear him. I saw his mouth move but could
not make out his words.

'I'm afraid your wife, Rose, has been found dead this morning . . .'

I sat there, not able to take it in.

'Sorry, what did you say?'

'Your wife, Rose, was found dead . . .'

It was as if I was floating out of myself for a little while.

I kept thinking, *but I got her letter this morning*; felt for it in my pocket. It was there.

Finally I asked, 'What happened?'

I don't know why, whether it was just that I didn't believe it, but I couldn't cry on that train journey back to Lagos. I watched the vegetation go by, heard the sound of the train running on the tracks, saw the people get on and off, but just didn't know how or what I was supposed to feel. I suppose maybe there was a little part of me that hoped that they had it wrong. That they were mistaken somehow, for some unknown reason. That she would be standing there at the station as the train pulled in. Standing there waiting for me, as she had been standing there waving me goodbye five weeks ago, that weekend we first made love.

I couldn't get any sense out of Sergeant Ibeh when I asked him what had happened. All he kept saying was that she had been found dead and I needed to go to Lagos to identify her, and I kept thinking, *but where is Uche?* Uche would know if it was her or not, or Emeka.

'How was she found?'

'I don't know,' said Sergeant Ibeh.

'What happened?'

'I don't know,' he said again.

'What happened to her?'

'I don't have any further information. As her husband, you have to go to Lagos; they are waiting for you.'

So I had boarded the train confused, not sure what I would find when I got there. Watched the trees, the bush and the sky go by through the window on that train. It was the longest journey I had ever taken in my life.

*

The next day, I stood in the cool morgue. Looked down at her. She lay still on the trolley. Her face was misshapen, I couldn't quite make out that it was Rose. She was dressed in the same uniform and shoes that she had worn five weeks ago.

And I kept thinking, *it can't be her, it can't be my Rose*. How does one go from being so full of life, as she was the day we said our goodbyes at the station, to lying dead in a morgue? I just couldn't believe it. So I kept looking at her, at the body. She was dressed like any of the nurses in this hospital, but her uniform was dirty. One side of her face was particularly swollen, with very dark bruises. At a quick glance she could have been any of the African nurses in the hospital. I couldn't put my finger on it, but I knew things weren't right. I looked down on the body until it became hazy due to the tears welling in my eyes. I felt the wetness on my cheeks as they flowed. I was crying but still I couldn't feel, and all the while I kept thinking, *my sweet Nkem*. And in the midst of the tears I knew that something just wasn't right. Why was her face so swollen? Her hair different? I knew her hair very well. That night we had made love, I had buried my face in her straightened locks; they were soft against my chin. I had put my nose against her head, breathed in, filled my lungs with the scent of the Vaseline she used, as we lay there in each other's arms. I had looked down on the top of her head, seen each individual strand, circled my arms around her body, pulled her in, cupped each breast, felt skin against skin, listened to her quiet breathing as it soothed me. This hair was different, each strand thicker, much curlier – it just wasn't like her hair that night.

I came out of the morgue shaken. Uche stood waiting. She looked drawn, her eyes red like she hadn't stopped crying. I hadn't seen her look like that before. Emeka stood beside her. We greeted each other.

'It just can't be Rose,' I said.

Uche burst out crying again, then turned and leant into Emeka.

I heard the hospital administrator clear his throat and he guided me into a room.

I had walked up to the hospital reception that early afternoon after coming straight from the station, gave my name. They ushered me into a room.

'We are so sorry for your loss, Mr Nwogo.'

'What happened?' I asked.

'She was discovered dead yesterday morning.'

'By whom?'

'She was expected on the ward; it was raining and when she didn't turn up we sent Uche to look for her in their room. But she wasn't there. The caretaker discovered her body in some bushes in the grounds some hours later. We found this note.'

The hospital administrator handed it to me. I took it, opened it. Scribbled on the torn paper were the following words: *I am sorry, but I just can't go on any more.*

I looked down at the paper. It was torn right after the words 'any more', like she could have written more.

'I'm so sorry, she must have jumped from . . .'

'This isn't her writing,' I mumbled.

'Sorry?'

I looked up, straight at him, and said, 'It isn't Rose. It isn't her writing.'

'But we've checked it. I wouldn't have handed it to you if we were not sure.' He got up, walked over to a filing cabinet and brought out some files. 'Look, these are the medical records that Rose filled in just hours before she died.'

He put the note beside the records. 'You can see it is the same.'

I was silent while I looked from one piece of paper to the other, tried to make out a difference. I stared for a very long time but could only make out a very minor difference in the way the 'e's and 'c's flicked up at the end, instead of staying level as in her letters to me, but this was not enough to say for certain that they hadn't been written by the same hand. Besides, her 'e's in the medical documentation were not consistent.

'We found this in the clinic beside the note, near the window under which we found her body.' He pushed Rose's wedding ring across the desk.

I looked down at it, then up at him. 'That is not Rose lying in the morgue,' I said.

The room was silent.

Uche showed me to their room, the very one we had slept in just over a month ago. Emeka had made his excuses earlier and left. Uche opened the door. I went in. Stood in the middle. Looked around. The bed was neat, still made. Everything had its place, all her belongings carefully put away, as if waiting for her. I looked back at the door, to where Uche stood. 'Aren't you coming in?'

She backed away, shook her head and ran away wailing.

My head felt light, almost like I was gliding. I sat on the bed, the door wide open, felt the cotton sheets beneath my hand, cast my eyes up at the ceiling, took a deep breath to control the emotions that threatened to overwhelm me. Then looked around again, tried to feel her presence, but it was strange: I just couldn't feel her in that room.

There were so many questions, and I searched the room for answers. Who was this Rose who they say took her own life?

I could see her that night, not so long ago, leaning in, her elbow resting on the table, her hand cupping her face, eyes sparkling into mine, that night we danced, we first made love.

That Rose, my Rose, just wouldn't and couldn't have done this: taken her own life. It didn't make sense. I felt for her letter in my pocket, the last letter she had written me, remembered her words joyfully tumbling over each other. This Rose, the one who wrote the letter, was happy here. How does one go from being so happy to taking one's life? It just didn't make sense.

I thought of our people in the village, her brothers, her father; wondered what I was going to say to them. To take your own life in our culture is a taboo, an offence against the earth, the gods and your people. What would they say? How was I going to tell them? Where was Rose? The one who wrote that letter. The one I fell in love with up there in our mango tree.

Her Pond's cream, pressed powder, comb, charcoal pencil and lipstick sat on top of three large brown suitcases; the cases were piled on top of each other and acted like a dressing table. I was frightened to touch her belongings. I heard her say, 'Obi, please don't move my things.'

She was always very precise, knew when I had moved her things even if it was only by a fraction of an inch. Those weekends we had shared in my hut I had come to know this much about her. Maybe it came from her years of boarding school. I am not sure, but there are so many things that I was not sure about in those days.

I bent down, looked under the bed; there was another case, and beside that a smaller one, more like a leather briefcase. I pulled it out, pressed on the catches, heard the clicks as each one released, opened it wide as I knelt in front.

Inside were documents, photographs. I skipped through to look at a black-and-white photograph of her in a studio. She sat at an angle, head held high, looking straight at the camera. Her hair short, a straight line shaved on the right side of her head, with round spectacles and studs in her ears, gazing back ever so studiously. She looked just like my dear beloved Nkem. It must have been taken shortly after her mother died, when her hair was shaved for her year of mourning. I picked up another, a school group photograph, searched through the faces to find her, to the left up in the corner. Her white colonial headmistress and teachers sat in the middle on chairs in the first row. The local teachers beside and behind them. I searched the expressions of the teachers in the front row, but it was difficult to make out their thoughts. One or two looked stern. I remembered the marks on Rose's back. The ones I had seen when we were children as we walked through the bush. The fresh pink scars which had poked out from the back of her dress. In that moment I wondered about the scars, which of these smiling women was responsible. Then wondered, did Rose enjoy her school days? We never really talked about that part of her life. How could I have known her all my life and yet not be able to answer this simple question? I put the picture down, picked another; she was standing with Uche and two men I didn't know, both dressed in white, holding rackets on a tennis court somewhere in Lagos. One of them had his arm thrown around her shoulder. All were laughing gaily at the camera. I looked at the pictures in front of me and saw the gaps in my knowledge of her.

I sat down on the floor beside the case, my back leaning against the edge of the bed, listened to the sounds outside the room of muffled conversations, and the opening and closing of doors in the hallway.

I saw a scarf hiding under some documents, pulled it out, held it to my nose, breathed in deep. It smelt of old mothballs, but her scent was still there, bold and alive like she had been days ago.

I rummaged through again. In among her belongings in the case was her gold puzzle ring with the jaguar on the front. The one she often fiddled around with. I don't know why, but I took this and placed it in my pocket. Picked up a partially filled-in, creased form; it was for the Cambridge certificate. I remembered lying on the bed watching her fill in that form. It seemed so long ago, but I saw her sitting there, at her desk, in our hut, as vividly as if it was yesterday. I put it down, rummaged through, picked up another piece of paper. It was her results; I had not known she had taken the exams. I put it back in the case and found an acceptance letter, for her to study medicine at Trinity College Dublin. This shocked me. I did not know she had applied. She and Uche had always been very bright, but maybe that was part of the problem.

It just did not make sense – why would she kill herself when she had been accepted to study medicine? Why would she kill herself when we were making so many plans for our future together? It did not make any sense whatsoever. I reached over, picked up a bundle of letters tied together by ribbon, opened them one by one. My heart pumped, raced, shattered as I began to read. They were love letters, addressed to someone whose name she had scribbled out in each letter, and I could only make out that the name began with a 'C' where she hadn't quite concealed it in one letter. I felt an ache, a pain at the core of me. Who was this person she was writing to? I thought of all the people I knew whose name began with 'C' and all I could think of was Emeka, as he was Chukuemeka. But surely it was not him. I read through each letter until I came across one that read:

> *To my darling C—*
> *I gave birth to our daughter yesterday. She is a lovely child. Looks like you. I wish you could see her. She is such a happy child. I wish things had been different between us, and there are so many things that I regret. Sometimes, I wish that I had never met you, that I had never fallen in love with you, then I would not feel this pain each morning when I wake or go to sleep.*
>
> *Love,*
> *Rose*

She wrote these letters but never sent them. I was not sure I really knew this Rose, was not sure if I wanted to know this Rose. And who was this man? It was obvious from this letter that he was the father of

Little Rose. Emeka came to mind again, and the day he ran out on to the road after her, dressed in his school uniform, as she went off to QMC Girls' College, the way she looked back at him, the tear in her eye as she drove away – but that was a long time ago, so I pushed it straight out of my mind. It could not be him. I had no idea who this man was, or even what he looked like. But I read a passion in those letters that I didn't think she ever had for me. It broke me. I folded them, and put them away where I had found them.

I made arrangements for her body and her belongings to be brought home, all the while wondering what I was going to tell our people.

'I don't know how I am going to say these things to our family,' I said to the hospital administrator.

He nodded.

'None of these things make sense.'

He nodded again.

'Mr Nwogo, I wish I was not the bearer of this news. The police have conducted their investigations and they have concluded that it is Rose, and it is suicide.'

I shook my head. 'But it still does not make sense. Please help me understand.'

'Mr . . . I understand you are in shock.'

'How am I going to tell our people?'

'I wish I could help but . . .'

'Rose would not have killed herself,' I said.

'I am sorry, but I have no choice in the matter but to accept the conclusion of the colonial police. The case has been closed.'

'Do I not get a say?'

He was silent, avoided my eyes and looked away.

'I knew her, she would not have done this.'

'I'm afraid the matter is closed.'

I realized from his tone and countenance that to fight against this judgement would be a fight not just against him but against the powers of the hospital and those of the police. I was silent for a little while with frustration and grief. I was nothing but a mere African man within their system, and I understood that beneath the surface, beneath the pleasantries, beneath the manners was somewhere you didn't want to go.

'I cannot tell her people this,' I said, beseeching the humanity within him.

His face remained like stone.

And I understood, got up from the chair, took one last look at him in hope. Then I bid him a good day and left his office.

Uche saw me to the train station.

I took some of Rose's belongings with me. Two lone, scratched-up brown leather suitcases that contained the most important of her items. It was all I could confidently take on the train. They seemed to sum up everything, sitting there on the concrete platform. The sum of a life. *Is that all a human life comes down to – two suitcases?* I thought.

It was a hot but grey day and we sat in silence while waiting for the train. I fought inside to comprehend, to find answers to the questions swirling in my head. I could not help myself, just had to know. 'Was Rose seeing anyone?' I asked Uche as we sat there facing the train tracks.

She was quiet for a little while before answering. 'I don't know,' she said. 'Rose was secretive about her affairs.'

'Uche, what happened?'

She bent her head and sobbed into her handkerchief. 'I don't . . . I don't . . . know,' she said between sobs.

'But why would she kill herself?'

'I don't know,' she cried. 'I keep replaying the last time I saw her over and over in my head. Trying to find what I could have said that could have changed things.'

'Uche, what happened to her?'

'I don't know.'

We were silent again. Uche sat clenching a handkerchief to her mouth, trying to hold back her tears.

I heard the train coming in the distance.

'I have made arrangements for the rest of her belongings and her body to be brought home,' I said.

Uche nodded. 'I will oversee it this end,' she said in a low and gravelly voice. 'I will follow the body home.'

I stood up.

Uche put her hand out, grabbed hold of my lower arm to stop me from moving forward to board the train.

'I am sorry,' she said, 'very sorry.'

I nodded. 'What for? It was not your fault.'

She removed her hand. 'I looked for her, we all did. At first I thought . . .' She paused, then continued, 'I thought all sorts. The police found the note.'

The train stopped in front of us. I walked forward, loaded the suitcases on board. All the while Uche stood on the platform watching me. I found myself a seat in the carriage by the window, did not look back at where she stood on the platform, for fear of breaking down. Heard the sound of the conductor's whistle, then that of the wheels as they began to turn on the track. Saw the platform begin to disappear as the train moved out, taking me back to the barracks, back to our people, with this terrible news.

Rose's body was buried three weeks later, in the public cemetery – not in her father's yard beside her mother and her other ancestors, or in ours, or in the church grounds beside her grandfather, who had first converted.

It was a quiet affair; only five of us attended: myself, her father, the older two of her brothers and Uche. We did it early in the morning, at the crack of dawn, before the rest of the village was up and about and anyone could ask questions.

But I suspect that somehow the rest of the village knew, for there were many whispered conversations that would suddenly end when I approached, and many of the villagers kept away – very few came to give their condolences, even though they knew she had died.

I, however, could not bring myself to tell them the full truth. Those abominable words would not pass my lips, for I just could not believe she had committed suicide. So I lied. Told them it was an accident whenever someone plucked up the courage to ask; even my uncles, who wanted to understand more when we were alone and could not be overheard.

So, that early morning, we buried her quietly, and the next day I went back to the barracks. There was much to do, much to sort out. There were rumours circulating that we could be shipped out to fight at any moment.

19

Jungle

Eastern Nigeria, Wet Season, 1943

OUR COMPANY COMMENCED jungle training towards the second half of 1943, sixteen months after Rose . . . No. After the body was quietly buried. She was not talked of again. The shame silenced us. But she filled my thoughts, which nagged away at me; I had no control over them. Sometimes, in the early days, I would smell her, that sweet mixture of Vaseline, talcum powder and the fragrance from her creams, and just as suddenly as I had smelt her, the scent would disappear.

And so I trained the men harder in order to dislodge the thoughts, worked longer hours in order to retire exhausted so I didn't think of her, but instead she invaded my dreams. Still, I continued working, training the various recruits as they passed through the training centre, and also attending to my work in the office.

Early one week, while I typed and filed away documents, I overheard the colonial officers speaking about jungle training outside their offices. They stood in hastily half-opened doorways, and behind closed doors through which muted and muffled conversations could be heard, checking their arrangements. We got word from the 81st West African Division already fighting in Burma, with which Ifeanyi, having returned from East Africa, had been sent out to fight. And which, believe it or not, Emeka had also joined. This did not make sense to me, knowing Emeka, but then, with Rose gone, maybe we all were not in our right minds. I don't know. Anyway, they sent word to our commander that we should receive training in jungle warfare and watermanship prior to embarking on our journey to Asia.

And yet, despite this, I still awoke in shock at four in the morning to the sound of the early-morning bugle which rang out loud across the barracks. My dreams of Rose abruptly interrupted, I barely had time to clean my teeth, throw on some clothes and get my things together, before they quick-marched us outside with all our gear and bundled us into military trucks.

I listened as each engine started up, smelt a little diesel from the exhaust fumes, and one by one we left the barracks, driving in convoy, into the darkness.

The drivers steered the trucks along the road with such assurance and determination that I drew some comfort from the fact that even though we, my comrades and I, did not know where we were heading, at least the drivers knew.

We rocked back and forth as the truck sped along, felt the cold morning breeze against our skin, and one by one we awoke from our daze.

And yet I was still numb inside; I was still trying to make sense of Rose's death. It seemed the world had moved on but I could not. I stretched to uncoil the knots in my upper arms, but there was hardly room between us. We sat thigh against thigh, arm against arm. I fixed my hat on my head and secured the strap, shifted my backpack, then picked up my rifle again from where I had leant it against my chest. We watched daylight poke through the horizon, then the shadows begin to turn into trees as we journeyed on. But still, out in the open, driving along in the early morning, rocking from side to side, I wondered where she was.

'Sir!' shouted Afam, Chuks's partner in crime. 'Where are we going?'

'Training!' I shouted back, as I watched the bush pass behind him.

'What kind of training, sir?'

I shrugged, looked away to the back of the truck at the rest of the team, barely awake, then back at his baby face looking eagerly up at me, waiting for an answer.

'Jungle training,' I shouted above the noise of the engine and the rattling and creaking of the truck as we drove over a pot hole. He smiled, nodded and looked away, as if he was too tired to ask any more questions, to watch the vegetation the truck left behind.

I thought of Rose's father. The last time I had gone home it was as if he had shrunk to half his size, a shadow of the man I used to watch and admire through the stick partition that separated our compounds. His wife's death and then Rose's had taken their toll. Now that Rose's younger brothers were gone, either to school or to Kano for work, he seemed alone, rattling around in their house. My uncles kept saying he needed a young wife to power up his manhood again, but I knew Rose's supposed suicide, that of his favourite child, had almost finished him. I had no choice but to tell him the truth about the death. Like me, he did not believe it, so had gone to the hospital to get answers himself, and, like me, had come up against a wall. I did not tell him that sometimes, at night, in my dreams, a small part of me doubted, questioned whether she was alive or dead; a small part of me dreamt that maybe the body we buried was not Rose's. I felt myself hoping that she was still alive. And then I would wake, sweat pouring off me, my rational self asking, 'If she is alive, why does she not show herself to you? If she is alive, who did we bury in the early morning? If she is alive . . .' And then the reality of my surroundings, of the barracks, would seep back into my frazzled brain.

And so I had called two of my younger brothers, tasked them to investigate, gave them money to comb Lagos, find out what might have happened to her, for I could not believe in this suicide. I awaited their letters, some correspondence on what they had found.

We drove a little longer over several miles of rough terrain, rocking back and forth, before the trucks finally came to a stop at the edge of very thick forest. I heard the sergeants disembark and shout out instructions as they walked up and down between the trucks. Then the release of the catches on the tailboard. We jumped down, assembled and then marched into the depths of the forest.

It was late morning when we finally stopped and they put us to work setting up camp: clearing the ground, erecting tents. The next day we began our training. We sat on the forest floor in front of blackboards while the Sergeant and the other officers set about instructing us. The Sergeant walked back and forth, stick in hand, pointing to the board, barking out instructions on how to survive in dense and tangled vegetation when cut off from the rest of our troops, and about jungle warfare, before moving on to instructions on watermanship. His moustache seemed to fan and flutter above his top lip as he shouted out his words.

We learnt how to rescue each other from the water, build a raft, construct a makeshift bridge and manoeuvre in a canoe. We learnt how to identify edible plants and fruits, how to track and trap animals, collect water and build a fire in the challenging terrain. And I hoped for rescue from the turmoil inside. It was not knowing what had happened that made it worse. I was convinced that Rose could not have done such a thing, yet there were still moments of doubt when I thought that maybe it was just me, that maybe Rose had taken her own life. But then I would remember her smile as she stood on the platform waving me goodbye that day, and I would take out her last letter, tucked away among my belongings, and reread her words which tumbled over themselves with joy and excitement.

I remember jumping in and out of the water, which somehow

began to bring me back to life. And as I trained, the war ahead began to feel real. I was no longer a trainer but being trained to fight in it, and I became scared of what might lie ahead.

We spent six weeks in the jungle. That first week Captain Miller took ill and was evacuated to a military hospital. He was followed by a steady trickle of other colonial officers. Even the Sergeant and young Lieutenant Richards fell ill. I watched as one after another they grew pale, sickly, and were taken out of the forest to hospital. We watched as the rest of the colonials left behind seemed to sink into a form of melancholy, particularly as stories about what they might have contracted disseminated among them. I looked on, watching them as they sank, wondered about what seemed to me this frailness they displayed. Tried to reconcile this with the image I had in my head of them as godlike creatures, but could not. In this environment they did not seem as strong, or even godlike, as I had imagined them, and I began to wonder about who these white men were, and why I had thought them superior.

After we left the forest we were made to line up and undergo medicals. They took blood. My tests must have been in order as I was deemed fit to fight. A few lucky ones, however, were lost to the unit. But mostly we got new officers, as our officers and NCOs were still laid up in hospital. These new ones were green, barely dry behind the ears. A few were South African. A few Polish. I watched the novices take control, shuddered.

We prepared to leave for Sierra Leone, where they had a bigger port, could dock bigger ships, for further training with the rest of our division and to board the ships for Burma.

And still Rose would not remain silent, she rattled away in my brain.

We assembled in Sierra Leone. The soldiers came from all around: the Hausas and Yorubas from the north of Nigeria, the Gold

Coasters, the Gambians and many more. We camped under Wusum Hill in Sierra Leone, but there were soldiers also camped in Teko, and at the barracks in Port Loko. There were so many of us, speaking so many different languages, including the white NCOs and officers, that it made my head spin.

And yet, stationed in Freetown, more colonials died of diseases: blackwater fever, yellow fever, meningitis, malaria, dysentery.

We African soldiers got to know each other well as we waited for the ship for Burma to arrive, learnt each other's marching songs, watched the local children peering through the fence, copying and mimicking us as we carried out our drills. Some of the children spoke English and one or two would run errands for us, and we in return would reward them with our rations of biscuits and sugared bananas.

'Men, are you ready?'

'Yes, sir!' we shouted in unison.

'Are you ready?'

'Yes, sir!!!' we chorused.

The powerful sound of thousands of us soldiers resounded around the camp. We stood facing the General and his officers, who stood on a makeshift platform in the distance.

'Well,' he said, speaking into the loudhailer. 'The time has come.' He paused, bobbing his head as if he was looking at each one of us. 'We have received word; the ship to take us to battle arrives tomorrow.' He paused again, searching our faces. 'Japan has invaded Burma and refuses to relinquish its hold. You are called upon to defend King and Empire. Tomorrow, we set sail for Burma to begin our mission. It will be a long and hard fight, but ultimately we shall win!

'Men, are you ready?'

'Yes, sir!!!' we shouted back.

'Sleep well tonight, for our mission begins tomorrow,' he said.

We watched as he left the stage, his officers following behind. We dispersed to our quarters as soon as we could. I was quiet but could hear the others chatting in front. Afam and Chuks, the young boys, were tussling and joking with each other as we passed the other tents to get to ours.

The air was thick and hot, heavy between us. We retired early and sought solace in our beds, but we could hear laughter coming from the tent next door, then a small argument coming from the one on our left, and beyond these sounds was a low hum of chatter, mostly in Hausa, coming from the other tents all around us.

I think the General's speech focused our minds. The excitement and adventure that had filled our days while we waited in Sierra Leone were finally silenced, and in their place we fed on a sandwich of anxiety and uncertainty about what lay ahead. I knew we all wondered in the quiet corners of our minds whether we would see our homes again. The tension jumped like static between us as we tossed and coughed in the dark; each sound seemed amplified.

'Sir, are you awake?'

'Yes.'

'I don't want to die,' said Afam.

'Afam, be quiet, nobody does,' said Olu, who had recently joined us. He lifted his slim, muscular frame on to his elbows to face Afam. 'If we don't go out to face the enemy over there, they will come and find us here.'

'This is the white man's war,' Afam said back to him. 'Why do we have to fight their war and go and die in Asia?'

'What choice is there?' said Chuks. 'We have run away how many times and each time they brought us back.'

'Even after this war is over, when they are free of the enemy, we Africans still won't be free,' said another.

'All of you shut up,' I said. 'We are here now. Whether it is by your choice or not, it doesn't matter now. The important thing is to make it back home alive. We will have to look after each other when we are over there.'

'Yes,' said Olu, nodding his head and lying back down.

'Now go to sleep, there will be a lot for us to do tomorrow,' I ordered.

'Yes, sir,' said Afam.

I turned, closed my eyes, but for a long while I could not sleep. I listened to the men's heavy breathing and snores, and when sleep finally came I did not dream of the war but of Rose, of why after all these months my brothers still had sent no news. I felt the tears on my cheeks in my sleep as I fought thoughts of her.

We set sail from Sierra Leone to Burma – or Ceylon, to be precise – in May 1944, aboard a huge liner.

It was a hot sunny day and the quayside was alive with chatter, a mass of soldiers, almost four thousand of us troops, kitted out, assembled and ready to board.

It seemed everyone in Freetown had come to say their goodbyes. We smiled at the palm wine sellers, and the young boys who had run errands for us during our short stay. Handed over our final rations of biscuits and sugared bananas through the fence to the schoolboys as we went by.

They waved and hollered at us as we lined up to board; the mid-day sun glared down and the sweat dripped out from under my hat, ran down my temples, collected under my chin to soak the collar of my khaki shirt. I felt more beads of sweat form on my back and under my arms, making wet patches in my armpits, and at the back of my shirt.

I looked up at the hugeness of the vessel in front of me, mar-velled at its magnitude, and felt as small as a soldier ant. Heard the chatter of the men around me; moved forward, getting ever closer to the gangway; wondered if I could turn back, run; turned around only to see the masses of troops behind, still to come. There was no going back. No choice but to move forward, move forward towards the battlefield in a foreign land. I felt the weight of my rucksack, a slight pain as the straps bit into my shoulders, shifted it to move the load. And then we were walking up the gangway, and I looked down on all that was happening below, all the while moving forward, closer to war.

We stood on the top deck with hardly any room to move, watched the shoreline disappear, the people left behind waving goodbye and diminishing into dots.

20

Away

Ceylon, Monsoon Season, 1944

WE LANDED IN Ceylon in June. The monsoon season, by all accounts, was almost in full swing.

It was not a safe journey, so we were escorted by the Royal Navy. We were told that Japanese submarines were in the deep waters, and so we often peeked over the side to see if we could detect signs of them through the murky blue ocean, but we could not. Instead we saw the clouds of white sea foam lap, bounce and spray off the sides of the vessel, and heard the sound of the wind as it gusted through the ship, the flap of a flag from somewhere up above, and the creaks of the liner as the water ebbed and flowed around it.

I watched the two destroyers and the cruiser as they sailed beside us, felt the wind on my face as I looked back towards home.

'They should be harvesting the corn,' said Olu as we stared out over the water, his voice wistful.

I looked over at him, at his boyish profile, which reminded me of one of my younger brothers, though I think there was only a year, maybe two, between us. He was the oldest child in his family.

His red-brown skin glowed healthy in the sun. Then I looked back out over the sea. 'Yes, indeed,' I replied.

'With so many of us gone, I hope the women have enough men to bring in the harvest,' said Olu.

'Indeed,' I said again, and at the same time we both heard Afam calling Olu on the deck below.

'Olu,' shouted Afam, 'Chuks has made a fishing rod. He wants to see if he can catch fish. Your people, are they not fisher people?'

Olu was from a small fishing and farming village by the coast, near to Lagos. He laughed. 'Excuse me,' he said, and quickly ran off to help with Chuks's and Afam's fishing adventures.

I thought of our people and wondered what they would think if they too could see the expanse of water and sky between us. As the sun disappeared, I shivered from the cold, and was glad we had beds to sleep in below. But mostly I wondered about Rose, about my brothers, what information they might have found, about the letter in her room, about the father of Little Rose. Who was he? Where was he? Maybe he had something to do with Rose's disappearance, her supposed suicide? There were so many questions, yet still no answers.

During the day I found a spot on the deck where I could doze, covered my face with my wide-brimmed army hat, but often a space was difficult to find with so many of us on board. Many succumbed to seasickness; even Olu, who was normally such a jolly fellow, seemed to struggle. I do not know why I did not.

Sometimes we played cards, sometimes Chuks and Afam made us laugh with their banter and quick jabs at each other, taking our minds off the ones we had left at home, and the battles that lay ahead. Once or twice we saw dolphins, whales, turtles and flying fish. It was the excitement of the day. We laughed and jostled as we went from port to starboard, trying to see it all.

To keep myself busy, I volunteered while on board to help the NCOs and officers teach English to the illiterate soldiers. Every morning we brought the blackboards out for the NCOs, and stood among the men ready to help translate as the officer stood in front pointing and teaching the Churchill Basic English.

I was not of great use to most, as the majority of our soldiers were Hausa and I had learnt but a few words of their language, but I tried my best.

Along the way, the ship docked at Cape Town, in South Africa. Only the white officers were initially welcomed and allowed off the ship. Many of my colleagues, and a few of the white officers, were so incensed by the situation that they caused a fuss. The port authorities eventually relented and allowed a few of us off, but only in groups of no more than two. I myself had refused to go ashore out of sheer stubbornness and pride. I was not going to step even one foot on to their land. I was glad that I decided not to go, for the few that did go ashore, including Olu and Chuks, returned quickly enough, telling stories of watching eyes and harassment by shopkeepers.

At that point, at the beginning of our journey towards war, a few did not make it off our boat, or out of the makeshift army hospital, as they died from pneumonia.

All sorts of ridiculous rumours spread among the locals as we disembarked from the ship in Ceylon. The colonial authorities fuelled the rumours of us having tails and eating people alive, in order to put fear into the locals, and the Japanese if the stories should reach their ears.

Our division assembled in India gradually over time. On our arrival in the camp, one of the high-ranking officers gathered us together, and gave us general information on the country and the war we had been brought halfway across the world to fight.

The 81ˢᵗ West African Division, already in the field fighting, were gaining a reputation for their bravery and skills; some were even seconded into special-operation Chindit units, who provided intelligence to our commanders, and so we were sent for more jungle training some distance from Bombay.

In August it was the beginning of yam harvest season back home, and as we trained, many of us worried again about the women and hoped there would be enough young boys left to help them with the harvest. We continued training and, by October, at the end of yam harvest season in my village, we were ready.

We rode on the train to Calcutta, en route to the battlefield in Burma. I was quiet as we went, the others chattering around me. I listened to the chug-chug of the train and caught quick glimpses of grassland, dwellings and people as we sped by, before meeting the expanse of hills covered with a mist that seemed to dance and skim over the land. It was hot in the carriage but the air coming through the window cooled us a little. India was nothing like we had thought it would be: the heat and the grassland seemed somehow familiar, but the people so very different. We were surprised by the number of beggars, the poverty and signs of hunger along the route, and as we got closer to Calcutta it seemed to get worse. It was not until we reached the city that we stood there as grown men wanting to cry. Ifeanyi had sent letters, almost a year back, when he had passed through the city with his division at the height of the Bengal famine. But still we were not prepared. He had written in his letters of how they had to help gather the dead to be buried, and the barely living to be fed in camps, but still we were not prepared. Seeing emaciated men and women with skin hanging from their bones, and gaunt children sucking from dry, leather-like breasts, lining the streets in front of your very eyes is not something a letter can truly prepare you for. I stopped, stood there, wishing to help; we gave what we could but it didn't seem enough. We wondered why, if the colonials could ship us at great cost to fight the Japanese in Burma, they couldn't also ship in food to feed these poor people. It did not make any sense to us.

They quickly marched us on and we hurried to catch up with the rest to board the train to Chittagong.

Well, we thought we had seen the worst in Calcutta, but the Japanese had bombed the city of Chittagong days earlier. We walked through the city stealthily, clutching our guns, checking the skies, listening out for any sound which might indicate that the Japs had decided to return. The city was virtually impassable as we stepped carefully to avoid jagged edges of metal and rubble, and booby traps, and more, for heads, legs, all sorts of body parts would suddenly appear from under bricks and debris as we moved forward.

And when we made camp that night I could not sleep, for my head was filled with the horrors we had seen during the day. I eventually fell asleep thinking of Rose. I dreamt of our single night together. I dreamt of it in order not to think of what I had seen during the day, to take away the nightmares. In the morning I thought I smelt her beside me, before the reality of where I was and where we were heading came flooding back to me.

'Rose,' I cried.

I hoped my brothers would soon send word.

Our division, the 82nd West African Division, was sent to the Arakan Mountains to relieve the 26th Indian Division, which was being withdrawn to rest and train for amphibious operations on the coast, and to chase and push the Japs south out of Burma.

On nearing the Burmese border, we heard bomb explosions, saw flashes of fire, fiery plumes sending out big balloons of black smoke high into the sky. We flinched with each loud bang, the air smelt of strange gases, and mixed in, I thought I smelt blood. War was finally there in front of us. No longer a destination. We had arrived, and I remember thinking, coming into the battlefield, *I am not ready*, as we heard the big bangs going off in the sky above. We were away from everyone and everything we knew. I felt alone in that moment, heard another explosion up above and prayed, *God, please don't let me die here.*

Two fellow African soldiers, who had been there a while before we arrived, came out to greet us. To my surprise and great joy, when I looked, one of them was Emeka's brother Nonso.

'My friend!'

We forgot ourselves, quickly hugged each other tight. I could smell war on him. He smelt of a mixture of earth, days of sweat and cordite; deep, but sharp, with a sweet undertone of burnt sugar and ash.

'How have you been?' I asked, looking into his eyes to get an honest answer.

But he cast his eyes away. 'Good, good,' he said. 'Look, there is not enough time for this. Come, when we reach camp we can talk.' We followed the other soldier, a sergeant who was in a hurry to get us back to base. I came to know the other man as Sergeant Ibrahim, a Hausa man, a northerner, who I later found out was the NCO for my squad. It was a great relief to see them, especially to come across Emeka's brother so far from home, and so we followed them into camp.

'How is it going?' I asked stupidly, as we manoeuvred through the bush.

They laughed as we all flinched from the sound of an explosion in the distance.

'As the white man would say, "swimmingly",' joked Nonso.

I said no more.

Reaching camp, they gave us food, then took us to the camp

stores and kitted us out with utensils and other supplies. Afterwards we were allocated to different platoons. Chuks was the first to be separated from our small group to another squad. Olu, Afam and I formed part of Sergeant Ibrahim's squad.

That night Emeka's brother and I managed to catch up. I told him the news about Rose, and he nodded as if he already knew. He told me a little about the battle in East Africa, that he and a few of the troops from the 81st had been transferred back from the Chindits when it was disbanded, and also what to expect out there in the jungle. We hugged once more before parting again, for he was helping specifically at this camp due to his experience and language skills. He had learnt to speak Yoruba while living in Lagos, and knew Hausa from childhood as his family had spent a little time in the north.

The following day, before dawn, we were mobilized for battle. The auxiliary group followed behind, carrying on their heads the large loads of equipment needed for the fight. We established headquarters and were tasked with capturing the town of Buthidaung, and extending the Arakan front lines further south.

21

Killing

WE MARCHED ALONG the Maungdaw–Buthidaung road, through the two long tunnels which the Allies had captured earlier that year. The tunnels were dark, damp and filled with rubble, but we sweltered in the heat once we emerged into the sun. All was quiet except for the sound of our boots crunching the dirt as they clunked on the ground, the clink and clank of our equipment as we marched along. Our commanding officer, one of two white men in our platoon, could also be heard somewhere ahead talking on the field radio, communicating back to base, or possibly with the other platoons that were in front or behind us. We kept to the sides of the road, listening as we went, ready to take cover and fire back if needed. Sergeant Ibrahim, our squad leader, was just in front of me. Young Afam, now our grenadier, was behind. Olu was on the other side of the road pointing his automatic rifle towards the trees as we marched by.

I kept looking up at the sky. There were birds circling above, giving out little squawks as if they were trying to tell us something about the fate that lay ahead.

The night before, Sergeant Ibrahim had gathered the nine of us in his squad after he had said his evening prayers and we had eaten.

Olu and I were already sitting there conversing, while taking apart our guns to clean and check their mechanism. He suddenly stood before us, tall, dark and slim, a proud Hausa man with tribal marks just below his cheekbones, his left foot resting on a log. He was older, I guessed almost forty, with a fatherly presence that made you want to listen.

'Tomorrow we go into battle,' he said, looking at each one of us. 'Some of you I only met a few days ago, and mostly we have neither religion nor language in common.' He paused, stared straight at me, and it felt like he could see right into my very soul. 'I don't care if you can read.' His eyes continued his search. 'Or if you drink.' His eyes continued on their travels between us. 'What matters is that you can shoot straight. That we have each other's backs out there. Do you understand?'

'Yes, sir!' we said, staring up at him.

'On the battlefield we have one thing, and one thing only: each other. We are all we have to get us out of this alive. Do you understand?'

'Yes, sir!'

'May Allah protect every one of us,' he said, then sauntered away to attend to other duties.

There was something in the way he had spoken and walked away that put fear into me. I looked around at the rest, from Afam to Olu and the others. In that moment I wished I had listened to my grandmother way back then, when she had told me to run. As he said, we had neither tribe nor language in common, but these were my brothers. They relied on me as much as I relied on them.

I mulled over the conversation from the night before as we marched along, heard a rustle in the trees, pointed my gun quickly towards it. A bird flew out and up into the sky, and so I calmed my beating heart, pointed the rifle down; the metal somehow felt sweaty in my palms. My backpack was heavy, dragging me down; I hitched it up and continued with the rest. And I kept thinking, *what am I doing here?*, for it all felt surreal out there, so far from home, and I couldn't wait for a rest, for I was tired already.

And as evening fell and we drew closer to Buthidaung, we came off the road, got into position. Some of our division took to the hills surrounding the town. Our squad to the bush. Our white platoon leader painted his face black as we hid. He looked a strange sort of black, a black I had never seen on any Black man, with white-pink eyes and pink lips that suddenly poked, flickered and glared back at you from amid the black paint on his face. I later came to understand that this was for camouflage and to avoid sniper action, for the white men were targets in the jungle. The Japanese killed the white officers among us first, as they were the ones who were fully instructed on where we were going, and so to kill them meant the rest of us could potentially be left directionless. I later came to resent the fact that not many of our men had been taught to be officers, as our own experienced soldiers, like Ibrahim, whom I had come to respect, were far superior leaders to the whites they sent our way.

As I followed Ibrahim that day, I had a sense that the officer in front of him was green, even though I had been under his command mere hours. This was confirmed as I watched Ibrahim once or twice diplomatically intervene to steer us back on the right course. But even seeing the interactions between Ibrahim and the officer then, for some reason I still clung to the belief that the white officer surely must know better.

I heard the crunch of branches beneath my feet and the sound of wildlife high up in the trees as we crept towards the town of Buthidaung. I looked up, then down and around, searching carefully as we passed through for signs of the enemy hiding in the grass. Then we were almost there, scaled a hilltop, hid in among the trees; from there we could see the town below. We waited.

At first light we began to hear the machine gunfire and mortars, and we pushed forward in the grey of dawn. I was suddenly filled with adrenaline, heard the radio communication between our NCOs and the platoon leader become ever more frantic with directions. We repositioned ourselves quickly, running low, hid as best we could in the vegetation and fired back at the Japanese soldiers across the way; in the bushes, in the trees, I was not sure. We saw sparks coming from a small wood. Heard the ta-ta-ta of the machine guns. We fired back. Afam, our grenadier, got up quickly on to his knees, threw his grenades in their direction, and fell back down beside me on my right. I heard the grenades explode as they landed, and ducked. Looked to my left, and found Sergeant Ibrahim beside me. I watched him lift himself, aim and shoot one of the Japs down from the trees. I followed his lead and shot down another. My heart pumped so loudly I thought it was going to explode in my chest. Ibrahim shouted at me to move, surround them on the other side. And so when he got up low and ran, I ran with him.

The artillery and tanks of the Indian tank brigade rolled in.

We took Buthidaung on the second day.

My dearest Rose, if you can hear me, wherever you may be, my dearest love, I have an urge to let you know, to tell you how much I loved you, lest the unthinkable should happen.

Rose, war is a strange thing. A very strange thing indeed. We captured a Burmese town today, and as we aimed, and fired, and chased those Japs away, advancing forward as they fled, there was something that took over. I thought I would be scared, worried about being killed. But that's not the way I felt at all, Rose. I didn't think of dying once. It didn't even cross my mind in those moments. I was so focused, Rose, focused on doing as I was commanded, making sure I played my part, making sure we all got out of there alive that there was no time to think of death. It was only afterwards, my dear love, that it hit me.

Well, I hope to come back in one piece, count the days and pray I make it home. I rub the talisman you put around my neck that day and pray I make it home.

It hit me, after the battle, when they lined up some of my comrades' bodies on the ground. Looking down on those young men, their still African faces, one or two with the tribal marks of their people, it hit me that it could have been me lying there. They would not be buried according to the ways of their people. They would never see home again. Their mothers could be at home, pounding yam, seeing to their chores, hoping against all hope that their sons would be the lucky ones, the ones to come home, not knowing they were already dead. That their bodies were to be buried in a foreign land, thrown into the ground that day. Killed in a war they most probably did not willingly choose to be in. It was them today, could it be me tomorrow?

I spotted the body of a young man among all the dead Hausa soldiers. I did not know him well, but I knew he was Igbo, like me. I had no camwood to rub him down, but I had a little chalk; for some reason I had stored it in my rucksack from the days of helping teach English on the ship. I fished it out, bent down and marked his hands and head as my people would have done to send him on his way to the next life.

Lying apart from the bodies of my fellow Africans were the bodies of three white officers riddled with bullets. Seeing them lying there dead shook me. It was alien to my mind that white men could die just as easily and quickly as us Africans.

I hurried on, as Sergeant Ibrahim was calling me.

And so we took and secured Buthidaung on the Kalapanzin River. We built a bridgehead on the east bank, establishing control of the Maungdaw–Buthidaung road. A road that had been contested for three years.

We heard the buzz of the engines first, as the Allies arrived with equipment and supplies, then the trucks emerged triumphant from the bush. Everyone gave out a loud cheer, and we got to work assembling the pontoons. We shifted wooden sleepers and metal road-bearers to the bank, under the hot sun, to help with the launch of the crafts into the water. We manoeuvred, shirtless, back and forth, with only our felt bush hats to shade us from the sun.

I stopped once or twice, wiped the sweat from my brow, having dropped a load which clanked and cluttered as it settled, and looked up. The birds glided majestically high up in the bright blue skies. The bushes on the other side of the bank swayed a little in the breeze. It was a beautiful day.

And I wondered, briefly, when we would get word from home. When, or even if, letters from my brothers would arrive. And if they did, what news would they bring? As I stood there looking at the sky, I prayed that despite my fears, despite the thoughts I battled at night, I would finally get news of Rose, to help clear away the muddle inside me, for at the time I was sure of one thing: that Rose could not have killed herself.

One of our white officers, a South African, shouted out instructions and pointed as we worked. I could see Ibrahim was irritated by him, as sometimes he got in the way and the loads were heavy.

We manoeuvred a pontoon into the water, filled it with artillery guns, crates of ammunition and supplies, launched the river craft downstream. The men sitting in the canoe-like pontoons carefully steered them with their paddles. Then we loaded another pontoon, drove a tank from the Indian tank brigade on to its platform, and set it on its way. We worked like this for days, briefly watching each raft set off, making sure all was steady, drifting safely on its way, to provide supplies to the Indian division waiting patiently downstream in the Mayu Peninsula. They needed the supplies for their advance south, to capture Rathedaung and Kudaung Island from the Japs.

Meanwhile, one of the Nigerian battalions from our division was sent south on foot to clear the villages and surrounding areas parallel to the river of Japs. Another battalion was sent downriver into the *chaung*s to build a bridgehead. We got word that they had succeeded. A day later it came under fire from the Japs. I remember looking up into the sky. I heard the faint hum of the engines first, so I looked up to see British planes flying overhead and knew they were carrying out airstrikes on the Japs downstream, knew the battle must be tough for them to bring out the planes. I wondered how many we might have lost, and when we would be called on to drop what we were doing to support the fight there.

But they let us finish, then gave us our orders: to take the village of Seinnyinbya to support the fighting downstream. Our platoon set off in assault boats in the early morning, down the Kalapanzin River to where the waters meet; it was still dark. Three men paddled on the left, and three on the right, while our white officer sat in front and navigated; he held what I thought was a compass tight in his hand, and a map with a torch, both shielded to hide the light in the morning darkness. Our officer set off with a verse of 'Row, Row, Row Your Boat', and those of us who knew it sang along with him; the others attempted to learn it with their awkward English. We laughed and teased each other as we glided through the water. There were other canoe-like crafts, with African soldiers, in front and behind, drifting along the side of the riverbank to take advantage of its cover. Once we were clear of secure ground, we fell silent. All I could hear was the sound of the paddles quietly sloshing and splashing through the water. Sergeant Ibrahim and Olu sat in front, Afam and another young boy in the middle. I sat towards the back with others looking out, guns at the ready, searching for any movement among the shrubs on the banks. And as dawn spread we caught glimpses of river mist dancing over the paddy fields beyond, a lone water buffalo drinking quietly from the river, and, every so often, abandoned grass huts which sat on stilts rising out of the water.

We disembarked on to the muddy bank, headed towards the village of Seinnyinbya in order to attack the Japs from behind, as they were putting up a fight and pushing some of our men back north. As we entered the village we came under fire, retreated for cover, but then drove on, and while I lay there cowering from the bullets, reloading my rifle, one of our men, a Hausa, tall and slim like Ibrahim, got up calmly and walked slowly around. Not a single bullet grazed him. It was as if no one could see him but me, as if maybe the talisman he wore was protecting him. He had shown it to me during the days after we had taken Buthidaung, late one evening as we sat eating. He said his wife had given it to him, told him to hurry back home, and he intended to do so. I remember at the time clutching the one around my neck, the one Rose had given me so many moons ago when we had said our sweet goodbyes at the train station in Lagos. I clutched it, hoping mine would also protect me and bring me home to my people.

Well, he walked towards where a Japanese soldier was hiding in the trees, sniping at us, pointed his gun up into the branches and shot the Jap dead. His body landed with a thump on the ground. If I hadn't seen it with my own two eyes, I would not have believed it. That fellow was my hero. He was later awarded a medal. I wanted to be brave, to get a medal just like him.

We continued to forge forwards, took control of Seinnyinbya. The remaining Japanese soldiers were now sandwiched between us and our other battalions.

I admired him, our brave soldier. But I don't know what made him so brave. Maybe that was just the way he was. Or maybe he had been fighting for too long, maybe he was tired – that's what Sergeant Ibrahim said when I asked as we sat eating our dinner. He told me war can exhaust you if you let it. He meant mentally, not physically. He said the constant searching and hiding from the enemy can take its toll on your mind, can wear you down until you are too tired to feel fear.

He had been fighting longer than the rest of us, transferred out from the 81st, our brave soldier. Well, I still don't totally understand his bravery. All I do know is I found his talisman on the ground the day he finally died.

We buried him, our brave soldier, on the outskirts of the village where he fell.

22

The Chase

IN THE MORNING, just before dawn, we prepared ourselves for the trek across open fields, and over steep jungle hills, into the Kaladan Valley. Our task was to move towards Myohaung and relieve the 81st West African Division.

Their division was making its way down the Kaladan River, which ran parallel to the river we had battled over and crossed. The 81st had been chasing the Japs south, out of Burma, towards the coast and the Bay of Bengal.

So, that morning we waded cautiously through the muddy marsh of the paddy fields, and the twisting and winding waterways which snaked their way through the land. We were followed by the auxiliary group who carried on their heads all the equipment we required. I was looking forward to meeting up with Ifeanyi, but first there were mountains to climb. We were lucky that it was not yet monsoon season to worsen our trek. We moved tentatively across the open fields, trudged through the waterways, which were in some places waist-deep; the reconnaissance unit was already waiting in position in the jungle, a platoon behind us hiding in the vegetation to provide cover.

Our backpacks were heavy, our hands sweaty as we held our

guns, looking around for signs and sounds of Japs as we went across the open fields. Our units moved in a bounding, then overwatch motion with each other. We could see the jungle with its steep mountain ranges in the distance. I mentally readied myself for the long trek through it, and was glad once we reached cover just before nightfall.

We settled down, established a secure defence position, dug out our trenches with our knives to sleep fully clothed, applied our mosquito repellent, and took up our gun posts for the night, ready for action, while the monkeys chattered loudly high up in the dark trees.

We got news from base camp that our commander had been sent to hospital for an ingrown toenail, but there was something not quite right about the news. It was as if our white officer knew more than he said when he told us. Anyway, not long after, we had a new British commander, Major-General Stockwell.

We led the advance. The auxiliary group came behind, carrying head loads, as we followed a path made by the Japs. Our unit trekked through the jungle, up into the hills. We would march for over an hour, followed by a short period of rest, before starting up again. We gasped our way to what we thought were the hilltops, only to find another stretch upwards even steeper than the one we had just climbed. We were all exhausted. The auxiliary group groaned under their heavy loads and I was glad I was not the one having to carry them. On reaching the summit, we looked out on the surrounding country and saw its wild beauty. Many shades of green billowed out as far as the eye could see, and monkeys hooted high up in the trees. Their sound echoed and bounced off the hills. We were awed at the wonder of nature, before being brought back down to earth as we looked over to find a drop just as steep as the one we had climbed. And as we descended, our muscles ached from the effort of having to prevent ourselves from going too fast down the paths. In some places the loads had to be taken off the heads of the auxiliary troops and lowered down the slopes using rifle slings and rope.

It took us some time, but we made it through the jungle, and the steep climbs, to the west side of the Kaladan Valley. It was January 1945, and we suddenly realized that we had missed Christmas and New Year.

But the real fight still lay ahead.

I never thought . . . Well, there are many things I never thought I would do, or become, growing up in my small village not far from Onitsha. I never thought back then that I could become a killer of men, like my grandmother called it way back before the war began. Even when I joined the army, war seemed so far away. But do we truly know ourselves? Do we know what we are really capable of? We all think we do, that is, until we find ourselves in a situation we did not foresee, staring down the barrel of a gun. Even now, thinking about what happened between us, what led me to that moment, I could cry. But I am too weary now. If I could go back, change things, undo my mistakes, truly follow my heart . . . But the question is: would it have changed anything? Or would I have been caught up in the happenings of this world? I am not sure.

23

Reunion

Burma, Cool Season, 1945

As WE MET up with the 81st West African and the 25th Indian Infantry Divisions, I was ever so glad to see my old friend Ifeanyi, and surprised to find Emeka with him, for although I knew he had joined the army, with everything that had happened we had lost touch, and Ifeanyi had not mentioned him in the latest letters I had received six months ago.

We came under the command of the 81st Division, and together we took the city of Myohaung. It was not an easy task, so they sent in the planes.

Then we went in, crossed the *chaung*s, approached the city from the west. I stabbed my bayonet into a Jap hiding in the bushes, plunged my knife into another who jumped from nowhere as we entered a bombed dwelling looking for signs of life. We stumbled over rubble and bodies left behind by the planes, kept moving and taking cover from the enemy fire as they retreated. But the adrenaline, the will to survive, to get home, kept pumping through me, so I kept moving with the rest, and we drove those Japanese out.

Sergeant Ibrahim was awarded the Distinguished Conduct

Medal for his gallantry. I was happy for him. But truth be known, I was beginning to feel . . . I don't know, cannot find the words . . . maybe numb.

We swam in the river; I had my first bath in almost six weeks.

I heard the splash as my feet broke through the surface of the water, and a sharp chill pinched my skin and rushed through to my brain. I felt the cold wetness engulf me. Then nothing, just a muffled hum as I fell deeper into its fold. I opened my eyes to darkness, looked up, saw the diffused light above, began to flap my legs, pushed myself back up to the surface, up into air, and light, and sound. To begin to feel . . . maybe a little human again.

There were others splashing and playing in the water. So, I swam to the side where I saw Ifeanyi deep in conversation with two Indian soldiers, and sat beside him on a rock. I looked out on the rest of the African and Indian soldiers; some were to the side soaping up, rinsing themselves, others racing each other.

'Rahul here was telling us about independence and this fellow called Gandhi,' said Ifeanyi as I joined them.

'Gandhi?' I asked.

'My friend, you never heard of Gandhi?' laughed Rahul, then turned. 'Sanjeev, tell our African friends about Gandhi.'

Sanjeev started to tell us about his hero, then in the midst of the conversation Rahul turned to me and said, 'Are you people not wanting your independence?'

'It's not something I've thought of,' I replied.

'Never mind him,' interrupted Ifeanyi. 'Of course we want independence. We have been talking of it for years. Our friend from back home, Michael, in the medical corps, joined an African independence movement while studying in America and was keen for us to join one back home, and Emeka over there used to work for the *West African Pilot*, a nationalist newspaper.'

'Well, it is all the talk in India,' said Rahul. 'They say that the Indian army have negotiated something with the British for when the war is over, so we hope it will hurry up and end soon!' He laughed again.

Ifeanyi nodded in agreement. 'I cannot wait. There is so much that this war has opened my eyes to,' he said, 'and so much I want to do when I get home. I am determined I will join the fight for independence.'

I listened to Ifeanyi and knew without a doubt that he would have much to give. Even now, looking back at that conversation, I lament a great loss; if only things had not gone the way they did.

I watched on, looking at Ifeanyi, Sanjeev and Rahul, wished I had something to add. For like Ifeanyi, in the short time I had been in Burma, there had been so much that this war had opened my eyes to and I was still trying to process it.

Before this war I had thought that we, Africans, were backward. Had even looked upon the white man as better. But I had seen so many of them fall ill from pneumonia, malaria, from all sorts of disease, unable to go on, shipped out to recuperate in places made especially for them, while we remained fighting. I had heard their insults, their quick lowly assessment of us, and yet they could not manage any more, or do any better than us. Had watched the green officers, the men sent our way, unable to lead, crumble with fear, while our much more experienced and knowledgeable soldiers were sidelined. I had thought that the rest of the world was so much more advanced, but seeing India, and the Burmese people, the way their women carried heavy loads on their heads, similar to our own – their village life was not much different to ours and yet they were talking about independence. The bravery and gallantry of our men was all the talk; we were just as capable, and in some instances I had seen with my own two eyes, better, as we had stood our ground and destroyed the Japanese on the battlefield despite the insufficient equipment sent our way.

I walked away from the conversation and went over to join Emeka, who was shaving by the riverside. And I began to realize that it was not that I thought the white man superior to me, for I did not believe this deep down inside. Did we not have the same God, and were we not taught by Reverend Nwachukwu that we were all created in God's image? The problem was that I believed in my own inferiority. The problem was a lack of belief in my own capabilities. The problem was the chain on my mind. The shame I carried inside in my Africanness, as had I not been taught that we were savages? That belief that whatever the colonials did was better? I needed to break free of that shame. And for the first time I thought of independence, and there was a desire in me for change.

'Oh boyo,' said Emeka as I sat down beside him.

'I have missed you,' I said.

Ifeanyi must have finished his conversation, as I looked around and there he was, walking towards us.

Emeka paused, then said, 'I have missed you both,' as Ifeanyi reached our side.

'How have you both been?' I asked.

Emeka was quiet, went back to looking in the mirror and shaving.

'Well,' said Ifeanyi, laughing wearily, 'what can I say? War is war, and four years of it is bound to leave its mark. I will be glad when we head out of this place in the next few weeks or so.'

'I remember the last time the three of us were together like this,' I said.

'It seems a long time ago,' said Emeka.

'It might have been the day we buried Rose's mother. Do you remember?'

'Yes,' said Ifeanyi, 'Rose was still alive . . .'

Emeka cleared his throat, gave Ifeanyi a look that I did not quite understand at the time. I looked at Ifeanyi, opened my mouth to reminisce, but for some reason the words would not come forth. I just couldn't speak about Rose. I thought of my brothers, of what they might have found out, and instead I said, 'They say our letters came with the drop this morning.'

'Yes,' said Emeka.

'Letters from home,' said Ifeanyi wistfully.

'Home,' said Emeka, lost in his thoughts.

And a melancholy descended on us. I knew we were all thinking the same thing: would we ever see home again? For nothing was certain from hour to hour out there. We could laugh and joke with a comrade in the morning and within the hour they could be dead. I wondered for the first time what would happen if I didn't make it home. Who would find out what had happened to Rose? For I knew it was due to my insistence that they still continued to search. And Little Rose – who would look after her?

Ifeanyi was the first to jump up and break the mood as they called us for breakfast.

'Come,' he said, forcing himself to sound jovial, 'let's go and eat.'

He leaped off the rock, and we followed, Emeka and Ifeanyi jostling with each other, like they did when we were boys, back home in our village, in our fathers' yards.

We had a good breakfast that day. They took a risk and lit a fire. I didn't know it would feel so good to eat hot food, food which you see the steam rising from. I think they had sent English sausages. A wash and a warm breakfast.

Heaven.

They gave out our letters, which had arrived in the drop. My hand shook as I sat on the ground and opened mine up to read.

Dear Obi,
I hope this letter finds you well, and in good health. Please send
my regards and good wishes, if you can, to the others, if you should

ever meet up with each other over there in Burma – especially Emeka, who refuses to answer my letters. I understand that you are in different divisions and regiments, and located far and wide. I don't know if this letter will reach you, but I write anyway in the hope that it will. Your brothers have been asking for information about Rose again but to no avail.

Obi, I loved her as much as you and your family, but I hope you will be able to focus on the fight at hand and come back to us safely. Please, I implore you and hope you will let the matter go and send word to your brothers to call off their search. It is creating major problems with the colonials at the hospital – please, for your sake and ours, please accept what has happened and come back safely to us. Your family send their love. We all pray for your safe return.

Yours faithfully,
Uche

I scrunched up her letter in my hand, went over to the smouldering fire and threw it into the last few embers, watched it glow as it burnt, turning from white to black, then swung round to join the rest of my platoon; it was time to head out. Emeka and Ifeanyi were in the platoon just ahead.

We pressed on, secured the crossing of the Lemro River, chased the Japs south, down the Arakan, through the fields, into villages which fell to us. In some we found atrocities. We entered one village to find a woman staked to the ground, arms and legs outstretched, raped to death. I threw up. What is it about us humans? How do we have the capacity for so much kindness and yet do so much evil?

*

One day we ran low on supplies. Radio communication was made, but by then our officer was not in a good way; he was shaking and shivering with fever. Ibrahim took control of our unit in every way but name. We got out the battery-operated radio, powered it up with batteries supplied in the last drop.

'Mayday, Mayday.'

'Come in . . .'

'We have an officer down.'

I was grateful for Ibrahim and his experience. We cleared a patch of land away from our main platoon, as communicated by Ibrahim, put up a flare and waited for the helicopter to fly over with what we needed. In exchange, we handed over our semi-conscious platoon leader, who was airlifted out and replaced with another. But this time, and to our pleasant surprise, we got young Lieutenant Richards, who we knew from our Enugu training days, and who should have been our platoon leader in the first place if it hadn't been for him falling sick after jungle training. We were glad to see him, grateful that it wasn't another rookie sent our way, and that he knew at least how to talk to us, even if it was in just a few words of Hausa and Igbo. We were relieved to have a leader at last who knew what war was about.

'Good to have you, sir.'

'Good to be out here with you soldiers again. You men are gaining quite a reputation,' said Lieutenant Richards, his green eyes twinkling back at us.

'Thank you, sir,' said Sergeant Ibrahim.

That was the last time we had the opportunity to carry out an airlift. But, more importantly to me at the time, more letters arrived in the supply drops. My hand shook later as I sat on the ground in my freshly dug-out trench and opened up the envelopes to read the letters sent by my brothers. There was still a little light left before sunset. I swear the letters smelt of home.

Dear Obi,

We hope this letter reaches you and finds you well, and that you received Uche's letter explaining the troubles and backlash she faced in Lagos due to our enquiries.

We have received numerous letters from you about the errand you sent us on to Lagos, and although this is not the way I wished to discuss these matters, the tone of your last letter has forced me to put pen to paper. I hope this will once and for all put these thoughts you had about Rose not being one to take her own life to rest. As we told you before we left, we did indeed find no evidence for your view when we went to Lagos. It is important that we face the facts; the truth is, if Rose did not take her own life then it means someone else did, and no one here can see or has found any evidence of such a thing. Who would want dear sweet Rose dead? We know this is not the news you wanted to hear but please, please, please, we implore you to leave these things behind and think only of Little Rose, for she needs you more than ever.

Obi, we loved Rose as much as you; she was like a big sister to me, and I, like you, also do not want to believe what has transpired. Please let this rest, focus on the fight at hand, for we need to turn our minds to doing the best for Little Rose.

Our family miss you and our grandmother sends her love. She is getting older, and her eyesight is failing, she prays each day for your safe return, says she wants to see you before she passes from this world. Well, we all pray for your return home, soon, we hope.

Your loving brother,
Chiedu

I wanted to tear up the letter in my hand, but I didn't. There were so many questions swirling in my head. Questions I wanted to ask them but couldn't. 'Damn this war,' I said, sitting there after our meal having a quick rest. It was frustrating being so far from home. Not able to carry out this investigation myself. But I knew my younger brother, and he was as suspicious as me, which was partly why I had chosen him. However, for him to send me such a letter . . . I folded it carefully and put it in my pocket to read again when I had more time to think and reply, then picked up my gun to pull apart and clean, before we set off again.

24

Talisman

WE FOLLOWED THE Japs into dense jungle. Lieutenant Richards led the way. I remember deciding out there in the jungle that I really did quite like him, particularly when he tried at least to speak to me in his broken Igbo, and to Sergeant Ibrahim in a little Hausa. I knew Ibrahim seemed more relaxed, not so watchful, like he was constantly trying to pre-empt problems, as he had done with the last officer. Sergeant Ibrahim was such a seasoned soldier, so any officer whom he relaxed with must have been OK. Back when we were training in our Enugu barracks, Lieutenant Richards had remained separate from us. I always remember him standing with the colonial officers pointing and directing at a distance, but out here in the jungle it was difficult to maintain that separation, so we all got to know each other better than we would have in normal army life.

I could hear the crunch of branches beneath my feet and the sound of monkeys chattering high up in the trees. As we made our way deeper into the jungle, the vegetation grew thicker, until I could barely see more than twenty yards ahead. It was difficult to know where we were, or where we were heading, so I kept close to Sergeant Ibrahim, never let him out of my sight, stopped him whenever I couldn't see Olu and Afam.

But it was the leeches that got to me. They burrowed deep into my skin; it was a fight to pull them off; they wouldn't let go unless you lit a cigarette and burnt them. So Sergeant Ibrahim handed me a few of his Lucky Strikes to burn them off. That's how I got into this nasty habit of smoking.

As for the bugs and ticks, they were even worse; they seemed to find their way to your private parts. You had to be careful when pulling them off not to leave their heads behind.

Sometimes we came across a stream or water source, and filled up. We added chlorine to the water to kill the bugs, or our water purification tablets which brought up all the gunk to the surface. We cleared the gunk from the top, then closed our eyes and drank.

Each night we set up our defence position, and at dawn patrols were sent out to clear any snipers from the trees. When they returned, Lieutenant Richards would give the order to move camp.

It was slow progress.

We had to cut and sometimes smash our way through thick vegetation. And even then we had to be careful, as any noise could alert the enemy to our whereabouts. In some places we could hardly see more than fifteen feet ahead, but we kept going with the sweat dripping off us, soaking our shirts right through, and sucked on salt pills to replace what we sweated out. Sometimes I just had to remove my shirt, but the ticks and bites from mosquitoes the size of bees would force me to put it back on again.

We only managed to move forward two miles one day before settling back down to camp for the night again. We were exhausted; the heat and humidity tired us out. But still the Japs had the upper hand. We heard them making monkey sounds, knew they could be waiting, lurking in the bush, planning to counterattack. So we travelled with caution.

*

Later, in the darkness, we could hear the Japs carefully making their way through the night. We stayed as quiet as we could in our trenches. They had sent out jitter patrols, trying to find our position, and from the sounds of things there were more than two of them. Then they started firing their light machine guns into the dark, swinging from left to right as they went. Sparks darted everywhere. All I could see was small specks of light flashing against the blackness of the night. We were disciplined and let them pass. But I could not sleep. I thought of Rose and the letter from my brother while lying there quiet in my trench. I stroked my leather talisman. She had given it to me that day at the Lagos train station. Hung it around my neck for good luck and to bring me back to her. I remembered that morning we parted. Her lips soft, sweet. I had waited a lifetime to taste them. I had held her warm body against mine. I shouldn't have taken the talisman. I should have insisted she kept it for . . . for . . . for her own protection. But here it was, around my neck, and so I held on, and rubbed it, and prayed, and hoped I would get through the night, as the sparks rained above my head.

The next morning we were ready to move on again, to continue chasing the Japs down the Arakan. We waited for the patrol to return before first light. Stood in our stand-to positions, holding our fighting loads. One hundred per cent alert and ready. The patrol returned. We set off. We only managed three miles that day.

In the morning I awoke with thoughts of my people on my mind. The sweet but sour taste of the *udala* fruit in my mouth, for it was February and *udala* season back home. Memories of my grandmother perched on her wooden stool, tearing its golden-orangey-red flesh apart to reveal the juicy white pulp inside. Sharing it out to us, her grandchildren, as we sat at her feet enjoying the lazy evening breeze.

For some reason it felt strange that that memory of my

grandmother should have come to me in my dreams. I hoped she was OK. I knew her prayers were keeping me safe. The thought of her praying for me kept my spirits up.

The following day unfolded just as the previous day had. We moved into another position, but the Japs were tricky. Each night they came out on their jitter patrols, and each time it was worse than the last.

We were going to have to ambush them at some point, I thought. And in the midst of wading through that jungle, chasing those Japs down the Arakan, I often wondered what it would be like to have a bed, and get some good sleep. To be back in Rose's arms and smell her sweet scent again. Not the stench that followed me around, as I had not bathed in weeks. I awoke in the same clothes, went to sleep in the same clothes; as for the foul odour when I dared take off my boots, it is best I don't talk about that. Instead, I preferred to think of Rose's smell. That sweet mixture of Vaseline, talcum powder and the scent of her Pond's cream.

I fell asleep remembering.

In our rest times the others talked about women, but I did not talk about Rose. Not at all. Not to them. We shared tales of happy times back home, of our people, and the loved ones we had left behind. We talked of the sweetness of our foods. I spoke of the wonder of the *ube* fruit, famous in my parts. A small dark-purple fruit, a little like a miniature avocado, in season across the waters in my tropical paradise as we sat in the jungle quietly speaking, in what seemed to me at that time like hell. And sometimes the rest spoke of their wives. Sergeant Ibrahim had two, and seven children.

'And what if . . . you don't . . .?' I asked softly. We sat close, only the two of us. I on the forest floor looking up at him as he sat on a dead branch.

'Spit it out. What if I don't make it home?'

'Yes.'

Then it will be Allah's will. But I will.'

'How can you be so sure?'

'Like you, I also have my talisman,' he laughed.

Sergeant Ibrahim always laughed, and tried to keep up our morale. Then he teased me about my stubble, as they all, except Afam, had beards.

We had not come across a secure water source in days and our supplies were running low. We needed an airdrop as soon as yesterday, but the Japs were everywhere. We still heard them in the trees, imitating monkey sounds. We remained silent and planned our offensive while Lieutenant Richards sent out a reconnaissance unit to gather intelligence.

We camped near by, lit no fires, made no sound, then hid in the bushes watching. We ambushed them at dusk.

They did not know we were there; we took them by surprise. The other platoons went in first. We followed. A few, including Lieutenant Richards and myself, guarded the entrance to the camp, taking cover in the bushes, in case other Japanese soldiers were around on the outskirts.

We killed twelve that day. Heard when Lieutenant Richards received the news over the radio that we had lost five of our own. I worried it was someone I knew, felt the bottom give way in my stomach, but thank God, and to my relief, it was not Olu, or Sergeant Ibrahim. Another team gathered the bodies. Our team searched through the Japs' camp for intelligence. Came back, looked down on the bodies, and there was Chuks. I closed his eyes, said a prayer, took his gun; we buried him as best we could and kept on moving. All the while I was wondering about his mother, all the while regretting not having helped him escape when we were back in our barracks in Enugu.

*

That night I sat in my trench looking at my trembling hands. Those hands, my hands, hands that had once held Rose with love, that had gently caressed her body, those same hands that had taken a knife and stabbed another human being to death, that had taken a gun and shot a man dead. It was them or me. Their life or mine. It was war.

Still, I could not help but wonder about their lives, their families, but I quickly shooed these thoughts away. Such thoughts could not be allowed to fester, lest I went mad right there and then.

A day later we came across a little river, and a good patch of land to receive our long-delayed airdrops. We cleared an area. Lieutenant Richards sent out a communication, then a signal. And we waited for sounds of the plane, and sight of the supply boxes parachuting through the sky. That night the Japs came again, firing their guns as they passed.

> *My dear brother,*
> *I read your letter and it has left me with much to mull over. Things here are getting tougher. I do not know if I will make it out of here alive, but I want you to have all my worldly possessions to distribute among the family. You have always been honest and I trust you to do things according to my wishes. I should receive a substantial amount from the army; please look after this and use it to contribute towards our grandmother's and Little Rose's upkeep. I would like her to go to school, study hard, like her mother. I don't know if this letter will ever reach you, but just in case by some miracle it does, please carry out my wishes and give my love to everyone.*
>
> *I must apologize for the state of this letter for my hand just won't stop shaking, and the rain just hasn't let up today. I am trying my best to keep the paper dry but it is not easy. You really cannot imagine what it is like here. What it's like to be so far from*

home without a warm and dry place to sleep. What it's like not to
be able to have hot food or rest for days. What it is like to see your
comrades fall. Unable to get up, their legs shattered, lying there on
the steep jungle floor. What it's like not to be able to wait, to have
to push on, because they are not fit enough to climb and you cannot
carry them. What it is like to have to leave them behind, maybe,
later, to be eaten by wild animals. Dear God, today we left Olu.

Your—

That night I cried. I could hear the Japs firing their guns in the distance. I cried silently as the rain pelted down, lying in my trench, in a pool of muddy water. I looked up into the dusk, squeezed my eyes to see through the rain, and the sky still seemed to have enough tears to last a lifetime. I clenched my gun tight as the rain hammered down; still I was at the ready. But the others didn't hear me.

That night I shut my eyes, heard the mortars in the distance, fell asleep under the rain wishing to die. And I cried, and cried.

At first I was confused, could not make out the sound, but I heard them. Heard them as they came, the little rattles tied at their ankles clattering and chattering, like the sound of the Umuada that night my mother died. They came silently at first, just the sound of the rattles, as they arrived en masse from all around and surrounded me. They were dressed in our cloth, like the Akwete fabric that our women weave, with traditional beads around their necks and waists. The chalk marks to see them into the next life still on their foreheads and arms. Rose came forward. Stood in the centre. Then they disappeared, leaving her standing alone. I closed my eyes tight against the sight, the tears still shaking my body. I felt her kneel down beside me, felt her hand on my head, soothing me, trying to stroke away the pain. She hugged me tight. I knew it was her, I smelt her fragrance. She soothed and rocked me while the mortars exploded over my head.

'*Obi, we heard your cry. Your mother waits for you, prays for you. She says it is not yet your time. Your grandmother is holding on for your safe return. Each day she looks to the trunk road to see you walking up the dirt path. Hold on, please hold on. She wants to meet you while she is still alive. I hung my talisman around your neck that day we parted . . . hold on.*'

I cried.

'*I cannot bear to see you like this. There is too much pain in this world. Forgive me, my love, forgive me. It is not your time. Open your eyes. I am here, my love. Open your eyes.*'

I opened my eyes to the world, peered up into the black night, listened, could not hear gunfire. The rain was gone, all was quiet, all were asleep, but there she was: my Rose, kneeling inside my trench, crouching above me, staring down into my eyes, holding my face, her eyes filled with tears. Above her, the Burma sky, filled with stars, silhouetted her face.

'Am I dead, Rose?'

'*Shush.*'

'And you? Are you alive?'

'*Shush.*'

I moved over, made room for her, and she climbed in beside me.

'This is no place for a woman.'

'*And this is no place for a man.*'

She wrapped her arms around me.

'Rose, what happened to you?'

'*Shush, sleep.*'

I fell asleep with her arms wrapped around me, and in those brief moments as I closed my eyes, I turned to face her and hold her in my arms. I forgot about war, about pain, about loss . . . about Olu.

25

Water

THE NEXT DAY, they woke us quietly, much earlier than usual. I sat up and looked around. Rose was not in my arms. All that was left was the indentation of my body on the groundsheet over the muddy earth. I got up and packed up the plastic sheet and my other possessions, hurried as they gestured silently and we moved position.

Not long after, all hell broke loose. We looked back to watch the sparks flying up into the air as the Japs bombed the site we had moved from but forty minutes earlier. We heard the explosions and wondered if there was anything left alive in our old position. But we kept on the march after the main party of Japs down the Arakan. Left a platoon behind us to deal with them.

I dreamt of my grandmother again. Could not sleep. Tossed and turned. And as I dozed off, Rose came to me again.

'*Why do you fret?*'

'I don't know, she is on my mind.'

'*Your grandmother sends her love, says you should hurry and come home. She is waiting for you. Does not want to pass from this world without seeing you.*'

'Rose, what happened?'

'*Shush. Go to sleep.*'

'Rose, why did you not love me?'

'*Obi*,' she said, reaching out to stroke my face, '*but I did.*'

'Did you?'

'*Yes.*'

'Then what happened?'

'*Life. Now go to sleep.*'

'And Little Rose – who's her father?'

'*I did not come to you to speak to you about these things.*'

'Then why did you come?'

'*You called.*'

I was silent, then I said, 'Rose, do you remember when you were a little girl?'

'*Of course.*'

'There are so many questions between us that went unanswered. So much, looking back now, that I did not and still do not understand. You asked me once, did I think you got into QMC Girls' College by accident? At the time it puzzled me. What did you mean?'

'*Just there were many battles I had to fight that I did not speak of, that you did not notice.*'

'What battles?'

'*Sleep.*'

'No, speak to me. Make me understand.'

'*This is not the time or place.*'

'Is there really ever a time or place for such conversations? Please, tell me why.'

'*I think it is you who needs to speak,*' she said, then looked around the camp, '*out here in this hell.*'

I glanced up at my comrades but all was quiet in their trenches, so I continued. 'What were your battles?'

'*You know . . . it has always been a battle for the real me to be seen and truly heard, a struggle between who I was in our culture and who I was in our colonial world. Neither truly saw me.*

'But Rose, I saw you.'

'Did you, Obi? Did you really?'

'Rose, who is Little Rose's father?'

'*You are.*'

'Rose, you know what I am asking. Who is her father?'

'*I always think of you as her father, as you have always cared for her. Promise me that if you get out of here alive, you will look after her,*' she said. '*Promise me that at least.*'

I felt her fear, her anxiety, coughed and said, 'Yes. I promise.'

'*Make sure she is OK.*'

'Yes, of course. Tell me this, Rose: who is her father? Is it Michael?'

'*No.*'

'Then who killed you? Was it Ifeanyi?'

'*Don't be ridiculous.*'

'Was it Emeka?'

'*Stop asking me these questions.*'

'Rose, are you dead?'

'*You know the answer.*'

'Rose, who murdered you?'

'*Did you not hear I killed myself?*'

'I know you. Who killed you?'

Then she disappeared.

The next evening I settled down in my trench and waited for her again.

'I knew you would be back.'

She sat down beside me. '*Did you?*'

'Yes, there is just too much that we need to talk about.' We both sat up as we heard the Japs in the distance firing into the night.

'*Obi, what is it about men that they insist on killing the beauty in this world?*'

'I don't know.'

'*There are too many mothers left to mourn, each day they die a thousand deaths. When it comes to it, this is so unnecessary. To lose so much life, for what? When you get down to it, nobody owns this world; we came from dust and to dust we will return.*' She was quiet and then said, '*Obi, I pray you make it out of here alive.*'

'Rose,' I said, 'so do I.'

'*It seems to me that men will always find a way to kill each other. Maybe, if they had to bleed, feel the pain and the labour of bringing life into this world, maybe then they would respect it more?*'

'Rose, your talk is not helping.'

'*I'm sorry.*'

'I thought you came to take my mind off this place.'

'*I did.*'

I listened, but thankfully the Japs had moved on.

'*It is best you don't head in that direction,*' she said.

'Why?'

'*I just have a feeling. Just don't head that way.*'

'OK,' I said, mainly to placate her. 'So, tell me this: did you ever love me?'

'*Obi, yes. I still do.*'

'And Little Rose's father – did you love him?'

'*Unfortunately, I did.*'

'I know you don't wish to tell me who he was, but how did it happen?'

She was silent.

I pushed again. 'So what happened?'

'*Life?*'

I looked at her and decided not to push her further.

'The night we made love, what made you change your mind?'

'*Obi,*' she said, '*I have loved you since we were little children, but that night was the first time I saw you as a man. Not a boy pretending*'

to be a man, but a man who I cared about. I just knew that night that
you were who I needed in my life.'

'Corporal, who are you talking to?' asked Lieutenant Richards.

'No one, sir.'

'Then stop mumbling and go back to sleep.'

'Yes, sir.'

And when I looked around, she was gone.

In the morning we were ready to move again, waited for the
patrol to return in our stand-to positions within our trench, holding our fighting loads. Sergeant Ibrahim was standing outside the
trenches.

'Let's go.'

'But Sergeant, why are we heading in that direction?' I asked. 'It
is not the best route.'

'We've been given our orders.'

'But I heard the Japs last night; there was something about their
movements. Rose said—'

'Who is Rose?' he asked, looking at me strangely.

'Never mind, I just have a feeling. It is not the best route. Sir' – I
turned to Lieutenant Richards – 'I heard the Japs last night moving
in that direction.'

'Corporal, we hear the Japs almost every night. Besides, the
patrol has returned and they have determined the route is safe.'

'But sir—'

'The regiments from the 81st are ahead and have found a fresh
water source, and we need water like yesterday.'

'But sir—'

'Corporal, we are on the move.'

He brushed past me and the rest followed. I was irritated and a
little annoyed but had no choice but to follow.

*

So how did it begin? Well, that afternoon, having trekked two miles through the jungle, we met up with the platoon that had been in front of us at the river. I was glad to see Emeka and Ifeanyi again, although they were to move on in just an hour.

We, our platoon, sat separately, replenishing our water containers, while the other platoon remained further up. Although, for a brief moment, Ifeanyi and I exchanged some words, when he came over under the pretence of refilling his half-empty bottle and quickly washed his face while I knelt at the stream.

Then we ate our meal. I think it was beans out of a tin, washed down with tea that had come in the food drops that morning. I remember the liquid was hot and didn't taste of much. All was quiet. As usual, I sat beside Sergeant Ibrahim, who was telling us what he would do first if he made it home. He liked to tease, his way of helping us forget about the troubles of this war, even if it was for just a moment. So I was there on the ground laughing when Lieutenant Richards joined us. This was rare. The afternoon seemed a little weird. I was still uneasy about the route. But all seemed calm, too calm. I remember there was something at the back of my mind, niggling away, which hadn't left me since speaking with Rose that morning, but I just couldn't put my finger on it. Maybe that was it, maybe that was what I was feeling: as the colonials liked to say, 'the calm before the storm'.

'So what's amusing you?' asked Lieutenant Richards.

'Nothing, sir.'

'We were just talking about what we would do when we get home.'

'You, sir, what's the first thing you would do?' asked Ibrahim.

Lieutenant Richards sat down on the log beside us, directly opposite me. Although we had become somewhat closer, most times he did not sit and chat idly with us, but that afternoon he took a seat.

'I don't know, maybe take a long, long bath,' he joked, slapping his right shoulder as an insect buzzed and landed.

'Do you have a sweetheart, sir?' asked Sergeant Ibrahim.

There was a look that crossed his face, almost haunted. I think we all saw it.

'I did, but it was not to be.'

Then he quickly composed himself, and shifted the conversation away.

'And what about you?' he directed his question at me as he pushed himself to the edge of the log, as if he was going to get up again.

'Me, sir?'

'Yes, you.'

'I did have, sir, but it is a long story.'

'Well, maybe one day you will tell me about it, but meanwhile I must get back to my duties.'

And just as he stood up, he seemed to be violently attacked by three insects that set upon him, buzzing around his head, then his body, before one went inside his shirt. I got up from where I was sitting to help, and that's when he pulled off his shirt. And I saw it, dangling from his neck.

'Got the bugger,' he laughed.

He was standing there shirtless, his identity tag around his neck, and right next to it was a ring – the other part of the jaguar puzzle ring. But it wasn't the ring that had me. It was the first time that I had actually looked properly and focused on his features, and I knew I had seen that face before.

'Sir, where did you say you were based before coming to Enugu?'

'Lagos. Why?'

'Nothing, I was just wondering. And, sir, where in Lagos were you?'

'What's with the twenty questions?'

'Nothing, sir. Sir, I've never known your first name. Do you have a Christian name?'

'Casper. I don't have all day, Corporal, to stand around answering your pointless questions,' he said and walked away.

I couldn't seem to think straight. I was all of a muddle inside. His name began with C, like in Rose's letter. And I kept looking over to where he was now giving orders to the other soldiers.

'Rose, is he the one?'

She did not answer.

'Is he Little Rose's father? Rose, is he the one who killed you?' I could not feel her presence, only silence. 'Rose!'

I followed him to where he stood at the edge of the bank. Watching over the soldiers in the stream below. Giving orders to fill up with as much water as they could.

'Sir, the ring around your neck?'

'What?'

'The ring? Where did you get it from?'

'Is this really necessary, Corporal?'

I put myself in front of him, blocked his way, wouldn't allow him to leave. We stood there on the bank, glaring at each other.

'Tell me, sir, where did you get it from?'

I brought out Rose's ring to show him. The other part of the puzzle.

Lieutenant Richards recoiled suddenly, and began to tremble.

We stood there staring at each other.

Then he manoeuvred and walked around me, away from the bank.

I turned and watched him stride away. I didn't know what to do; I was frozen there in my thoughts.

'Obi, are you all right?' shouted Emeka from across the way, watching me standing at the edge of the bank. I did not answer. I was lost trying to calculate and recalculate. I thought of Little Rose

and the paleness of her skin, the strangeness of her hair and the letter among Rose's possessions.

'Rose, is he the one?'

She didn't answer.

'Is he the one, Rose?!'

'Are you all right?' asked Emeka, coming towards me. 'Is who the
one? Who are you speaking to?'

Anger was boiling up inside me. I turned around to follow
Lieutenant Richards when suddenly gunshots rang out from the
opposite bank. I ducked to take cover. Threw myself on the ground.
I couldn't make out where the gunshots were coming from, as they
seemed to be from different directions, and all the while I couldn't
believe it. *He killed her. He killed Rose*, I thought. I was sure of it, for
I knew Rose would not have killed herself.

I looked down the slanting riverbank to see the others scram-
bling up to escape the gunfire, but there was no cover down there.
Some fell by the riverside where a second previously they had been
shaving, their blood turning the water red. Some fell on the slope
as they rushed to get away, the back of their shirts torn apart by the
force of the bullets, red soaking the fabric and the ground beneath
them.

Lieutenant Richards grabbed his gun, got up and ran ahead,
shouting orders at the rest of the troops further up the bank. They
hurried around, grabbing whatever weapons they could, keeping
low, while the ta-ta-ta-ta of the gunfire rang out above them.

I tried to get up. Crawled forward, only to throw myself on the
ground again. The gunfire intensified, so I lay there face down,
smelling the damp earth, covering my head with my arms, the cool
metal of my gun pressed against my right cheek, and yet, as I lay
there cowering on the ground, listening to the bullets flying over
my head, despite the death happening around me, all I could think
of was that he had killed Rose, all I could remember was Rose lying

in the morgue, all I could see was Rose smiling at me, all I could smell was Rose.

Then the gunfire stopped. Silence.

I lay on the muddy ground, head low. I dared to look up, wondering about the silence, what it meant, if I should get up and run. I checked the trees, the bushes, spotted Emeka in the distance crouched low to the ground, Lieutenant Richards beside him and Ifeanyi standing, as if surprised, just ahead of him, near the edge of the dense jungle, pointing his gun at a Jap standing inches away. Both stood frozen, suspended in time, looking at each other for what seemed an eternity, but I know in reality it must have been a mere second, if that.

Then the gunfire started up again, breaking the momentary spell.

I saw them both lift their rifles higher. Both fired. Blood, skin and organs splattered out. Both fell like trees.

Ifeanyi lay on the jungle floor, the leaves and twigs beneath him, looking up at the Burma sky. Blood soaked his shirt, formed a pool on the ground around him; the Jap lay dead on the opposite side.

I knew, as he lay there, that he had a hole where his heart used to be.

I bent my head, looked away. The sight of him broke something inside me. In that moment I was sure I was going to die out there in that jungle, miles from home, fighting in that godforsaken war.

I looked at the dead bodies that carpeted the jungle floor, but I could not see anyone's face. Then I spotted Emeka still on the ground, cowering from the gunshots, Lieutenant Richards beside him. Something snapped inside me.

I saw him, Lieutenant Casper Richards, cowering from the gunfire raining down on us, sparks flying. I could just make out his face as he looked back towards us, his body tight to the ground.

I felt for the trigger with my index finger.

I saw him put out a hand and signal to the other troops.

I held my gun, the bottom held steady against my shoulder,

pointed it at Lieutenant Richards. If he had only listened. We should have gone the other way. My finger trembled. The flashes from the gunfire filled the air.

I took aim, steadied my nerves, the sweat pouring down my temple.

I lifted myself slightly, aimed at him. I heard, felt, the pumping of my heart, and my finger began to tremble as I pressed down. A heart for a heart, I thought. I closed my eyes, pulled the trigger, heard it fire.

I bent my head down to the floor and screamed, and the words 'For what does it profit a man' filled my head, but then I lifted myself to check, to see if he was dead where he lay, but I could not see, so I lifted myself higher, and that's when I felt the full force of the bullets hit my back. I dropped my gun, lay with my hands outstretched on the ground. I felt the blood gushing out, my body soaked with my own blood.

I turned to lie on my back, looking up at the trees and the sky.

'Am I not a man?' I said on the jungle floor, looking up into the blue Burma sky. Then I cried for Rose.

I turned again to see what I had done, to take one last look.

To my surprise, Lieutenant Richards got up from where he lay, rushed over to take cover in the bushes.

'Rose!'

Then, darkness descended.

26

Floating

A ND THAT IS how I came to want to take the life of another in
cold blood. How I came to lie on the jungle floor, crying out
for Rose, looking up at the Burma sky, wondering if I was alive or
dead. How I came to take the life of so many men, until I could not
feel, was numb from it all, and yet, at the same time, screaming
inside for escape.

I, Obi, the one who my dear Rose once called green. Nobody
really knows where their life and desires will lead them. It was a
simple desire for Rose that led me there. A simple desire to possess
her and her love. Isn't that what we all want? To love and be loved
in return. Looking back, I now realize that to love my fellow man
as myself would have led me down a better path.

And this is where the story should end, but nothing is ever that
simple. There are always twists and turns along the way. Unexpected truths that need to be discovered and revealed.

I must have been out for maybe five or ten minutes. I am not
sure, and it is not clear to me why I was still alive.

I opened my eyes, looked around.

I heard a comrade beside me groaning in pain.

'Take me, Lord,' he cried.

I heard him struggling for breath, gasping, then one last breath and he was gone.

The Japs walked among our bodies. I heard their boots crunching on the damp soil. *It is just a matter of time; if they don't get me, then the loss of blood will.* I closed my eyes again and played dead.

They were ransacking equipment and the pockets of my dead comrades, looking for guns, documents or information that would give them details of our operations.

They got closer, speaking among themselves. Then one stood above me; his presence blocked the little shards of light from criss-crossing my face. He shouted back to a comrade, stooped to rummage through my trouser pockets, got up again, but didn't touch my upper half, as there was too much blood.

He must have wanted my gun, for then he kicked me, rolled me off my rifle, did it with such force that I didn't stop rolling, and as the land sloped I just kept going, down the bank. Splash, into the water. I felt something hit my side. I was half on, half off a log in the water. It was cold, the current strong. I heard the Japs still rummaging above me. Next, I was floating head down in the cold water. I was somewhere out of my own body. Then I thought I heard Rose scramble in behind me. Help me lift my head out of the water.

'*Obi, hold on.*'

'Rose,' I whispered, 'I'm cold.'

'*Just hold on.*'

I heard her splashing around. I put my head on top of the log, out of the water, and I was adrift.

'*Just know that I love you, always loved you.*'

'Rose, I'm so cold.' I felt myself floating away. And I heard her shout after me.

'*Take care of Little Rose.*'

'Rose!'

And then I was being dragged down the river, and she was gone.

27

Awake

I REGAINED CONSCIOUSNESS SLOWLY. Lay there, staring up at the ceiling. Wondered where the hell I was. I was sure of two things: one, it was daytime; and two, I was not in the jungle.

I heard a cough to my left and turned to see a man gazing back at me from where he sat on the bed next to mine. He had two vertical tribal marks on each cheek.

'You're awake,' he said, beaming at me.

I nodded, furrowed my forehead, a question hidden in each crease.

'We were worried there for a while, my friend.'

I looked around at my surroundings. I was in a large hall with a few men scattered in beds on either side of the aisle; I assumed it was an army hospital.

'It was touch-and-go for a little while,' said the man, 'but the doctor will be pleased to see that you are awake.'

I looked down the aisle to see a man, dressed in white, pushing a creaking trolley towards us; occasionally he stopped to drop off something or other.

'Our medication is on its way,' my neighbour said, looking in the direction of the trolley.

I nodded again, but could not say a word. My mouth was dry, lips stuck together. I attempted to part them and push myself up on to my elbows; that's when I felt the sharp pain and lay back down.

'Not so fast, my friend,' he said.

'How long have I been here?'

'Two, maybe three weeks.'

I nodded again.

'My name is Babatunde.'

'Obi.'

The man with the trolley reached our side and Babatunde collected two little containers from him. There was water on the table between our beds.

'Here,' he said, then lifted my head to put some tablets in my mouth, followed by water.

I swallowed the pills but there were many questions agitating around in my head.

'Where are the nurses?'

'There are few around here,' he laughed. 'This ward is for African troops. One might pass by later.'

I looked around to see if I recognized any of the others.

'Where is the rest of my platoon?'

'I don't know.'

'My sergeant? Ibrahim? Where is he? And Emeka, is he alive? Where are they?'

'Take it easy.'

'Did they make it?'

'I don't know,' he said, and waddled back to his bed. 'All I know is that we, my friend, are the lucky ones.'

I lay back down and stared up, hoping against hope that they were still alive. That they had made it out.

'Get some rest.'

I heard Babatunde's words, felt the strength drain from my body, and drifted off to sleep again.

'Obi,' said Babatunde, 'wake up. They have brought food. Wake up.'

I heard his words through the fog. He shook me gently, lifted my head, put a pillow behind my shoulders.

'Take,' he said, holding a plate out to me. 'Have you got it?'

'Yes. Thank you,' I said to him as I took the plate and spoon, and began to eat. I watched him limp back to his bed to eat his own food, and I was suddenly grateful to him. 'Thank you,' I said again.

'It is not a problem. If we do not look after each other, who will?'

I smiled. 'The nurses? When do they make their rounds?'

'Late morning. But until then' – he looked around at the other soldiers – 'we try to look after each other as best we can.'

I looked around the room, lifted my eyebrows to question this.

'There are not enough Black nurses and the few we have are also deployed to help out with the prisoners and sometimes with the white wards,' he said.

'The doctors?'

'They come every now and then. But you, my friend, I think you will be OK, you have come through the worst. Your first day here I did wonder, but you have too much fight in you. Have you finished?'

'Thank you,' I said as he took the plate from me and put it on the table between us.

'Now sleep.'

'What if the nurse comes?'

'Don't worry, I will wake you. I have been looking after you these past weeks, making sure you took your medication, feeding you, and I am excited to see their faces now you are roused.'

So I lay back down and obeyed, still wondering how I made it out of the jungle.

*

I heard a scream. It jerked me out of my sleep.

'It is OK,' said Babatunde as he looked down the ward towards the noise.

I turned to see the commotion at the far end. There was a man screaming in his sleep and another beside him trying to wake him up.

'Go back to sleep,' said Babatunde. 'We all have nightmares of our own now.'

I lay there listening to the man until his shouts turned into sobs, then felt a wetness on the side of my face, felt it slide from my eyes on to the sheet below. I felt it again. I turned away from Babatunde, scrunched up the bed sheet into my fist, pushed it into my mouth and bit down hard, and I prayed that Emeka was still alive, then silently cried myself back to sleep.

'Your wounds are healing nicely,' said the doctor.

'Doctor Nwosu, do you know what happened to my platoon?' I asked. 'My friends, did they survive?'

'I am not clear exactly,' he said, 'but your company sustained heavy losses. Your friends, what are their names?'

And so I told him, and waited for word, but none came.

I healed, a little each day, got stronger, eventually sat up without the sharp pain.

Made it out of the ward for a little exercise, walked in the grounds. And that's when I found him, Sergeant Ibrahim, sitting there having come outside for air and a smoke.

We were excited to see each other and hugged as we cried. He was fully recovered, waiting to be transferred out, and we spoke about that day, about what it was like in those moments as the gunfire rained down on us, how he had thought he was going to die, how he made it out of the jungle and how he had been convinced that I had died. And then I asked about Emeka. He looked away. And I knew. He was gone. They were all gone. Only Sergeant Ibrahim and myself survived.

Before we could finish talking, Sergeant Ibrahim was called away.

I heard the sound of the soldiers talking in their beds around me, but could not make out the words, saw men pass by but could not have told you who they were. I floated, somewhere between this ward and the battlefield, and wished to go back. I thought of the things I could have done differently that day: made the officers listen, made a fuss, directed them more forcibly in the other direction. 'Why me?' I cried and wished to be back in the jungle, to lie among the leaves and twigs, with the bamboo stems criss-crossed above my head, the sound of gunfire ringing out all around me.

The day came when Babatunde stood beside me saying his good-byes. At first I could not speak. I saw his lips move, and a part of me understood, so I nodded, opened my mouth, and I heard myself say some words of farewell, but it was not me. I was floating outside my body, watching the two of us. And inside there was a low murmur, almost like a hum; it had been with me since that day in the hospital grounds. Sometimes, when I lay down at night, when all was quiet, in the dark, I could make out the words beneath the hum, whispering. Only loud enough for me to hear.

Why are you still alive? Why did you survive?

I turned, and twisted, and curled up, and rolled among the bed sheets, trying to silence the words, to dislodge them from my brain. I thought of Rose. Why was she silent?

I wanted to get back to the fight, tried to heal quickly, hoped they would send me back soon. Craved to feel the enemy's bullets once again, feel them pierce my body, shatter flesh and bone, for the vegetation to creep, entwine and pull me into the dirt where I belonged. Where Emeka and Ifeanyi lay, lost in a foreign land.

And as I lay in my bed, my mind set on heading back to the battlefield, for the war to settle the score, we got word of surrender.

At first, we thought it just a rumour.

Then one of the men burst into the ward with a newspaper in hand.

'We're going home,' he roared, as he ran down the aisle. 'The Germans have surrendered, the Japanese are sure to follow suit.'

There were sounds of hope throughout the ward. Those who could sit up, sat up, those who could get up, got up, as we accosted him with questions. He held out the paper to us, but not all could read, so he sat on the bed, the one Babatunde had vacated, and started to read aloud.

I got up from my bed to stand behind him, to check and confirm the truth of his words as he read. I looked at the top of the paper where the date *8 May 1945* was written.

'Praise to Allah,' said one of the men to my right.

'Praise indeed,' said another.

I sat back on my bed, silent again, wondering at his words, not sure how soon the Japs would also surrender, for my experience of them out in the jungle was of a people willing to continue till death, to die in honour rather than surrender.

Then I thought of home; I saw Rose standing on the veranda, looking out into the distance. Saw Ifeanyi, Emeka and myself playing football in the yard. We were all gone, in some way or other.

Rose had once said, 'Obi, you always see things in such simple ways.' Now I understood her words, for the world is as complex as it is simple, and I was not sure how this person I had become would fit back into the world I had left back home.

28

Waiting

THOSE OF US well enough were transferred to a makeshift camp in central India, some miles northwest of the port city of Madras, to wait for the vessels.

We joined the other African regiments, while more trickled in, one by one, sent at first for a respite from the war, for some of them had been fighting with the Chindits and in the Arakan since 1943. They drifted in from the battlefields, glad to be alive, their white officers by their side.

I searched for Emeka's brother among them. I don't know why, but I had a need to know that he was alive, that even though Emeka would not make it home, at least Nonso would.

And when I found him, he was not the young man I had encountered in the training camp back in Enugu. But, then again, none of us were. He had injured his foot, and was unusually silent, which frightened me. I sensed that all was not right with him, and I wondered how his mother was going to cope with him, for she was but a simple village woman, with no understanding of how to deal with what this war could do to a man's mind.

At first we thought going home was imminent. This filled me

with dread; this pushed on my insides, threatened to expand until I exploded into fragments, pieces of myself.

I looked across the vast, dusty, open land surrounding the camp, which seemed to stretch out as far as my eyes could see, with only the sight of small green shrubs in the distance, and an occasional wispy dry bush floating by, carried on the wind.

The hot sun blazed heavy on my back as I crouched looking for signs of life, but there were none to see. I felt loneliness looking out across the vast land outside the camp and I thought back to the days when we were young, running through the fields and each other's yards.

I had not envisioned then the turn our lives would take. Emeka was buried somewhere out there in the Burma jungle. As for Ifeanyi – well, I did not want to remember. I could not stop the tears from streaming down my face as I crouched there. I thought of our people, about what they were doing back home in our village at that moment as I stooped, contemplating life. I saw the view of our village from the top of our little mango tree, the sound of Rose sucking on her mango beside me. Her blue dress scrunched up around her thighs. The sound of children running in the yard below, and my grandmother sitting under her favourite pawpaw tree shelling pumpkin seeds. And then I sensed her, my grandmother, felt her spirit hanging on for my return. And knew she was still in the world.

We were truly isolated, with only a railway station some hundreds of yards away to give us respite. Sometimes, we took the train into town to visit the temples, rode on elephants and watched the snake charmers before returning to the solitude of the camp.

A few soldiers, the more educated African NCOs, attended dances put on for the Allies, where they met pretty Indian ladies, and returned to talk with excitement about their experiences. A few less cultured returned telling tales about the ladies of the night. I still had too much pain in my back for such vigorous activities, but the truth was, with all that had happened, I was not in the mood for any kind of joviality; it was a step too far. I wanted to be punished for not making them listen, for not forcing them to take a different route, and I waited for the punishment to come.

We tried as best we could to occupy ourselves in camp: we played cards, exercised and debated about African independence.

Still I waited, Rose did not come, and I began to doubt my memories of her at night in the jungle. Maybe I had dreamt it, maybe it was not real. I cried out to the sky, 'Rose! Why are you silent?'

June turned into July and July into August. We were still waiting. We questioned, among ourselves, when we would be going home.

On 6 August 1945, we got news that the Americans had dropped an atomic bomb on the Japanese city of Hiroshima.

We could not believe it, the cruelty of such an action. Three days later they dropped yet another on Nagasaki. I saw the pictures in the papers; whole cities were reduced to rubble. We saw photos of the dead lying among the wreckage, in another a gigantic plume of dust billowing up into the heavens. We were silent at the sight of these horrors. I walked away to get some air, to gather myself.

'Why?' said one of the African soldiers to my back and the space I left behind. 'Are they not civilians? Human beings?' he shouted after me.

'How many dead?' asked another, standing beside him.

'The article says the bodies are too numerous to count,' said another.

'But why?' he asked again.

And so I went outside to look up towards the sky, to look for Rose, but she was not there.

'Why is there so much wickedness in this world?' I asked the sky, then heard my words echo back at me, heard the answer in the echo and hid my face in shame on behalf of the human race.

The Japanese surrendered shortly after, and we rejoiced in the fact that we all surely would soon be heading home. So we waited, and waited.

The ships came, but there was no space for us.

We looked around and our white officers had slipped away, boarded the ships towards home.

We questioned, 'When are the ships coming for us?'

'They are reserved for the white soldiers, the British. Once they have been sent home, then your repatriation can begin.'

'Surely, you can send us home as well. We have loved ones waiting for us, too.'

And so we waited, and waited, out there in that isolated land, away from home, the ones we loved, with only dust and sky to keep us company.

'I did not ask to be in this war.'

'Most of us didn't, son.'

'You came to my village and took me, forced me here, and now I have fought and survived, you leave me out here in this godforsaken place and will not send me home?'

'There was no space for you on the ships. Britain needs British soldiers.'

'And what? Africa does not need us?'

As each ship came in and left without us on board, I wondered if I would find my grandmother alive. I prayed and asked her to hold on.

Then the rumours came, spreading through the camp, that they were holding us there to send us out to fight in the Malay peninsula. It must have been the last straw because that's when the unrest came.

A small group broke out, having had enough, and confronted their commander. It did not end well. A fight started among another group of African troops, and another refused to eat or obey orders until they were heard. Miraculously, by November a ship had been found. Those involved in the trouble who were not court-martialled were the first to board the ship with other African troops. I wasn't among them.

My turn finally came in January. We boarded the trains to the port of Madras, and the troopship home.

29

Just in Time

Nigeria, Dry Season, 1946

WE ARRIVED IN the early morning; the Lagos coastline loomed heavy in the distance. The sun rose and I breathed a long, deep breath as the ship sailed towards it. It was almost two years since I had last seen the port, and I wondered what I would find and how our people would react to the me that had returned.

But still, we were the lucky ones, the ones who had survived; I thought of Emeka and shuddered, thought of Ifeanyi and wondered what I was to say to his people. Thought of their mothers – would I be able to confront the devastation that would surely be in their eyes? Others joined me, stood beside me silently. I gripped my walking stick tight as I watched the coastline come ever closer.

We had all lost friends and the guilt hung between us; it hid in the folds of our silence as we stood there, stopped our tongues as we looked on. I knew, like me, it kept them awake at night, tossing and turning until we could do nothing but give up on sleep.

There were many people on the quayside waiting to greet us, and much buzz as those families that could, that lived in Lagos, fought through the vendors and port workers to find the faces of their loved ones as we filed off the ship. I had no one; it was too far for my people to travel, even if they had known I was arriving home. There were wails of joy as wives caught sight of their husbands coming down the gangway, brothers recognized the faces of their siblings, children saw their fathers. I looked sideways at the crowd as we marched by. We, the injured soldiers, were at the back of the rank and file, as we moved much more slowly, so we heard when the wails of joy began to change to something else, as there were no more troops left to disembark except us, and it became clear to some that their nearest and dearest were not among us, and could therefore be among the ones who might never return.

'Is there another ship?' I heard one woman ask in desperation. 'Maybe he is on the next one?'

'Yes, madam, maybe,' answered a man standing beside her. 'You didn't get a letter?'

'No. They don't send letters to many of us. We have to wait to see if they come off the vessel to be sure.'

'Then maybe he is on the next one.'

We boarded the trucks that came to collect us injured troops and headed for the barracks. Our new-found heroes, leaders, the brave ones, like Sergeant Ibrahim, who were fortunate to make it home, led the way. On entering the base, it felt abandoned, the atmosphere subdued, not frenzied like when we were shipped out from Lagos and then Freetown two years previously. Few white colonials remained. Our arrival woke the barracks from its stupor and we settled in for the night.

A part of me was glad to be on my way home, and yet the guilt inside tightened its grip; it rode me, and no matter how much I tried I could not shake it off. The sight of Emeka smiling at me that morning and Ifeanyi lying on the ground out there in the jungle as I aimed my gun at Lieutenant Richards kept interrupting my thoughts. And each time, I clenched and unclenched my fists at the treachery of life. I tried to shake off the guilt, shake the longing for Rose. Sometimes, in my moments alone, I thought of ending it, to stop the ache that gnawed away in my head and heart. Then, just as I thought I could bear it no more, she came to me: not Rose, but my grandmother. She came in my sleep that first night back home on African soil, sat down beside me.

'*Why are you not coming home?*'

'But I'm on my way.'

'*I am waiting.*'

'I know, Grandmother, I will be home soon.'

'*I cannot wait for ever.*'

'I know, but hold on a little longer. I am almost there.'

'*Hurry!*'

I woke trembling, a sense of urgency hanging over me.

We boarded the trains headed towards our home barracks, left Lagos and many of our comrades behind. And as we got closer to home I felt the urgency in her call get stronger. We spent a night in Enugu, and in the morning, that last day, we lined up in the open air with the others to collect our gratuity pay, for services to the Empire.

The clerk behind the desk looked at my papers, counted out my money and placed it in my hand.

'What about the rest?' I asked, for I knew that the white privates we had come across in the camp in India had received four times the amount.

'What rest?' interjected the colonial officer sitting beside him, overseeing all that was happening.

'We were told that we would get an army pension and enough money to buy good farming land if we went out to fight.'

'I'm not sure about that,' he said, crinkling his brow. 'This is what we are authorized to pay.'

'But just before we went to war we were told . . .'

'I know nothing about what you were told. Take it up with the appropriate department; the private here can give you the details. As you can see, we have too many to get through today and you're holding up the queue,' he said, pointing back at the men waiting behind me.

'But, sir.'

The fellow behind me cleared his throat. So I looked at the long queue of men, and back at the colonial soldier. His eyebrows rose, almost questioning.

'OK,' I said, grabbing my walking stick and moving along. 'Let me have the information.'

The private scribbled some details on a piece of paper, gave it to me with my demob papers. I took them from him so as not to be a nuisance, then folded the money and papers away into my pocket.

I stepped back, unsteady on my feet, for there was still pain in my back when I moved in a particular way. I stood up as straight as I could in my uniform, with shoulders back, and gave one last salute as a soldier.

'Goodbye, sir,' I said to the officer, a half-smile on my face.

'Don't spend it all at once,' the officer joked after me.

'No, sir, of course not, sir,' I shouted back, waving the stick in my hand at him, my belongings heavy in my other hand.

I walked away, my head filled with memories of that day, eight years before, when I had lined up in the open air to sign up for duty. I put my cap on, nodded my head one last time at my comrades and headed along the path towards the gates.

I walked out of the barracks into my new civilian life. I wanted to cry, but held it together, threw my belongings over my shoulder, steadied myself, waited for the sharp pain to subside. Looked left, then right, unsure which way to go. Waited like I was expecting a command before taking action, I was so used to them.

I had been in the army for eight years and had grown used to its rules and regulations. Out there in the world again I felt vulnerable, shaky with the making of decisions.

I felt my grandmother again, and knew I had to hurry. There were things I had to ask her, things I needed to know before her passing, so I got my bearings and hitched a lift towards the truck park, near Ogbete and Coal Camp, to catch a mammy truck heading towards Onitsha. I did not stop off to see my father, for my grandmother's call was urgent.

At the truck park, while I waited, I bought fruit and peanuts from the vendors to sustain me during the long journey, and could not believe the prices. It then began to dawn on me that maybe even the money I had in my pocket was not going to go as far as I had originally hoped. When I first joined the army, an orange would have cost me but a third of what it was currently priced at.

While I was away, inflation and shortages had definitely taken their toll; I could see it all around. And although there were no dead bodies and bombed-out buildings, like in Burma, the war had left its mark here too.

We boarded the green mammy truck, which smiled broadly like a puffed-up African bullfrog. The inscription 'In God We Trust' written in large letters on the back. It rumbled along the winding road of Milken Hill, circled up the hillside, towards the heavens. We looked down the steep drops into a forest of trees and foliage, and held our breath as we caught glimpses of death. We were grateful once it circled around and reached flatter ground. From then on it was just us and wilderness, with the truck jolting us from side to side as it sped along, past reams of bush and waving palm trees. I poked my head out of the open side, closed my eyes, felt the breeze on my face, tasted dust; heard my grandmother calling me, and snapped my eyelids open, only to see the road snaking its way into the far distance until it merged with blue sky. I heard her call again, brought my head back in, twisted myself to look out of the back, just to check, only to see a trail of red dust following, riding the wheels, as if it couldn't bear to say goodbye.

Occasionally, we passed people. Some carried loads, others were dressed in their Sunday best, as if they were heading somewhere important. One, maybe two, rode along on bicycles, before disappearing on to, or appearing from, dirt paths hidden in the bush, and I knew then we must be near a village.

As the truck rocked along, I closed my eyes again, heard the voices of men debating in Igbo up front, the conversation of the two women beside me, the cluck of a man's chickens sitting two rows up to the left, and my grandmother still called, and I kept saying to her, 'Hold on, just hold on,' like Rose had to me.

'Mister?'

A little boy sat beside me at the back, squashed between me and his mother, who was deep in conversation with her neighbour.

'Have you come back from the war?' he asked. His eyes big and wide as he looked up at me.

I looked at the boy, no more than nine, and thought it was pointless to say anything else as I was still in uniform, and so answered, 'Yes.'

'Welcome, sir,' he said. 'My brother went but he didn't come back.'

I thought again of Emeka, of Ifeanyi, then said, 'I am sorry.'

He was silent for a second, looked down then up into my eyes. 'Well, we thank God that at least you came back.' I didn't know whether to smile or not, for there was a battle inside me, but I gave up, half smiled back, offered up some of my fruit, which he took.

'Thank you, sir,' his mother said on his behalf.

I nodded and looked back out of the opening.

We arrived late in the morning. I banged on the side for the driver to stop. He dropped me off at the side of the road; the little boy and his mother passed down my belongings.

217

'Take care,' shouted the little boy as the truck started up and continued on its way to Onitsha.

I turned around, looked up the hill to see the tops of our tin roofs in the distance. What would I find? What would they make of me? For I was not the same Obi who had left over two years ago to go to war. Then I thought I heard my grandmother, so hurried up the dirt path, ran as fast as my injuries would allow, sweating as I made it through the cornfield home.

I stood for a moment, just outside our compound, drinking it in. It was years since I had last seen home, and I wanted to cry, to kiss the soil.

I walked through the fence opening, heard the children's laughter go quiet, saw them looking at me as I walked further in. I knew initially they wondered who I was.

But then one of my little brothers said, 'Go, go get Mama. Quick . . . it's Obi.'

'Obi?'

'Yes, Obi. Our brother.'

One of the children squealed, the rest rushed towards me, pulled me further into the compound.

'Obi's home!' shouted one of the boys, and ran to the back to alert the women. 'He's home.'

The womenfolk came rushing out to check on the validity of the boy's statement. My father's second wife, Nnenna, was overcome; she collapsed to the floor crying and the rest had a job trying to get her up.

'Obi, is that you?!' she howled.

'Yes, Ma!'

'We thought you were dead. Is it you?'

'Yes, Ma.'

And there was much wailing and crying. It brought the neighbours out; the children ran to tell as many as they could.

'What took you so long?' asked Nnenna.

'I came home as fast as I could.'

'But the war ended months ago. When we finally got word about Emeka and Ifeanyi we thought . . . we prayed . . . but we thought . . .'

'I am home now.'

She came towards me, hugged me tight. 'Welcome,' she said, her eyes brimming over with tears. 'We did not cease praying for you. Your father even went to the barracks looking for you, but there was no news, and with each passing day we thought . . .'

'Well, I am home now. Stop crying. Where is my grandmother?'

They were silent.

'Where is she?' I repeated.

'Obi, she just couldn't wait any longer. She kept holding on but just couldn't . . .'

I took my bag from my shoulder and put it down on the ground. 'Where is she?'

They looked towards her hut. I clapped my hands outside and entered. It was dark and I went to the bed where she lay and looked down on her. She looked asleep. I sat down on the stool beside her, held her hand; she was still warm.

'She couldn't wait any more,' said Nnenna. 'She went this morning, not long ago.'

I nodded.

'She hasn't been well for some time.'

'I know.'

'She's been holding on for months.'

I nodded again.

There was nothing else I could say; I was too late. I sat beside her, held her hand. I saw her loading our heads to go to market, shelling pumpkin seeds under her favourite tree, singing and soothing us to sleep when times were hard. This hut held all those memories and more. Memories of my older brother and sister. Memories of how pretty Rose looked on our wedding day, and of her cradling and feeding Little Rose. A few of Rose's belongings were still neatly packed in a corner. The two women I had loved the most were gone, the two men also.

'Lord, what is this life about?' I said, looking over the stillness of my grandmother's face. I felt like half-cut rope holding on tightly to the remaining strands. That connection to the old world she was born into, a world in which Nigeria did not exist, was slowly being severed.

She looked peaceful, almost smiling, and I wondered whether the Umuada had come to meet her, like they had come to meet me out there in Burma. My limbs felt heavy. I hadn't enough energy to push myself up from where I sat.

Nnenna cleared her throat behind me. 'At least you're home in time to help bury her,' she said.

And I laughed.

'She wanted that.'

'Did she?' I asked.

'Yes. She said she was holding on for you to bury her, that she wanted to be buried well.'

I laughed again; knowing my grandmother, I knew this to be true. I heard her speak into my ear.

'*Bury me well.*'

I laughed once more. 'So, I made it home just in time.'

'We sent word to your father and he should be home tonight.'

We, the men of her line, gave her the best send-off we could. We buried her like an honorary man, a soldier. We laid her in state, killed a cow, fired bullets into the morning sky in salute of her life. People came from all around to say their goodbyes. There was no quiet early-morning burial for her. She would have been proud.

30

An Interruption

Eastern Nigeria, Wet Season, 1946

I WOKE TO A dull ache in my back, lay still on the bed waiting for it to go, and listened to the old familiar sounds. The women sweeping the yard. The bark of our dogs. The sizzling sound of frying food. Nnenna calling her children for breakfast. I knew at long last I was home.

I went for a short walk; there was nothing else to do. Avoided the main routes, because I was not ready to face too many questions from our people. Searched for a little land, but there was none I could afford. Ruminated and worried over how long the gratuity pay from the army would last, especially with inflation reducing its value.

So I unfolded my papers, sat at my desk. The one Rose had bought after we were married. Lingered for a while, remembering how the light from the lamp would caress the side of her face as she sat and wrote. Thought I smelt her. Looked around, but she was not there, shook my head to shake out the memories. Breathed in hard. Exhaled. Then wrote a letter to the army using the address I had been given.

I hitched a lift into Onitsha to post it, bought a little liquor to

221

ease the underlying pain in my back, and returned home to anxiously await the army's reply.

I woke in the middle of the night, sweat pouring off me, just couldn't work out where I was for a little while.

'Obi? Are you OK?'

It was my father's second wife, Nnenna, who slept in the hut next door. I could make out her shadow standing on the other side of the curtain at the entryway.

'I'm fine.'

'It's just that I heard you calling out in your sleep.'

'I'm fine, go back to sleep.'

I heard her walk away, and settled back down in the bed, squinted up at the ceiling, but I could not shake the feelings, the agitation. Thoughts of Burma were riding me again; I saw Ifeanyi and Emeka in front of me, cutting their way through thick bamboo, the sound of monkeys chirping up above; they were smiling back at me, their guns secured on their shoulders, the sweat glistening off their arms, as we hacked our way through the thick vegetation. Then Olu lying on the ground, unable to get up. And bodies with bullets through the middle of their heads, bodies with limbs blown off, and bodies, and bodies . . . I lifted my rifle. I woke again screaming.

I got up, got the liquor from my jacket pocket, sat on the side of the bed, and I drank, gulped it down. There was fire in my throat. I drank till I felt no more pain.

In the morning my head throbbed. I tried to peel back my eyelids, reached halfway then closed them again. Waited to adjust, for the nausea to go away, then opened them again. My blurry vision soon focused. Right above my head was a child's face looking down on me.

'Morning,' she said.

'Morning,' I said back.

'Are you my father?'

At first I was confused, but as I looked up at her the confusion faded. She was a pretty little girl with a smile like Rose's, skin the colour of light toffee, and eyes like her father's. I was not sure how to respond.

'They say you are my papa.'

'Who?'

'My cousins, and Auntie Nnenna. Is it true?'

I shifted and sat up in the bed.

'Auntie Nnenna says I should bring you this.'

She handed me a white enamel cup, with dents and chips in various places.

I took it and drank the hot liquid.

She smiled.

'Rose!' shouted Nnenna, her voice coming from the direction of the kitchen. Little Rose turned and ran out of the hut.

I wanted to stop her, call her back, find out more, but I heard my father's wife call again so I let her go.

I dressed smartly, pulling on my pressed khaki uniform. Then tugged on the bottom of my jacket, puffed out my chest for a better fit, and fixed the collar in the speckled mirror which leant against the mud hut walls. I left the compound, stick in hand. This time, I was able to go for a longer walk around the village. Besides, there was nothing else for me to do, no work to be had or farmland I could afford.

The village was not as I had left it. It was as if it too was trying to recover, struggling also to get back on its feet.

I waved at old family friends as I rambled along. A few stopped, some gestured as I passed, shouting, 'Welcome home!' One or two invited me into their yards, but I smiled, made my excuses and kept walking. Even my father's former friend, whom he had fallen out with years back at a village meeting, lifted his hand to his temple in a salute, and raised his right foot high in the air to stamp it hard on to the powdery ground; the dust billowed up between us.

'Welcome home, son,' he said, a little unsteady as he brought his hand down.

'Thank you, sir.'

'The village is in mourning for its lost sons and yet jubilant for those of you who are back. We thank almighty God for your safe return home.'

'Thank you, sir,' I said.

'We will be glad for you to join us one evening; come when you are ready.'

'Yes, sir. I will one evening,' I said, moving on.

But I was quiet when I walked past Emeka's parents' home. There was a silence in their yard, and his mother and brothers were nowhere to be seen. She must be hiding away in her pain, I thought. So I shuffled past quickly, my head low.

I stopped under the shade of the main village tree, leant against the trunk, and watched our old school from afar. The one in the centre of our village, where we also went to church on a Sunday, singing hymns out loud with childish, shiny Vaseline grins, secretly pushing and shoving each other in our seats.

Reverend Nwachukwu, our old teacher and priest, was no longer teaching but was still the vicar of our village, and so I watched the new teacher and the village children from a distance, listened to the children reciting their lessons. I heard them but I also heard us, Ifeanyi, Emeka, Rose and Uche.

'. . . two times two is four, two times three is six, two times four is eight . . .' and so they continued.

I walked around the village looking at everything, and everything seemed so much smaller than I remembered. A simple, neat little village, naive about the world beyond it. It seemed too small a place to contain so much damage.

And as I walked, exploring the sights, I didn't know why, but there was a sudden need within me to speak to Emeka's brother

Nonso. I didn't know what I had to say to him, or even if he would be in, but I needed to know how he was faring, to understand if it was just me struggling. And yet, at the same time, I did not want to, did not want the reminders of what had happened out there in the jungle. But there was no one else, no one who could possibly understand, who could comprehend. So I found myself walking back in the direction of their family home, in search of understanding.

I entered their yard; there was tension in the air. Their mother sat on a wooden stool on the front veranda, a calabash bowl in her lap, cutting okra; I assumed for soup. There was no one else around and the way in which she seemed to stop her cutting, only for a second, meant she was already aware I was hovering in the entrance. So, I put my stick under my arm and clapped my hands twice to draw her attention, bowed my head in greeting, walked further in and sat down on the step beside her feet; the spot where she signalled for me to sit by pursing her lips in that direction.

'Do you want something to drink?' she asked, wiping her brow with the back of her hand, her hair pulled and parted into four square sections, threaded with cotton.

'Water,' I replied.

She turned to call one of the children from the back to bring the water.

A little boy appeared. 'Thank you,' I said and took the cup from his hands.

'My grandson. Emeka's sister's child.'

I nodded.

'Uncle, welcome,' he said and backed away quickly, disappeared inside the house again as if he sensed that out here among the adults was not the best place to be at that moment.

I took a sip, then spoke. 'Mama, I hope this day finds you well?' I asked. Although, from her countenance, I had a feeling that all was not well.

'As well as can be expected.'

'I came looking for your son . . . and . . . Is he home?'

She was quiet, looked down and continued to cut okra into her bowl.

I turned my body to look directly up at her.

'Mama, are you OK?'

'Please forgive me,' she said, lifted her head; a lone tear fell from the corner of her eye. 'Obi,' she added, and forced a weak smile on to her face. 'I wish I knew.'

'Is all well?'

'Obi, my boy is not the same boy that went away.' She paused then asked, 'Obi, are you the same?'

'What do you mean, ma?'

'I mean, Nonso was always a sweet child, and if you did not know him before, you may not initially notice, but at night, that is when it comes out. I hear him talking to himself in his sleep, tossing and turning in the bed, and sometimes he wakes—' She paused again, as if something had suddenly occurred to her. 'Obi, do you also wake screaming?'

I was quiet and looked away.

'He is angry all the time. At night he drinks and staggers back home. That is not the son I knew. Yesterday they had to pull him off someone for fear of what he might do.'

'I am sorry, ma.'

'It is in his eyes. It scares me. It's as if he is controlling himself and if I were to push too far he would definitely, possibly . . . I am frightened. Obi, tell me these things will pass.'

I hung my head between my legs, said nothing, for I had nothing to say.

'I only tell you these things because I have been sitting here praying for someone to talk to, and I think the gods, they sent you, for as I was praying, in you walked. I know you understand because you know what went on out there in Burma.'

'Mama, I am sorry . . .'

'There is no need for sorrys. Obi, I knew I would have to mourn Emeka, but I did not know I would have to mourn the one who returned as well. Obi, does your family mourn you?'

'Please don't speak like this, mama. Don't ask me these questions.'

She was silent for a second, as if she was thinking, trying to solve things in her head, then continued, 'I miss Emeka, my first-born. I wish he was home with us now; he would have known what to do. He was always such a sensible child, like his father. I do not know how to handle Nonso. It is just me here, a widow, no husband to help me. My son and I are strangers living under the same roof. I don't know how to help him, how to take away his pain,' she cried.

I didn't know what to say, so I was silent.

'Are you the same? Do you sleep at night? And when you do, do you wake screaming? Please help me understand.'

'Mama, I have to go.' I got up quickly from where I sat.

'Obi!' she shouted after me.

I walked, limped, moved as fast as my stick would allow, out of the compound on to the path which led me home, and all the while as I shuffled back through the village I could not see anything for the glaze of tears in my eyes. I did not hear anyone for the fever of thoughts running in my head.

'Papa,' shouted Little Rose as I rushed past her into our yard.

'Leave him,' said Nnenna. 'I think he needs to be by himself for a little while.'

I entered my hut, sat on my bed, stared into my thoughts; it was like watching a film. I shook, sweated, felt the droplets trickling down my cheeks.

God, what is there to say? How can you make someone understand?

I looked up at the thatched roof, through my blurred vision, and I was shaking, remembering, crying. And when I could not take it any more I bent down, reached under the bed, rummaged and pulled out a revolver from the bag I had hidden. Sat down on the floor, my back against the side of the bed, looked down at the gun in my hand, felt the weight of the cold metal, pulled back the trigger, heard the click as the cylinder started to rotate. My hand trembled as I fought the urge to lift it to my temple and pull harder. I said a prayer, hoped they – Rose, Emeka and Ifeanyi – would be on the other side to greet me, began to lift the gun, my eyes squeezed shut.

'Papa.'

I stopped midway.

'Papa,' said Little Rose from outside the hut, 'are you all right?'

I quickly moved the gun, hid it under the bed. 'Go away.'

'What are you doing?' she asked. I could see her shadow, her ear up against the thin fabric in the entryway.

'Go away and play.'

But she did not listen and popped her head through.

'Papa, are you all right?' she asked. 'Can I come in?'

'Didn't I hear your auntie tell you to leave me be?'

'Yes, but I wanted to check that you were OK.'

She walked further into the room and leant against the desk; she was just slightly taller than the chair. We stared at each other.

'Did your auntie not tell you to leave me?'

'Yes,' she said now, staring down at her feet.

'Well, you've checked, now go. Shoo.'

'Papa,' she said, still staring down at the ground. 'What was my mother like?'

'What?'

'Auntie Nnenna says she was pretty. Was she?'

I was at a loss. It was not a conversation I had been expecting to have or wanted to have, but as I looked at the little girl there was something about her that compelled me to answer. 'Yes. She was very pretty.'

Little Rose moved from the desk and came to sit down beside me on the floor. 'And did you love her?' she asked, staring up at me. There was a longing for answers in her eyes that surprised me.

'Yes, very much so.'

'Good,' she said. 'You will take me to church on Sunday.'

'What?'

'Church. You will take me.'

'Church?'

'Yes, church. Will you?'

And as I watched this child I sensed that for whatever reason, me taking her to church was important, and so although I hesitated, I said, 'Yes.'

'Good. Then everyone will be able to see I have a father. Ebele, my friend, will be shocked to see you.'

'Will she?'

'Yes, she says that I have no father and that my mother committed an abominable act. She says that's why the rest of the village treats me strangely. Papa, what is an abominable act?'

'It's when . . . What do you mean, the rest of the village treats you strangely?'

'I don't know, they behave strangely towards me. I hear their gossip. I know what people say about my mother. I once overheard someone say as I passed, "That's Rose's daughter, you know, the one that committed the abomination." I thought that's why some treat me like I am a leper. What is abomination? Auntie Nnenna refuses to tell me. What does it mean?'

I heard her auntie Nnenna calling her.

'I'd better go.'

'Yes, you'd best.'

'Sunday, then?'

'What?'

'Church. You will take me to church.'

'OK,' I said to get rid of her.

'You promise?'

I looked at her. Her eyes were desperate with a yearning, and I sensed that it meant more to her than her outward self wanted to let on, and so I said, 'I promise.' And as I watched her run out, it began to dawn on me – although it seemed a simple thing to connect, I hadn't – that my almost actions a moment ago would also have been an abomination and would have had a subsequent impact on everyone else. Another one to bury in the public cemetery.

31

Unanswered Questions

'**Y**OU'D BETTER HURRY, the service will start soon.'

'I'm coming,' I said, trying to keep up with the child.

She ran ahead into the church to find a seat on the back benches and I followed.

The new junior vicar, appointed to help Reverend Nwachukwu with his growing parish, entered from the side dressed in his black cassock, white over-garment and stole. I heard the scraping of the legs of the wooden benches against the concrete floor as everyone got to their feet, and once again when they took their seats.

And as I sat there, I noticed a few in the congregation twisting and straining to look at me sitting there in the back.

'Take your hat off.'

'What?'

'Take your hat off,' said Little Rose, a little amused.

And so I did. But one of the older women in the congregation, sitting in a row in front, slightly to the left, continued to stare and smile at me.

'That's Auntie Adaora,' said Little Rose. 'She has many daughters and is looking for husbands for all of them.'

Little Rose smiled and looked forward, swung her legs on the bench beside me.

She was wearing a blue cotton dress, not much different to the one her mother had worn that day I fell in love with her up there in our mango tree, and before I knew it Little Rose had hooked her arm through mine and leant her head against me. I looked down at the top of her head and remembered the day we, Rose and I, stood at the front of the church and baptized her. It came flooding back to me. Rose had dressed her in a lace gown, one she had sat up all night sewing. Little Rose had opened her mouth wide as Reverend Nwachukwu poured the water over her head, and let out a strong cry. It had seemed to me at the time that even then this child was very much like her mother.

Rose's words echoed in my ear.

'*Promise me . . . you will look after her,*' she had said out there in the jungle. '*Make sure she is OK.*'

And I had nodded, agreed. When she had asked, it had seemed like such a simple request, but so much had transpired since then, and I thought of the war, of all our dead men, of Emeka lying out there in a foreign land, of the guilt, of the blood on my hands and the gun hidden under my bed. To live, to die: that was the question. This earthly journey . . . *Dear God!* I cried out. *Help me understand, help me make sense of it. Rose, wherever you are, I hope . . . I hope . . . Dear God, is it not too late to hope?*

Then I heard the vicar say in Igbo, 'For what does it profit a man to gain the whole world and forfeit his soul?'

And I knew he was talking to me.

'Are you all right?' asked Little Rose.

'What?'

'Are you all right?'

'Fine, why?'

'You're gripping the Bible very hard, like you could tear it in half.'

'Oh, sorry,' I said, and released the Bible from my grip.

The congregation stood to sing. I stood with them, and I too began to sing. I remembered the words, the hymn came rolling off my tongue like paper off a roll; everything came back to me so naturally, as well as the prayer responses, like I hadn't been away.

I could see the three of us – Emeka, Ifeanyi and myself – together again, mischievous, sitting in the last row, like I was now, fidgeting and quietly jostling each other. Michael was up front with his father and Rose would usually be with Uche, doing her best to ignore us. Then afterwards, the six of us outside, our childish play; our laughter rang in my ears. Despite everything, we were happy. The memory disintegrated before my eyes, and I thought of the gun lying under my bed.

'*Promise me . . . you will look after her,*' Rose had said. I looked down at the child; she seemed happy singing along to the hymn, then she looked up at me, and I forced a smile. I thought of her words to me a few days ago.

'They say my mother committed an abominable act . . . What is an abominable act?'

And I thought again of the gun under my bed, thought of our people, the effect it would have on my family, on Little Rose, and I thought of Rose.

'*Take care of Little Rose,*' Rose had whispered in my ear as I floated down the river.

Once again there was a fight within me. I knew it was again a fight between Rose and me. I felt her.

After the service, outside in the yard, many came forward to talk to me and welcome me, including Auntie Adaora, who insisted that Little Rose should go and play.

Once Little Rose was gone, she invited me to her home. I hesitated politely, and was saved as others came forward, busybodies; some enquired about my uniform, others questioned me about the army and where I had served. And as they questioned me I noticed Little Rose in the distance playing with other children. There was something odd about the way she interacted with the other children in the churchyard; she was on the periphery, awkward in her stance. I called to her, and made a note in my head to find out more about it later.

'Why did you not play with the other children?' I asked as we made our way home.

'What do you mean?'

'I noticed that you were not in the middle of the game, more on the outskirts of it. Why?'

She shrugged her shoulders.

We walked in silence and then she said, 'Sometimes they don't want to play with me.'

'Why?'

'They tease me, say I am odd-looking. That I don't look like my family. That I am *anyali*, albino.'

I listened and nodded, wondered what to say to the child. 'What do you say to them, when they say these things?'

She shrugged her shoulders again. 'Not much. Sometimes I ignore them. Sometimes I fight.'

'You fight?'

'Yes,' she said, looking defiantly back at me.

I laughed, for I knew she was truly Rose's child.

Little Rose smiled back and skipped on ahead.

We continued the walk home along the dirt path in comfortable silence.

I looked for work, but there was none to be found. I went as far as Onitsha but there was no work there either. Things were tough, tougher than I had imagined. The country still had not recovered from the war, and I was beginning to run low on funds. I did not know what I was going to do.

I chased up my letter to the army but they had no response to give me.

Nnenna, my father's second wife, asked me for more money for the child. I gave it to her, but this was not sustainable.

There was a veterans' club set up by some ex-soldiers; they met up not far from the village. I decided to find out more and possibly attend.

It felt good to be among them, to know they silently understood, not to have to explain the confusion, or the little changes in my behaviour since my return. But at the same time they also scared me. Emeka's brother Nonso, the one with the wild eyes, was among them, and like many, he was a hothead.

One day we sat joking, playing cards, and what little money we had we pooled to brew some local inebriant, and so we drank, drank until we could not drink any more. Emeka's brother was the worse for it. I don't know what one man said to him, but suddenly he jumped on him. We had to pull him off; there was murder in his eyes. It took four of us to restrain him. I swear, if we had not been there, that man would now be dead.

I took him outside.

Nonso looked at me and said, 'How do you turn off the impulse to want to kill?'

I looked back at him, not knowing what to say.

'I mean, that's what I've been trained to do. That's what I know how to do. I did it well. How do you switch it off?'

The truth was, as much as we were a solace to each other, we were drowning, and drowning men cannot save each other. I was beginning to believe that there were a few among us who would never recover, and that we had been abandoned. We were trying, in whichever way we could, to find a way back to who we had been. But our people did not understand, and some of our ways were beginning to become more of a nuisance to them, especially as most of us were idle because there was no work to be found. And still, of an evening, I found myself staggering and singing along the dirt paths home, full of drink. It was a relief from reality, a way of quietening the dull hum from the gun that lay under my bed.

I came back from my search for work early that day and for once I was not drunk. Maybe it was because it was still early, or maybe I was growing tired of such an existence, I don't know. I just know it was unusual for me to be home and even more unusual for hardly anyone else to be there as well.

At first when I entered the compound all seemed quiet. It was only on walking further into the yard that I heard the faint sound of a child crying. It confused me at first, as I was not sure where it was coming from, but on listening closely I was sure it came from somewhere within the compound, and so I went in search of its source. I found the child hiding in the kitchen, head resting on her knees, squeezed in between the wall and the kitchen stove.

I stood looking down on her at first, and called her name.

She continued crying, so I bent down to her eye level.

'Little Rose,' I said and gently placed a hand on her shoulder, then on her head, patted it cautiously. 'Are you OK?'

She continued to cry, so I pulled her out from the space that she had squeezed herself into and held her in my arms.

'Shush, little one, what is all this?'

Her crying got deeper and she began to shake with it.

'Shush now,' I said. 'Why are you crying so?'

'They say . . . they say . . .' she said, taking in big gulps of air, the tears streaming down her face, 'that . . . that my mother killed herself.'

I did not know what to say to her. What does one say to a child on these matters? Matters that I myself had not come to terms with. I breathed in, tried to figure out what best to say, chose my words carefully.

Then I heard her say, through tears, the words muffled against my shoulder, 'Why did she not love me?'

My heart broke on hearing her words. And I too began to cry at this terrible mess we had left behind.

'If she loved me, she wouldn't have done such a thing.'

'Shush, child, your mother loved you very much.'

'Then why did she kill herself?'

'She did not.'

'Then why do they say she did?'

'Because they don't know any better. Your mother did not kill herself.' I went to tell her that Rose had been murdered, but thought better of it, as I suspected that telling her this information would make things even worse. I pulled her off my shoulder, squeezed her tight, looked directly into her eyes; she looked back into mine, and I said, 'Trust me, your mother did not kill herself, she loved you very much, did not want to leave you.'

'Did she?'

'Yes, she did.'

The child's tears began to dry up and she lifted the back of her hand to wipe the remainder away.

'And you, did you love her?'

I laughed through my own tears. 'Very much. I think too much. You know, she was a wonderful woman. Spirited, like you.'

The child lifted her head as if deep in thought, turned to me and said, 'Is that why you come home drunk?'

I was quiet for a little, then said, 'Maybe.'

And I felt that the child had so much more she wanted to ask, many things churning in her brain, but I was not ready to answer them – no, the real truth was that I was not able to answer them yet, I needed time to formulate the answers, to uncoil the confusion, examine them, before I would be able to give her the answers she truly needed. So I got up and said, 'Come, let's go for a walk.'

She too got to her feet and cautiously followed me out; we walked out of the compound, along the dirt path, towards the trunk road and the vendors that sold her favourite *udala* fruit. We bought enough for the rest of the household, including bananas and groundnuts. It was a bright, hot day, and she was happy again and skipped ahead. We greeted the other villagers who passed us, and I was sure all they saw was a father walking with his happy child, not the sadness and devastation that lay beneath, or the questions and answers that needed to be worked through. And as she skipped back and forth, I resolved to make good my promise to Rose, to take care of her. Even as I said these things to myself, there was something in me that was uneasy. But meanwhile we were father and happy daughter, returning home with treats for everyone.

She laughed and rushed ahead.

32

Hope

Eastern Nigeria, Dry Season, 1948

How time flew! One Christmas and New Year came and went, and then another. Little Rose was doing well, and I still accompanied her to church on a Sunday.

My father came home at the weekends saying there was work available at the mines. It was not something I wished to do, but nevertheless I needed to consider it, as if I continued spending money at the rate I was, I would soon completely run out of funds. Nnenna had been asking for more money again. I did, only briefly, contemplate approaching Rose's family next door to ask them to contribute, but thought better of it, as this would only begin to raise questions, maybe open up things I was, at the time, not ready to deal with.

We got news that there were riots in the Gold Coast after the colonial government shot dead three veterans during a march for better treatment.

We were very angry at this news, and at the conditions we faced at home. My father said the miners were quite vocal and they had rejected the colonial government's mass literacy programme as they said all it would prepare children for was a life of menial labour. He had got quite political and was involved in a number of projects set up by the colliers' association he belonged to, building our own schools and supporting maternity clinics. He said they intended to carry out a 'Go Slow' strike the following week.

'Papa, where are you going?' asked Little Rose.

'To my meeting.'

'Will you be back late?'

'I don't know.'

'Remember you promised to take me to church tomorrow.'

'Yes, Little Rose.'

Even at the veterans' club there had been a change in the atmosphere, or maybe the change was in me, for although I drank, I was more in control. Some of the veterans were talking about organizing themselves to protest against the army and to demand the things promised them before they had gone out to fight.

Still there was no response from the army to my letter; it had been over a year, almost two, and at the time I was beginning to wonder if they ever would reply.

I was sober when I got home from the meeting. Hadn't been sober at night in a long time. I lay on my bed listening to the crickets chirping outside and the quiet chatter of the wives as they conversed together, having sent the remaining children to bed. It was hot with little breeze, but that night I did not hear the gun under my bed calling. I knew it was there but it did not call, yet the guilt still rode me.

There were so many questions I wished I had asked, so much I wished I knew, but Rose no longer visited, hadn't visited since the last time I had seen her, threading through the water to whisper in my ear. I had thought I had asked her all the things I wished to know out there in the jungle. But that's the problem with life: you can never really ask all the questions you need to ask until you have distance, and by then, like in my case, it is too late. I still did not know the details of why Lieutenant Richards would have killed Rose. I wished I understood what could have driven him to it. But maybe we never really get the answers we want, maybe that is the way it is supposed to be, maybe the only real answers are the ones we give ourselves, that life reveals with time.

An old colleague of mine sent word that the Enugu barracks was looking for civilians to do clerical work, and as I had no desire to go back into the army as a soldier, nor join my father at the mines, the work was ideal. So I hurried and applied.

We left for Enugu early in the morning, my father and I, the day before I started work at the barracks. As we travelled down he was full of talk about the marches happening all around, but in particular what was happening in the Gold Coast. There was stronger talk of independence; things were still tough, shortages were many, and people were growing increasingly frustrated, especially now there was no war to blame things on.

It was strange to be in Enugu again, working back at my old barracks, only a few miles away from where my father resided. In the old days when I was in the army I had rarely visited, but my father and I had now developed a different type of relationship. I did not like him as a father, but I found — somewhere between his visits home and my rare visits to Coal Camp to see him — that I actually liked him as a man. He believed in community, and was what you would call a kind of activist in those days, which later began to rub off on me.

It was good to have money coming in once again. It was like I hadn't been away, and there were still soldiers who remembered me from before.

Little Rose was doing well, thriving, and each time I went home, the more she reminded me of her mother, but seeing this did not fill me with pain as it once had. I tried as best I could to help out Emeka's mother, tried to make up a little for being the one who had lived. But the truth is, no matter what, there are just some things that can never be mended. She was ever so grateful, and in those moments I wondered how she would react if she knew the truth. If I had the courage to tell her what had really happened out in the jungle, that maybe I could have saved them if I had made them go in a different direction. But then I stopped myself, as I knew this would break her, and no good would ever come of that.

33

The Hilltop

Eastern Nigeria, Dry Season, 1949

IT WAS DRY season and it had not rained in weeks. The hot sun slapped me across my forehead as I removed the hat from my head. Hot winds blew through, brushing the small hairs on my arm, and lifted the surface layer of terracotta dust off the ground, swirled it up into the air, dispersed it everywhere, so that the old tree that stood to the right, just off the main path into Coal Camp, the little vegetation that poked and waved from the ground, and the thrown-together shanty houses made of rusty tin were all coated in it.

That Friday morning, I woke and could not feel the pain in my back. I lay looking up at the ceiling, orientating myself, for even three years after returning home, I could sometimes, not often, get confused about where I was, particularly if I woke quickly from what I called my Burma dreams. I thought I had been dreaming of Ifeanyi and Emeka again, young as we were then. We were joking around by the stream, in an attempt to keep the nightmare of all that was happening to us at bay, and for some strange reason my father appeared among us. That was when I woke up, and resolved that it was time to visit him. So I walked the four or five miles to Coal Camp.

There were rumours that there was to be yet another 'Go Slow' strike for the back-pay owed the miners, as striking by downing tools and leaving the site was illegal, and so I set off in the hope that I would find him milling about, not too focused on work that day.

As I was reaching the entrance to my father's quarters in the camp, a convoy of police and Hausa troops, unfamiliar to me, and whom I suspected must have been shipped in from the north, whizzed past me in military trucks. I ran up the hill towards the mines where my father worked. They were a fair distance away.

I heard the miners' chants first. When I got to the top the troops had disembarked from the trucks. They stood with rifles in their hands, facing the miners.

I looked for my father among the men; they faced the armed troops and police, strips of red cloth tied around their arms and on their helmets. They chanted and danced, the white captain shouting at them to stop and get back. The men continued in protest. The captain shouted again, the gun shaking in his hand. I moved slowly towards the crowd, watching as I walked, looking for my father among the miners, and there he was in the middle of them, dancing back and forth. I heard a shot, saw my father's friend Sunday fall to the ground, saw the white captain shoot again, heard the command, and the round of fire from the troops. The men fell one by one, it seemed in slow motion. I watched my father fall to the ground, the blood flowing, and there was chaos.

I crouched down as some men were shot in the back, as the firing continued for several minutes; I ran to my father once the firing ceased. I found him on the ground, the blood pouring out of him.

I heard one man say, 'I surrender, please, I surrender.'

The white captain looked at him and said, 'I don't care.' Then walked away.

The troops climbed back on their trucks and left us there.

I watched as they drove away.

We carried those we could down the hill to try to get help.

Others who had heard the gunshots came panting up the hill, including women looking for their husbands.

I carried my father's body down to his quarters, crying for help, for a doctor.

He died in my arms.

34

My Father

I BURIED MY FATHER. Laid him next to my grandmother, across from Rose's mother in the next yard. The only one missing was Rose herself. The others – Ifeanyi and Emeka – we could do nothing about. As for Michael, he was still in America. Uche came home to say her goodbyes. It was good to see her. She was to leave for a nursing job in England later that day. We sat beside each other in our yard. She approached me straight after the last bit of dirt had been thrown over the body and we sat waiting to be fed.

'So what time do you leave?'

'This afternoon.'

'It was good of you to come.'

'I'm sorry, everything was already arranged by the time I knew.'

'Yes, of course, don't worry,' I replied.

Then we were quiet as we looked out on the rest of the people, at groups that had come to bid my father farewell. The miners had sent their representatives as well as our village council, and other groups my father had belonged to. They were all enraged and spoke quietly in corners about what should be done next, below the beat of the drums that hailed my father as a man among men, so as not to offend. It surprised me how respected my father, a poor man, had been in his life. I wished I had paid more attention when he had been alive. And for the first time in my life I resolved to follow in his footsteps, to seek out justice for him and the others.

'Your father was a well-respected man, who spoke truth where it was needed,' said Uche.

'Yes, indeed,' I said and wished I had known this man of whom many spoke. But that is the problem with life being so close; it can sometimes limit our perspective. To me, my father was my father, the one who barked and loved the cane, especially for us boys, but then I realized that to others he was so much more than this. Sometimes we need to step back to see the whole picture of who a person really is, see them through more eyes than just our own to get the full measure.

'I've been meaning to ask you things that have puzzled me about Rose, but never got the chance. The two of you were very close . . .'

'Were we?' she asked.

Her response seemed a little odd, especially as they had both lived and shared a room together in Lagos.

She stopped, gathered herself. 'Sorry. Yes, you're right. But we were closer as children than we were as adults.'

'Do you know if she was seeing anybody in Lagos before she died?'

'Not particularly, for Rose had many men in love with her. They saw her beauty and her poise and came under her spell. But Rose was complicated, she had thorns.'

Uche looked sideways at me, like she wasn't sure if she should go on, so I nodded.

'She had a way about her. She was like the sun: the further away you were, the more she shone, but the closer you got, the more she burned.'

'What do you mean?' I asked, for I was taken aback.

'Don't mind me,' she said. 'I just mean she had a charm that drew you in.'

'Was any of the men in love with her a Lieutenant Richards?'

She looked a little shocked that I had mentioned his name. 'Yes. But that ended long before the two of you married.'

'Did it?'

'Yes.'

'What happened between them?'

'Just that when his family found out how serious he was about her, they moved him quickly as far away from Lagos as they could.'

'But to Enugu?'

'Maybe they didn't realize she was Igbo. I don't know. Rose was devastated. Heartbroken.'

'Was she?'

'Yes. I think she loved him, but . . . I don't know, sometimes, I wondered . . . what made her so, so . . . I suppose nobody knows someone's full journey. But all you boys were in love with Rose.'

'I suppose we were,' I replied.

'Well, I'd better go. I just wanted to give my condolences before I headed out.'

And she got up, gave me a half-hug and walked off.

It seemed like everyone in the village had come to pay their respects. Reverend Nwachukwu got up and blessed the food. He seemed old, very grey, much like how I felt at the time. It was too much to bear, all the loss, too much in my short life. I was tired of it, and yet I knew there would be more to come, but not so soon.

I had seen so much death out there in Burma, and then at home, and having put my father in the ground, that I was so very wary.

But this must be the lesson this life is intent on repeatedly teaching me – that nothing and no one is permanent. We are here but for a short moment, borrowing time on this earth, and all we can do is try to live the best we can, be the best we can, despite it all. For everything else that we place so much importance on – the things, the possessions – are but a mirage that fades away in the wind once our life is gone. Because all we are left with, at that point, is who we are and what we truly meant to those we leave behind.

I am glad I got to know my father as a man, to judge him truly through my adult eyes, and seeing him through these eyes was so different to seeing him as a child, for I loved the man I came to know my father to be, but hated the father that he was.

There was much to do, running up and down to make sure all the guests were fine, but in the midst of doing this I was so drained, so tired of everything and everyone, that I had a need to get away. So I walked out of my yard, down to the trunk road, through the fields of corn and sugar cane. Walked along the road towards Onitsha, put out my hand for a lift as I went along. To my surprise, ten minutes later, a lorry carrying logs stopped to let me climb up. I sat on top of the covered logs, tightly chained in, felt the warmth of the breeze on my skin as we drove along. Disembarked near Onitsha market.

It was busy as always. I walked past Vicky's, which to my surprise was still there. I thought of us, that last summer, when Ifeanyi, Emeka, Michael and I had come to while away the time before our lives changed.

I don't know why I headed for the riverbank, or why I took a seat on the slope to watch the people below waiting for the ferry to come across and the boats to take them to places further afield.

I just knew I needed to get away, from our village, the busyness and rowdiness of mourning, from where we had all grown up, and the only place that called to me was the little shanty eating-place, Vicky's. The view we all used to like to sit beside and quietly watch. So I made my way there without thinking, or understanding why.

And as I sat there drinking in the day, I saw Uche waiting for her boat to arrive below. She turned to look up the slope. I waved at her. She saw me, left her luggage for someone to keep an eye on, and made her way up the incline towards me.

'What are you doing here?' she asked.

'I just needed to get away. It was just too much.'

She sat down beside me, both of us looking out on the Niger.

'I know what you mean.'

'Do you?'

'Yes.'

'Uche, what went wrong?'

'I don't know.'

'I have done things in this world I wish I could go back and change. Wished I had made better decisions. Watched the pain of my decisions hurt so many others. Uche, I have murdered with these two hands.'

'I know. I know what you mean.'

'Do you?'

She was crying, deep sobs. 'Yes, I do.'

I took out a cigarette, lit it and smoked.

We saw her boat come in below, and the captain begin to direct the men to load the vessel.

'Your boat is in,' I said.

We stood.

'Do you have an address where you're going to in England? Might want to send you a letter or two.' I laughed. 'You never know, I might even come over to visit Buckingham Palace and all those other palaces they have over there.'

She rummaged in her bag for a pen, scribbled on a piece of paper, then handed it to me.

'You'd better hurry before it leaves.'

She nodded, gave me one last hug and walked back down the slope of the riverbank to board the boat.

I stood watching, took one last drag of my cigarette, blew out the smoke slowly through my pursed lips. It curled and swirled in a cloud in front of my eyes. I took one last long look at the cigarette butt, brought up my index finger and flicked it towards the water, and watched as the boat began to pull away from the docking point.

I took the paper out from my pocket and looked at the address Uche had written.

There was something strange about the writing, not right. I thought back to that terrible day at the hospital, to that room, and the scribbling on Rose's suicide note.

I am sorry . . .

I looked down at the paper Uche had given me, and underneath the address she had written, *I'm sorry.*

I was confused.

Back then, that day in the office, I had told them that it wasn't Rose's writing, had been convinced that it wasn't her writing, but the chief nurse had brought out the medical files they claimed Rose had filled in. I looked down at the paper, then up at the boat moving away.

'Uche!' I shouted. 'Uche!' I yelled as I ran down the incline. Stood on the riverbank, the stretch of water between the bank and the boat getting wider, me standing waving the paper at her. 'What is this?'

'I'm sorry, Obi, so sorry,' she called, standing at the edge of the boat, crying as it sailed away. 'It was an accident.'

I looked down at the paper in my hand.

It was her. It was Uche all along. She must have written the note and filled in the medical records. She had killed Rose.

I watched, not knowing what to do, as the boat sailed away down the Niger into the distance. I sat down on the incline, felt the light breeze fanning across my face. 'It was her.'

And I looked on, not knowing what to do, as the barge glided away through the calm waters, the sun beginning to set, the band of orange-yellow glow splitting the sky and the river, the tears streaming down my face as the boat disappeared.

35

An Answer

London, Summer, 1995

I DIDN'T SEE UCHE again till almost some fifty years later, in London, a day before I also made it across the city to visit Michael, who lived an hour away somewhere in the suburbs.

Our meeting was by chance – at least it seemed that way – at some function put on by the Nigerian High Commission to commemorate Victory over Japan (VJ) Day. I was in transit from Japan where I served as a diplomat at the tail end of my career. London was awash with veterans to celebrate the fiftieth anniversary of the end of the war with Japan, but there were few of us Nigerian veterans in attendance, either because many of us had passed or because the cost of attending was prohibitive; besides, very few even remember our contribution and sacrifice these days. And there I was, suddenly facing her, looking at the ghosts of yesteryear. We both stood, grey-haired, walking stick in hand, transported back to that day by the Niger.

I remember it was a rainy summer day in London and I was shocked to see her, and for a while in our minds we were young again, remembering all that we were and had been in our younger years. Michael, Ifeanyi, Emeka and Rose ran between us, letting out shrieks of joy as we moved between each other's compounds. And when we came back to that day it was a surprise to register how old she was, but then again, I didn't have a mirror to remind myself of how old I had become.

After the day she sailed away, I did not know what to do. I was burdened with what she had confessed to me and with my own guilt. I tried to report what she had done but the authorities did not take what I had to say seriously, especially with all the trouble I had caused over Rose previously, and so I left it alone. Instead, I threw myself into the things that I thought could redeem me, into the things that I knew Ifeanyi and Emeka would have done if they had lived. I fought for independence with such vigour and energy that when it finally came, I was lost. I joined the civil service, determined like so many of our generation to build our nation. As a young man I was filled with so much hope for the future. Things seemed so simple then. Did we succeed in changing our world? Well, we failed on so many counts, in so many ways, but I loved the image of the country we tried to create.

Michael also returned, to fight alongside us. We were young with fire in our bellies, but things do not always turn out the way you hope. He was a general in Biafra, and many years later returned to attempt a coup. He lived out his years in exile in England. He died three years after my visit to London, slumped in his chair, doing what he liked doing best: reading a political article on the state of Nigeria which riled him up, so his wife told me over the phone.

When you are young you think you have all the time in the world, but this life goes by so quickly that before you know it you are staring back at ghosts of your former selves. So we sat at a table across from each other near the window, droplets of rain sliding down the glass, and I asked the question that I had waited fifty years to ask.

'Why?'

She breathed in, looked out of the window, then back at me.

I poured her some water. She took a sip and began.

'It was not something I planned, it truly was an accident,' she said. 'That night I went looking for her it was raining just like it is now and I was angry.'

I watched on as she looked out of the window again to somewhere far away, watching as the rain slid down the glass pane. She gave a small laugh. 'You see, ever since we were girls there was always competition between us. I suppose maybe there was a little part of me that was always jealous of Rose. She always seemed to have more freedom and chances than me. Things always seemed to work out for her, even when she messed up so terribly. I, on the other hand, I never seemed to catch a break. I was brighter than her but she still went off to the best school. I didn't mess up like her but Emeka was still in love with her, despite the two of you being married. I convinced myself that with Emeka knowing the truth about Rose he would finally see me, but he didn't. That night I told him everything, about Rose's affair with Lieutenant Richards, about Little Rose and the mess between the two of you, and I went to go and comfort him . . . I was hopelessly in love with him and he just pushed me aside. I loved him and he pushed me aside.'

'But how did you . . .?'

'I was so angry. I think I had been angry with her for so long that Emeka's rejection was the last straw and I went looking for her. I found her in the clinic on the second floor of the hospital, cleaning and packing away things for the day, just before her duties on the night shift commenced.'

She went quiet again, her mind lost back in that day.

'And?' I prompted.

'We argued,' she said. 'I wish . . . We argued outside on the balcony near the stairs. I followed her there as she tried to get away. I didn't mean to . . . I didn't mean to do it. She tried to push me out of the way, and I was so angry. It had built up over the years. Then she said something. Don't remember exactly what, now. But it was in that cutting way. That way she could sometimes speak. I saw red . . . and I slapped her, slapped her with all that anger inside me, and she went backwards and over . . .'

'Went over what?'

'She went over the balcony. I ran down into the bushes where she had fallen, but she was all twisted, dead. I didn't know what to do. I was scared. I panicked. Wrote the note, made it look like a suicide. I'm sorry, Obi, really sorry. Not a day has gone by that I haven't . . .'

I nodded, for I understood. 'So why tell me now?'

She was silent again, did not say a word.

'Why now?'

She gave a sad laugh and changed the subject. 'How is the family?' she said. 'And Little Rose, how is she?'

I wanted to probe further but felt a change, maybe a distance, come between us that hadn't been there but a second before, so instead I said, 'Fine. They are all fine. Yours?'

'I have none, never got married, or had children. Couldn't bring myself to love again.'

I looked at her, saw her hands shaking, her frailness, sensed that the years had not been easy and could not find it in my heart to hate her, but only pity. I watched her walk away that day, knowing we probably would never meet again, but still it was a surprise when Michael phoned me up two months later to tell me the news. That she was gone. Cancer.

Maybe we never truly escape the hurts, the pains, and the teachings of our youth. Maybe that was what was at the root of it all. Maybe some of us never escape, no matter how hard we try. I see Reverend Nwachukwu back in our makeshift classroom, pointing at the blackboard, our faces eagerly taking it all in. Yes, maybe none of us escaped.

I have lived more of a life than I thought I ever would after the war, and now so many of us are gone. Looking to the future, I often wonder, will anyone remember us, see who we really were and the part we played?

That is the thing with the past: you have to see it from different perspectives, from different viewpoints, to truly see the people you really were, to understand and learn what needs to be learnt.

I looked at my watch. It was time.

'Dad, are you ready?'

I looked up at Little Rose standing there, a wreath in her hand.

'I didn't see you come in.'

'I know, you were deep in thought.' She held out her hand to help me up. We walked arm in arm down towards Whitehall to join the other veterans.

'You know, you children are my pride and joy,' I said to her as we walked along.

'I know, Dad.'

'I'm very proud of you all.'

'I know, Dad.'

'Don't tell the others, but I'm particularly proud of you and what you have made of your life and the grandchildren you have given me.'

She smiled as the sun came out to meet us. We stood with the rest.

'The world has forgotten them, Little Rose,' I said as we stood among the veterans and the strange looks came our way. I saw Ifeanyi, Emeka, Olu and Sergeant Ibrahim in front of my eyes. Cutting their way through the Burma jungle. Making their contribution, trying to forge a better world, the best they could, within the limits and despite the limitations of the time we had been born into.

'Please, when I am gone, don't forget us. Always lay a wreath in memory of us and the part we played, and for the ones that never came home.

'Always remember us.'

Author's Note

THE SEED FOR this novel was planted many years ago, one rainy Saturday afternoon as I sat with my grandmother watching the afternoon matinée on television. I had just learnt about the Aba Women's Riots in 1929 and was in the process of writing a play. My grandmother had always been a kind of feminist icon to me, an independent woman way ahead of her time, so I was delighted to learn that she had childhood memories of the riots. This also helped me to understand that her independence, her determination to live life on her own terms, was not unique to her generation but went back much further, and that the narrative of the powerless, down-trodden African woman was more nuanced, more complicated, than the one I had originally been fed. It was not a matter of one story fits all.

I remember sitting there that rainy afternoon in Brixton as we talked, grandmother to granddaughter, and I turned to see an old black-and-white war movie on the TV. I cannot recall the name of the movie, but what I do recall is that all the soldiers I saw were white, and I had been led to believe at school that all the soldiers who fought in the Second World War were white, so I turned, I don't know why, and asked in jest, 'Did any of the men from your

257

village fight in the war?' To my shock and surprise, she said yes. So we sat there, and she told me about her childhood and the young men from her village who went to war and the ones who never came back.

Since then, my grandmother has passed away, but the memories of that afternoon have never left me, and over the years I have always sought to find out more about the African soldiers who fought in the Second World War.

Fast-forward to 2018, when, after twenty years of trying to get published, I finally got a two-book deal for my debut novel, *The Book of Echoes*, and one more book – leaving me with the wonderful dilemma of what to write for my second novel.

Well, as I said, that conversation with my grandmother had never left me, so I decided that I would write a novel that would pay homage to our discussion and to those soldiers who had left my grandmother's village and never returned.

Little did I know at the time that I was about to embark on a journey of self-determination, which would continue despite the world going into lockdown around me as the pandemic took hold. I found new and inventive ways to continue my research. I read and listened to various accounts of growing up in Nigeria at the time, including the accounts of my best friend's father, Uncle Ukaegbu, who told me invaluable stories of his youth before emigrating to the UK as a young man. I discovered more about my family history as I interviewed older members of my family, such as my Auntie Doris, who is now in her nineties and was a good friend of my grandmother, and my Uncle Uju. They all helped fill in some of the gaps in Obi's story.

One thing I was eternally grateful for was being able to carry out extensive research via the Imperial War Museum before lockdown. I heard and read first-hand accounts from some of the men who went to war in Burma and who trained with and made up the 81st West African, 82nd West African and East African Divisions.

Through reading their stories, Obi came alive; he lived among them, fought beside them; he wanted to speak. And although this novel is fiction it does reflect some of the stories and experiences as told by these men.

I tried to remain as faithful as possible to the stories of the soldiers of these divisions. This was not always easy, particularly as most of this story was written during the pandemic and there were gaps in information for the 82nd West African Division. However, where there were gaps these have been filled in with information as given by soldiers of the 81st West African Division. This was done in order to make the story feel more authentic. For example, Obi's journey to Burma with the 82nd West African Division is largely based on accounts given by soldiers of the 81st West African Division, who travelled to Burma almost a year previously, as I found more 81st soldiers' accounts of their trip to Burma.

This novel reflects the stories and experiences as told by many of these men. Obi was right there living, breathing and marching beside them, and so was Rose, and the women they left behind. This novel tells the untold story of some of the Black lives that were lost in the Second World War and their community.

Notes

Tʜᴇ ᴅʀʏ sᴇᴀsᴏɴ in Nigeria runs frovm November to March, and the wet season from April to October.

Note that the word 'colonial' in the context of this book refers to representatives of the British state, or white officers, soldiers and settlers in Nigeria at the time.

This novel is set in the 1930s and 1940s. Many of the documents and accounts written at that time contain language that is not agreeable or acceptable today. Although it has been toned down for this novel, it seemed important not to pretend such language wasn't commonplace, or to lose the opportunity to see how the world we live in affects us and our world view.

Acknowledgements

I WOULD LIKE TO acknowledge those who have championed this book and without whose support it would not have been published. Firstly, I would like to give thanks to my late grandmother, who planted the seed of this novel in me, especially for the informal history lessons she gave me. To the Imperial War Museum and the soldiers of the 81st and 82nd West African and East African Divisions, whose stories have been invaluable. To my aunties and uncles, who helped me understand a little better what it would have been like living in the times this book is set in. To Emeka Keazor for his openness and helpfulness. To my agent, Niki Chang, for her initial feedback on this story. To my editor, Jane Lawson, whose input has been extremely useful, and also for her enthusiasm and championing of this book. And to Kate Samano and the team at Doubleday, who polished and buffed the manuscript and turned it into the book in front of you today. But most of all, I thank God.

THE BOOK OF ECHOES
Rosanna Amaka

Brixton, 1981. Sixteen-year-old Michael is already on the wrong side of the law. In his community, where job opportunities are low and drug-running is high, this is nothing new.

When Michael falls for Ngozi, a vibrant young immigrant from the Nigerian village of Obowi, their startling connection runs far deeper than they realize.

Narrated by an African woman who lost her life on a slave ship two centuries earlier, this powerful story reveals how Michael and Ngozi's struggle for happiness began many lifetimes ago.

Through haunting, lyrical words, one unforgettable message resonates: love, hope and unity will heal us all.

'A new classic' SARA COLLINS, author of *THE CONFESSIONS OF FRANNIE LANGTON*

'Filled with beauty and the power of ancestral connections' IRENOSEN OKOJIE, author of *NUDIBRANCH*

'Lyrical and affecting' *GUARDIAN*

'Powerfully redemptive' *INDEPENDENT*

'Powerful, impassioned, thought-provoking' *DAILY MAIL*